MIRACLE ON 134TH STREET

CHRIS STORM

CHRIS STORM BOOKS

ROBERT FROST: "For me the initial delight is in the surprise of remembering something I didn't know I knew.
I am in a place, in a situation, as if I had materialized from cloud or risen out of the ground."

1

CHAPTER ONE

"You gotta wear a suit." Dad had offered his usual unsolicited advice to Kelly the second he heard about her job interview. "Look professional, polished, but not too polished. And be smart, but not too smart. Listen, just answer their questions. Keep your opinions to yourself. We all know you got plenty of 'em. The bottom line is this: Try not to talk so much."

Well, Dad had certainly made the interview sound easy enough, but Kelly's outfit was the closest thing she owned to an actual suit. She wore a navy-blue wool blazer, black polyester pants, a white cotton blouse, and brown loafers. The blazer had belonged to her mom, and the last time Kelly wore it was one year ago at Mom's funeral. Kelly wasn't sure why she held onto that jacket. Some crazy idea that it would comfort her in some way?

Or maybe just because her mom loved that jacket so very much. The Irish wool blazer with a narrow lapel and gold claddagh buttons was probably the most precious piece of clothing her mother had ever owned. It had always looked sophisticated on Mom, but on Kelly, the jacket looked tight and wrinkled and quite miserable to be there.

Just like Kelly and Dad must have appeared at Mom's funeral.

Kelly had succeeded in forgetting all about that funeral until she pulled the blazer out of the back of her closet for the interview. Memories wafted with the musty mothballs. Smells could do that to you—remind you of something or someone, take you back to a specific place or time, good or bad. This time it was bad: the pungent floral arrangements filled with Christmas paperwhites that smelled like urine; the vulgar red hue of the poinsettias; the stiff wooden church pews; the buzz of the antiquated boiler that wouldn't shut off, making everyone use their printed funeral programs as makeshift fans in a New York City December.

Program fans that Kelly had stayed up all night creating while wearing that old wool blazer.

The front side of the program displayed a photograph of Kelly's mother at eighteen, the year she married Dad. Everyone always said that Kelly looked exactly like her. Mom was a pretty girl with wide green eyes and jet-black hair pinned up into a loose bun. In the photo, she wore a black dress with a white collar and a radiant smile. Like all her hopes and dreams were about to come true, and maybe they were. She was marrying her one true love, as she called Dad, and they were a perfect match.

Beneath the photo, Kelly had added a brief history of Mom's humble life: Irish immigrant, Manhattan seamstress, beloved wife, mother of one... On the back side, a little poem penned by Kelly herself at about two in the morning. There was something about the quiet solitude of the night, or maybe it was coming face to face with darkness, that gave Kelly the courage to fight back:

> *Death surrounds me, thick and smooth,*
> *And spreads his fingers over my moon,*
> *He turns out the light, and slams the door,*
> *And whispers that you are no more.*

But truth shines brightest in darkness gloom,
And breaks the lock and enters the room,
He takes our hands, and unites the two,
One strength,
One promise,
I will always love you.

Kelly had listed the author as anonymous because she wasn't supposed to feel that way. At least, not publicly. She wasn't supposed to fight death. How could anyone wage war against the inevitable? She was supposed to carry on, shoulders back and head held high, and shed some tears.

Maybe the poem was Kelly's way of telling everybody at the funeral exactly what death did to her. He stole. He lied. In fact, Kelly believed that death longed to cause excruciating pain.

And Kelly was angry.

She wore that blazer again today when she stopped at Dad's to give him the news—her job interview was this morning; there was no turning back now. It couldn't have been a coincidence that the jacket seemed to travel right along with every bad day. Kelly didn't want this job. In fact, she'd been trying to run away from it all her life.

But she needed the money, and she was discovering that dreams didn't always come true, that sacrifice was part of life, that reality had a way of making you feel like you were never going to be good enough, so you'd better settle for something, for anything you could get.

Dad rarely budged from his threadbare recliner and that reading lamp that illuminated only the left side of his face, making him look like some sort of disheveled detective from one of his mystery novels. If it weren't for those books, Kelly did not know how Dad would have occupied himself since Mom died. Whatever plot was building inside those pages was far more tolerable than what was happening in the real world.

Kelly took her usual place on the tapestry stool at Dad's feet, and he sank into his chair, releasing the footrest with a spring and locking himself into place. He already knew why Kelly had come.

Dad couldn't hide the grin. "So...you're going with Elite, are you?"

"Well, it's not like you didn't tell me about a thousand times that I should—"

Dad raised a flattened palm, a flashing red light that signaled a silent warning. "That is not what your character would say at a moment like this. We are at the crux of a beautiful story here, at the peak of a suspense-building plot wherein the daughter finally concedes to her irreversible destiny, upholding the family lineage, following in her father's footsteps, as well as her grandfather and great-grandfather before her."

All having been people from very different generations, Kelly wanted to remind him. Men whose only goal in life was to bring home a weekly paycheck, and there was nothing wrong with that, but this was a new world, a modern world. Was it so very wrong to want a little something more out of life? People were different now, weren't they? *We are supposed to follow our passions and dreams, aren't we?* Kelly knew the answer to those questions only too well.

She had chosen to pursue her passion rather than a paying job and enrolled as an art history major at NYU. She couldn't have been happier to land those summer internships at The Guggenheim. Well, not really internships—more like voluntary docent positions, without pay. But they became the highlight of her resume, or so she thought, until she discovered that hundreds—no, thousands—of art history students flocked to the city after graduation, all volunteering for free, all dreaming of assisting the curator of The Met or The Whitney or The Guggenheim, and all deleting one rejection email after another.

Kelly had no choice but to spend the next few years waitressing—actually, bartending and telling everyone she was waitressing, because Dad would have added pipe-smoking and a proper English tweed cap to his mystery-solving had he discovered his only child was serving cocktails in a tight black t-shirt and cutoff denim shorts.

But bartending wasn't paying the bills anymore. Three years ago, Kelly's life had changed in irreversible ways. She had no choice but to surrender her dreams to a much-needed reality: a steady weekly paycheck and health benefits. Maybe she wasn't so different from her dad and her grandfathers after all. Maybe being a personal driver was deeply embedded in her DNA and she had no real choice in the matter. Her life, her job, her relationships, all predetermined before she was ever born.

"Sad comes with happy," Dad always said. "You can never really know one without knowing the other."

So, when is the happy coming? She longed to ask, but didn't. In fact, Kelly and Dad seldom spoke about the sad part of Kelly's private life, and when they did, the conversation was a devoted-dad check-in. "So, how's things? Everything okay over there? You need anything?" This translated to "I can't help you, but I care. In my own way, I care, but I'm barely getting by on my own over here without your mom. You know that, don't you? I wish I could help, but I can't."

Yes, I know that, Dad, I know, and I still love you. That's why I stopped by today. That's why I'm sitting here on this worn-out stool, six inches from the floor, wearing some mismatched black and blue suit, staring up at you like a little girl looking for some sort of approval or something; I'm not sure what.

"The interview is at ten today," she said.

"On a Sunday?" Dad asked.

"That's what they told me."

"Hmpf. Something strange going on down there." Dad shook the thought from his brain until his face brightened. "Well, anyway, you belong at Elite. You know that, don't you, Kel?" Even Dad's hair seemed whiter. "Elite Drivers has always been the best. From the day Pops and Pa started until the day I retired, Elite was the best." Dad sucked in air. A big speech was coming. "Elite's got a reputation in Manhattan." Dad searched the ceiling, the sky beyond, someplace, any place, other than here. "Earned, not given, and the O'Sullivan family has got everything to do with that. When you land this job, and you'll get it, mark my words..." Dad fixed on Kelly. "Because of your good name, that's why. It'll be your responsibility now to make sure Elite stays the best. You do everything to keep it that way, and I promise you, Pops and Pa will be looking down from heaven..."

So that was where Dad had been looking.

"They'll be watching your every move, prouder than ever before."

Kelly seriously doubted that. Surely those people up in heaven, supposedly without worry or care, didn't waste their time monitoring every predicament Kelly O'Sullivan was getting herself into down here on this earth. Surely, they weren't up there biting their nails, hoping she didn't make all the wrong choices again. Please, if only somebody would tell her that Pops and Pa weren't up there thinking, "Well, would you take a gander at that? Our Kelly's finally got an interview with Elite, and by golly, this girl's going places. Let's hope she can handle it. I'm not going to sleep for weeks now. I can't eat a thing. I got to stand up here, peering over these clouds, watching her every move, hoping she doesn't screw it all up again."

Kelly regrouped, then returned Dad's gaze. "I'll do my best."

"I know you will, Kel." The squint of Dad's left eye now, like a little secret between them.

"You know..." Kelly began carefully. She didn't want to tell Dad, but if she didn't get the job—strike that; *when* she didn't get the job—he should be prepared. Kelly gave him a little something to suggest a different ending, a red herring, so he wouldn't be too disappointed. "The only problem is...they're looking for a guy...a male driver. I sent the application in anyway. What I'm saying is...it's a long shot."

"What's this nonsense?" Dad slapped the arm of his recliner. "That'd be illegal. It's the twentieth century. People can't get away with stuff like that anymore. They gotta take the most qualified person. Doesn't matter what you got inside your pants. Even I know that."

"Actually, it's the twenty-first century, and I'm sorry to say it still goes on."

"Is that what their job posting said? They're looking for a man? I say, take 'em to court."

"It's the rumor around town. They never hired a woman before."

"Then you'll be the first. You march right in there and tell them you're a better driver than any guy in town, and your dad says so. You prove 'em wrong. You might add that you will report this to the authorities...whoever deals with this kind of stuff. Go ahead and look it up ahead of time. Google it, or whatever you kids do today. Tell them you're going to report them if they don't give you the job."

"Somehow, I don't think that's going to make them hire me."

"Aw, quit being so dramatic all the time. You're acting like you're in a soap opera or something. This is real life we're talking about here."

"It sure is, Dad, and life isn't always fair."

Dad interrupted with his stop-sign hand. "Well, they never had an O'Sullivan woman apply for the job before. They'll recognize your name right away. I'm sure of it. You'll get that job. You just tell them who you are. Be yourself, like I said before, with a little less talking. Wait and see. Hey, I got an idea. You want me to go in there with you?"

Kelly felt the corners of her lips curl. "I appreciate the offer, but in case you haven't noticed, we both like to talk a lot, so how would I get a word in?"

"Well, at least you're listening to me for a change. That says something. So, listen to this: It doesn't matter if you're tall or short or fat or skinny. It doesn't matter if your hair is curly or straight or what color your eyes are. It doesn't matter if you pee standing up or sitting down. None of that makes you a good driver. None of that makes you good at anything in life. I never cared if your mom and me had a boy or a girl. But I gotta admit, raising a girl was the hardest thing I ever did." Even Dad was surprised by his remark. "Let me make myself clear here. I don't mind having a daughter." He shook his head. "No, that's not quite what I'm trying to say here." He blew air through his nose. "Oh, for heaven's sake, Kel. Let me put it this way: You're an O'Sullivan. That's all that matters. You got what it takes; now you march in there and prove it.

"And something more." Dad paused. "Don't ever underestimate anything that comes your way. Even the not-so-good stuff. If you let it, things have a way of turning themselves upside down and inside out, and all of a sudden, you find a miracle in the most unlikely place."

"Mom used to say that."

"Yes, she sure did."

Now it was Kelly's turn to squint one eye. *Maybe you're right, Dad. Maybe this one time, Elite will hire a woman, because I need that money now more than ever, and I finally understand why you did it—you and*

Pops and Pa. Why you took that miserable job and worked it seven days a week, twenty-four hours a day, on call, spring, summer, winter, fall, holidays, birthdays, graduations. You did what you had to do for your family, and I'm going to do the same. "Thanks, Dad."

Dad rested a firm hand on Kelly's shoulder, and she raised her hand to cover his. "You'll get that job," he repeated. "It's already yours."

Kelly kissed the top of Dad's head. A peck, like always, but this time was different. For the first time in her life, she was the child her dad had always dreamed of, finally becoming the fourth generation in her family to be a private driver with Elite.

***

Kelly started the mile-long walk to her interview. The winter sun frosted the piles of snow that lined the sidewalks and streets, like snow cones topped with chocolate sprinkles. Kelly waited at the curb for the light to change and stuck her hands in her jacket pockets to keep them warm as the chill from the Hudson River whipped inside her collar. She didn't own a dressy coat or a pair of leather boots or gloves. But she didn't really need any of those things. Not for a mile walk through downtown Manhattan.

Need and *want* had defined themselves in a much clearer way this past year. The light turned and the crowd stepped off the curb just as a cab spun the corner. His tires flung the icy slush at Kelly, but the sprinkles weren't chocolate. They were filth and grime from the thousands of dirty tires and boots. She stood at that curb, flicking the gray droplets from her fingertips. Her jacket was soaked, her loafers drenched. There was no time to go home and change, and even if she had time, she had nothing else to wear.

Dad had recited those rules so many times over the years, so proud that he had adhered to each and every one: "You gotta keep your eyes on the road, and stay quiet, like you don't exist. The only talking going on inside that car is the client on his phone. If you think he's talking to you, he's not. He doesn't care what you think. You nod your head if you have to, but don't say a word.

"When you pick him up, you pull the limo up to the side of the curb, you get out, make your way around the front fender, always the front fender, that way he sees where you are at all times. You open his door, you offer a hand to help him get out of the car, but don't act like he can't get out on his own. He doesn't want to be fussed over. He doesn't want to be treated like a kid—well, sometimes he is a kid, and that's another story altogether. Don't listen to kids. Don't talk to them either. They're conniving little leprechauns. It's usually a trap. Don't take them where they want to go, because they are always going to want to go someplace they're not supposed to, especially the teenagers. Remember, the kid isn't paying you. The dad is.

"And when you're standing on the sidewalk, waiting for the client to come out of his appointment, you open the door the second you see him, but never, and I mean never, speak to him in public. Sure, you can say 'good morning' or 'good night,' but no more than that.

"When he's in the back seat, do not check him out in your rearview mirror. Don't act like you can hear any part of his conversation or understand anything he's saying to whoever might be sitting beside him back there, even if it's not his wife, and it usually isn't. But that's none of your business either.

"The bottom line is this: The best driver is invisible."

Kelly merged with the pedestrian throng. "I am invisible."

2

CHAPTER TWO

E lite Drivers was not so elite after all, or maybe it had deteriorated since Dad worked there. The place was hidden in a back alleyway, like a speakeasy or brothel. Kelly uncovered what looked like an entrance behind two dumpsters. This had to be it because the street was narrowed by a couple of Bentley Bentaygas and an Audi A8, the typical automobiles used for chauffeur service.

Kelly knew all about cars because of Dad. He'd had an obsession with automobiles when he was a driver. It made perfect sense that a professional driver would be interested in cars. Kelly always believed that's why Dad loved cars so—because he was *supposed* to love them.

Her childhood memories included excursions to every parking lot auto show from Jersey to Brooklyn. It had been their family time, instead of that "Coney Island waste of hard-earned money," as Dad referred to it. They would stroll the long line of collector cars, usually displayed in big lots like Home Depot or Walmart, and Dad would give an in-depth history on every make and model. Mom was so proud of him. She welcomed his tutorials and shushed Kelly's interruptions. Mom asked plenty of questions, sometimes unnecessary and repetitive. Kelly understood what Mom was doing. She was lingering in the moment, respecting it.

Dad's car facts were still imprinted on Kelly's brain: "This 1959 Mercedes 220S Cabriolet was owned by Cary Grant. He drove it in the movie *North by Northwest*, fell in love with the car, and they gave it to him when the job was done. Now, would that be a hefty tip or what?" Kelly could almost see the Cabriolet—sleek form, silver sides, tan convertible top. She could picture Cary Grant behind the wheel, his arm wrapped loosely around some famous actress donned in dark sunglasses and a silk scarf, her hair billowing beautifully in the breeze as they sped through the cliff sides of Monte Carlo.

Dad always added, "If you can't afford to own it, the next best thing is driving it." On occasion, Dad would get a break in his daily schedule and stop back home for lunch. He would call Kelly and Mom outdoors and offer a brief tour of the vehicle of the day. But the very best part of that lesson was afterward when Dad would drive them all around town for fun. Mom wrapped a scarf around her permed hair and rested her elbow on the open window frame while Dad raised the radio volume as high as possible. The curious stares from onlookers amused Kelly, and she would offer a little wave from the back seat like a real celebrity. She always wore sunglasses for those jaunts, a cheap pair of Wayfarers from the drug store, so nobody ever knew it was just that little Kelly O'Sullivan from the Lower East, a driver's daughter.

Kelly pressed open the door of Elite Drivers's office, fully aware that even if she landed this job as a driver, she would never love a car as much as Dad. Art would always be her passion. But like Dad, Kelly didn't own what she loved. She just wanted to be around it, immersed inside it, a part of it somehow.

"Kelly O'Sullivan." She introduced herself to the skeletal figure hunched behind an old steel office desk. He was wearing a bow tie and a quite obvious toupee.

"Take a seat." He scratched his head and his wig wiggled. "I'll be with you in a minute."

Kelly sat in a folding chair directly in front of his desk, hands folded neatly in her lap, waiting patiently while he finished his work. She glanced around the room. Shelves stuffed with stacks of papers and ledgers, used coffee cups strewn about, a monstrous ancient computer monitor. The floor, worn, lumpy linoleum. The walls, seventies-style knotty pine paneling. Hanging behind the manager was a cheap print—the kind you might find at Target. It was an autumn forest scene, a pathway into the woods. Browns and golds and oranges forged a trail that slowly dissolved, smaller and narrower, into the distance until it was a sliver. Until it was gone.

"I'm ready." He broke her trance.

Kelly straightened, prepared for questioning, but none came. In fact, the man barely looked at her application, tossed onto his desk like last week's *NY Times*. He was doing all the talking, laying out the rules one by one, a little more simply than Dad had ever done.

"My current open position," he continued, "is for a CEO, his girlfriend, a teenage son, a dog walker, two dogs. They need transport twenty-four seven to work, school, activities, et cetera, et cetera. The head of the household is Marcus J. Irving, the CEO of CyberScape, Inc. You probably heard of him. Cover of *Time Magazine*, *Wall Street Journal*, that sort of thing. They live in a penthouse up in Central Park West. His office is Financial District, the son's school is Madison Academy..."

The manager's voice droned on and on with particulars that were unimportant and trivial until he said, "The past four drivers were either fired or quit. Couldn't seem to handle it. We can't keep anybody on this one, and—"

"I can do it," Kelly interrupted.

The manager took a big bite of his deli sandwich, chewed a little too long while surveying Kelly, then wiped his mouth with the back of his hand. "So, what makes you think you"—his eyes trailed her—"can handle it when no man lasted more than a day?"

Kelly knew what he saw: Some girl in a soaking wet wool blazer and polyester pants. A sad, tired expression. A lopsided, self-made black bob haircut. A little mascara, probably smudged by that splash of dirty snow, and crooked pink lipstick, awkwardly applied by the girl who rarely wore makeup.

People saw what they wanted to see. If this man was so shallow, so ignorant to demand a driver with specific body parts, then maybe that was his very problem. Whatever the reason, he was clearly in trouble. A very prominent, very rich businessman was going through Elite drivers like cups of stale coffee. Or maybe the CEO had switched to cheap martinis at this point and was getting ready to fire Elite, which had evidently proved to be not so elite after all.

"Let's be honest here," Kelly said. "The real problem is that all these terminations or resignations or whatever you want to call them are giving you a really bad reputation." The manager flinched, and Kelly pulled back a little. "Giving Elite a really bad rep that it doesn't deserve."

He lowered his sandwich, and a drop of mayonnaise leaked onto his desktop. He swiped the mayo with his pointer and licked it off. "Hmpf." He snorted. "Your application says you come from a family of drivers..."

So, Dad was right. Kelly's lineage finally held some significance. This guy believed, or hoped, that something within Kelly's DNA would enable her to manage the difficulties of the job. Some inherited gene would render her immune to her employer's personality flaws, life problems, psychological issues or whatever was going on inside the windows of that enclosed auto.

"That's right. My dad, my grandfather and my great-grandfather were all drivers for Elite. They had some very big clients like the one you're talking about here. But the difference is, they never had any problems. They got along perfectly fine with each and every one. You may have heard my family name, O'Sullivan?"

"Nope."

"Well, you can check your records. They worked here until they retired. They were good drivers, all three of them. I guess you could say it's in the blood."

"All men. So, what's that all about?"

And there it was. *Why, yes, how kind of you to notice. I am the daughter. So, the makeup worked after all?*

"Like I said." Kelly ignored him. "It's in the blood. Some people are good with autos, some people are good with..." She noted the financial statements on his desk. "Numbers, records, things like that."

He scanned her application. "Looks to me like you've been doing everything *but* driving. There's something here about working security at a museum."

Security? Uh, no, not exactly. I was a docent. "Yeah, but it didn't turn out like I thought."

"Can't blame you there. Why does the word 'boring' come to mind?"

Kelly glanced at that cheap print behind the manager's desk. She felt her face redden, her heart pound. What did this man believe? That being a driver was the very best job in the whole wide world, and she was lucky to have it? Art galleries brimming with colorful oils and pastels and watercolors, gloriously swept into imagery that evoked every emotion known to the heart of mankind, were dull? He waited for her response. Kelly clamped her lips. She could hear Dad's voice. *Less talking, Kel.*

Just then, she felt the buzz of her phone tucked inside her pocket. She checked the number and silenced the ringer. Another call from home. Her basement apartment in Harlem, West 134th Street. A garden apartment, they called it. The one-room studio had only one window at the far end that offered a sidewalk-level view of the steady traffic of feet. Only feet. Black boots and high heels and running shoes in the winter. Bare legs and flip-flops and sandals in the summer.

And then there was the water problem. That stubborn puddle in the middle of the floor. Before Kelly moved in, her apartment had been used as a cellar storage space. The walls were cracked, yellowed plaster. The floor, a rough concrete, and on rainy days, a small puddle collected in the center of the room. It seemed to be fairly clean but city water nonetheless. Kelly would step around it and over it and, on occasion, forge straight through the middle with a choice word or two. She mopped that puddle up over and over again but would never complain to the landlord. The rent was cheap, the neighborhood was safe, and she knew an apartment in Harlem could harbor worse secrets...lead paint, asbestos...rats.

And yet, inside that dismal apartment, even now, was the amazingly wonderful Mrs. Andrews, doing her very best to brighten Kelly's cloudy world.

The manager spoke with his mouth full of pastrami. He transitioned to a series of factual questions, verifying Kelly's date of birth, address, social security, driving record. He concluded the so-called interview with: "Like I said, I'm in a bind here. I need somebody who can handle it. I can't afford any more mistakes. We'll call you if we need you."

Handle it? As if driving an expensive car around all day filled with wealthy people who had no desire to become acquainted or speak to you whatsoever was the most challenging job in the city.

Kelly rested her elbows on his desk. She didn't even know this guy's name. He had never introduced himself. He made up his mind before she uttered a single word that she was unqualified. She had one last chance. "I'm sorry. I don't recall your name," she said.

"Mr. Johnson, HR VP."

"Mr. Johnson, with all due respect to Elite, and because of my father and grandfather and great-grandfather's utmost admiration for this company, may I please share what they taught me since I was a little girl? Three lifetimes of driver experience and service?"

"Sure. Why not?" A smirk slipped through the pastrami.

Kelly recited Dad's words. "I am not being hired to *handle* anything. Maybe that was the problem with your other drivers. I am an extension of the vehicle. I deliver the client to his destination, timely and safely. I don't strike up any conversation unless prompted, and even then, a nod of the head or a 'yes sir' will do. I am not their mentor, their teacher, their coach or their friend. I hear nothing. I see nothing. I remember nothing. I clock in, and I clock out. Period. Believe me, I can handle that. Maybe it's time you switch it up a little. You're telling me your past drivers lasted no more than a day. Maybe it's time to try a different kind of driver. The kind who is invisible."

He sank back into his chair.

Say nothing, Kel. Not a single word.

"You do come from a family of drivers," he said.

Stay quiet. You talk too much.

"But I can't afford another screwup."

She couldn't help herself. "You certainly can't. This is the CEO of CyberScape we're talking about here. He has friends, contacts. He knows a lot of people who need your driver service. If this news were to spread, even to one of his associates?"

The manager rolled his empty deli wrapper into a ball and tossed it into a garbage can. He scribbled on a crumpled yellow Post-it and slid it toward Kelly. "Be at this garage tomorrow morning, 5 a.m. The super will meet you. He'll fill you in, give you the keys, your daily schedule. You report to him from now on. A Mr. Perez. With any luck, I'll never see you again."

"So, I got the job?"

"Like I said. I'm in a bind here."

"Thanks so much. You won't regret this." The amazing Mrs. Andrews was up there in Kelly's Harlem apartment right now, playing soothing music and making everything so very wonderful, and Kelly finally had the means to pay her.

The manager was still talking. "...They'll give you a driver's uniform. Pants, jacket, hat. With any luck, they won't even notice you."

"Like I said, invisible."

***

By the time Kelly reached the subway station and transferred three trains to get back up to 134th Street, it was late afternoon, and Mrs. Andrews greeted her at the door with an update. It had been a bad day, much worse than she had revealed over the phone. The medication had not taken effect as quickly and was supplemented by a stronger drug that Kelly had been hoping to avoid.

"What do you think triggered it?" Kelly asked.

"Anything can be a trigger—a car horn, a strong odor, a change in humidity or barometric pressure." There was no way to know for certain. "But everything seems fine now."

Mrs. Andrews was right—everything was fine now, for a minute or an hour, or even a day. Kelly had a paying job, and she could afford to keep Mrs. Andrews. But new worries tugged at Kelly's heart, and she couldn't help but wonder: What if the new medications lost their effectiveness? What if side effects emerged? Kelly had read about medication plateau and tolerance issues. And she couldn't forget that her new job was on a trial period. What if her CEO employer, Mr. Irving, didn't like her? What if she couldn't *handle* the family after all?

And, once again, happy and sad were mixed together, swirling and blending in a cataclysmic collision like a myriad of paint colors swept across a canvas, until one could not be distinguished from the other.

3

CHAPTER THREE

The Irving Penthouse was located on the top floor of Fifteen Central Park West. Curious about her new boss, Kelly had done a quick computer search the night before. His building was a thirty-five-floor luxury high-rise in neoclassical style: limestone exterior, open courtyard and private motor vehicle entrance. Described as "The Architect Series," it was one of New York's most prestigious addresses and the coveted home of actors, athletes, CEOs and hedge fund managers. In other words, those few who could afford the hefty price tags over fifty million. People like Robert DeNiro, Denzel Washington, Mark Wahlberg, and Sting. But the jewel of the building, the penthouse, boasting three-hundred-and-sixty-degree views of the city and the park and valued at almost a hundred million dollars, belonged to Marcus Irving.

Irving owned the top floor of the garage, too—the entire floor. Following her instructions, Kelly rode the elevator until a polite *ding* signaled she had reached her destination. The doors glided apart, and the space that spread out before her seemed more like a luxurious lobby than a parking garage, with its geometric white stone flooring, high-gloss walls, and bright fluorescent spotlights. She stepped into

two perpendicular rows of collector automobiles, about forty in total, glittering before her like the shiny jewelry in Tiffany's storefront
windows. A 1964 Ferrari 250 LM, a 1994 McLaren F1 LM, a 1939
Alfa Romeo 8C 2900B, and the list went on. *If Dad could see this.*
She pulled out her mobile phone to snap a few photos when a voice
startled her from behind.

"Welcome."

Kelly spun around to find a very tall, very distinguished Black man,
slender and dressed in an expensive, carefully tailored suit with a red
silk tie and a matching pocket-handkerchief. "Oh. I didn't see you
there. Hi. Kelly O'Sullivan. They told me to report early. I took the
train down, then walked a few blocks. Luckily it was on time. Nobody
is really out at this hour. In fact, I haven't been out at this hour in years.
Not that I'm complaining or anything. I like getting up early." *Shut up,
Kelly. Just shut up.* "I'm the new driver. I'm looking for Mr. Perez."

"I am Mr. Perez, and I am fully aware of who you are. You are
number five in a long line of previous employees who either surrendered or abandoned me. Are you going to disappoint me next, Ms.
O'Sullivan? Or do I finally have someone robust enough to persevere
the arduous trials of navigating an automobile throughout the streets
of Manhattan?" He jabbed the air with an underhanded punch.

"Oh, I'm here to stay. You can be sure of that. I'm not going
anywhere. Other than driving around town, of course."

"In that case, exactly what do you think you were doing with that
phone of yours?"

Kelly surveyed the phone in her hand as if she were equally surprised to see it.

Mr. Perez continued. "Absolutely no photography whatsoever. Not
in my garage. Not in my automobiles. This goes without saying;
however, in your case, I will state the obvious anyway: absolutely no

photographs of the Irving family. I will not tolerate an invasion of privacy or..."

This man spoke as if he were a professor giving a lecture at a university podium, carefully choosing and precisely pronouncing each word. His temples were slightly gray, adding an air of intelligence, maybe some mystery. "You certainly don't appear any more resilient than your predecessors," he said. "But I am going to believe you are the answer I have been longing for because I have hope." He raised one hand in a salute to the sky. "And hope is a glorious thing. It shouts victory before the battle is ever won. It promises, at the very end of your story, all will be rectified."

"I like the sound of that."

"They all did." Mr. Perez's hand dropped to his side. "Until the day that their employment was terminated or they resigned or they disappeared from the face of this earth, never to be seen or heard from again, and I was summoned to take their place." His brows linked, and Kelly noticed they were neatly trimmed, quite possibly plucked.

"It is my duty to inform you," he continued, "I am not a driver, nor do I wish to be a driver. I have been the driver for this family for over fifty years, well before Mr. Irving was ever conceived. But"—he raised his index finger—"I am officially retired, and I have now accepted the prestigious opportunity as Inventory Supervisor. My driving days are finished and furthermore—" Mr. Perez's speech was suddenly cut short as his attention veered to Kelly's mismatched outfit. "I am not thoroughly convinced that person is you. However, finding no better candidates waiting in line..." He shielded his eyes, pretending to search behind her. "You will do. Now, go through the door into the back office, where you will find several suits. One will surely suffice. It does not have to be the perfect fit. This is not your wedding day, nor is it your funeral, and my local tailor will lend his artistry. Don the suit and the shoes, the hat and the gloves, and join me back here to receive your daily schedule." He pronounced the word "*sheddule*" with a hint of a British accent. "I am explaining your itinerary—are you listening?"

Kelly nodded, and Mr. Perez continued. "You will drive directly around the north side of the building to the front entrance, where you will introduce yourself to Mr. Jack, the doorman. This will be the one and only time you communicate with Jack because he does not wish to become any more familiarly acquainted with you than he is with, say, the dog walker or...the dogs. No insult intended."

"None taken."

"The end of each day will be determined by Mr. Irving himself, because the morning *sheddule* I give you may and probably will be altered and deviated from several times throughout the day. Some of these changes will work in your favor, and you will find yourself dismissed and home by 6 p.m. Other days, you will work until the early hours of the morning, have a nap on the sofa in the back room, and report here at full attention at 5 a.m. again, looking bright-eyed and bushy-tailed and extraordinarily thrilled to begin another day driving for the Irving family. Do you understand?"

"Yep."

"Please refrain from improper English. We are well educated in this establishment, and a 'yep' or 'nope' is sure to agitate Mr. Irving and myself. You do know proper English?"

"I have a degree from NYU."

"NYU. You don't say!" Mr. Perez clasped his hands. "Congratulations!" His hands abruptly fell to his sides. "I have had drivers with degrees from Columbia, master's from Amherst and Brown and Tufts, all in mundane subjects like English or ancient Greek studies or art history..."

Kelly must have altered her expression because Mr. Perez shot back, "Oh, I do apologize. It appears I have discovered your major. Welcome to the club. I have two degrees from Georgetown in ancient Greek and Roman history and a doctorate in Egyptology from Yale. Oh, to be a dreamer and a fantasizer...until the bills arrive. Now, go change into the proper clothing." He pointed to the steel door at the far end of the garage.

This was a lot of information to take in right away, but Kelly wasn't focusing on any of it. She was mesmerized by this man's every gesture, every facial expression, the inflection of his voice. Mr. Perez was an Ivy League graduate, an intellectual. But there was something more about him, something special. He made Kelly feel a little less embarrassed, a little less of a failure for surrendering to this position. She liked him.

"Well, what are you waiting for?" Mr. Perez said. "Go get dressed."

The back office was much what Kelly expected. A rack of jackets and pants and shirts. A shelf of shoes and hats and gloves. A desk with a blotter, a pen tidily placed within a pen holder, a cup of pencils, a calculator, and a porcelain teacup and saucer, all clearly belonging to Mr. Perez. The velvet sofa, draped in a faux fur throw, did not look uncomfortable, but Kelly dismissed this notion immediately. She would sleep in her own apartment; there would be no changing that. Even if it was only for a few hours, she must return home each night.

She slipped in and out of several pants and shirts until she found a close fit, then moved on to the shoes. For a minute she worried no shoe would be small enough. But she was relieved to find there were men on this planet with small feet and small necks and small waists, like her own. She found a necktie, a hat, and a pair of driving gloves, and when her new outfit was buttoned and zipped and tied, Kelly was relieved there was no mirror to gauge herself.

She stood a little straighter and squared her shoulders when she appeared before Mr. Perez, but he could not be fooled so easily. "Oh…I see…" He jotted a few notes. "Two sizes too big in the jacket. One size too big in the neckline, and the pants…" He flipped Kelly's jacket open and tugged at her waistline. "About an inch too big, but the length is fine. How are the shoes?"

"Fine."

"It is now or never to register any complaint with the clothing department. I shall inquire once more and only once. Are the shoes comfortable and properly fitted?"

"Actually, I guess about a half size too big."

"Very well then." More notes were made. Mr. Perez checked his wristwatch. "On to the *sheddule*."

Mr. Perez held a sheet of linen paper, the kind of expensive paper that would normally be used for a resume or an invitation to a formal event. "It is extraordinarily simple to interpret." His eyes flashed. "Even for an NYU graduate." His finger traced her daily itinerary. "Your first appointment is with Mr. Byron at 6 a.m. You will transport him to Madison Academy, where he will begin classes promptly at seven. He prefers to arrive approximately fifteen minutes early, which leaves him sufficient time to partake in the school breakfast since he refuses to dine at home. You will remain parked at the curb for one full hour to ensure Mr. Byron remains inside the school building and does not attempt a…now, what is the correct word here? I always choose the wrong one. It is not 'escape' but rather…oh yes, 'truancy.'"

Kelly had no shock to hide. She had been a teenager once, not so very long ago, and an expert at both truancy and escape.

Mr. Perez's finger inched across the page. "At 10 a.m., you will return for Miss Carolyn."

"Wait," Kelly interrupted. "What do I do between then?"

"Automobile maintenance, of course. You will clean the exterior and interior of the automobile, fill the gasoline tank. Driver maintenance. You may eat something, drink something, as in water or juice or coffee or tea only. I have encountered wrong beverage choices on a few occasions in the past, and I will not tolerate it. Do I make myself perfectly clear?"

"Of course."

"Miss Carolyn drinks Fine and—"

"What's that?"

"A Japanese product naturally filtered below Mount Fuji, rich in minerals and pollutant-free. Mr. Irving, iced coffee, a double espresso over ice. Mr. Byron prefers Diet Coke. All beverages will be fully stocked or found in the Sub-Zero, over there." He pointed to a refrigerator against the wall. "And please do not ask me what Coca-Cola is or how it is made, because I am certain it is a very convoluted chemical mixture that I refuse to pollute myself with and—"

"I don't drink it, either."

"Thank you for blurting out your trivial personal fact. Focus on the driving, Ms. O'Sullivan. I feel quite certain that that responsibility will be more than sufficient to consume your every available thought. At 10 a.m., Miss Carolyn will be off to her Body Pump class or perhaps her Soul Cycle or maybe a Swedish massage. She will inform you where she would like to go. We never know for certain. The mysterious creature changes her mind like a spring zephyr swirling into shore from the Atlantic." Mr. Perez's hand danced through the air like that of a symphony conductor, then stopped short. "But that is her prerogative, isn't it? And we are more than pleased to accommodate her ever-changing whims.

"At noon, you will retrieve the dog walker, Ms. Claire, and both labradoodles, Peter and Nicholas. It will be time for their two-hour stroll through Central Park. Mr. Irving demands it. Claire walks the dogs around the neighborhood the remainder of the day. The dog walker is from the rural Midwest, cornfields and such, and prefers you to follow her pathway around the circumference of the park, keeping her in clear view so she is not accosted or molested or—"

"It's broad daylight."

"First and foremost, stop interrupting. Had you waited patiently, you would already possess the answer to your question. I am fully aware that the park is safe at that hour, and I see you are privy to the same information, but Miss Claire is not, and because she is the caretaker of Mr. Irving's two prized possessions, she ranks high above us in the organizational chart, and you and even I, I am afraid, will do well by following her every command. Now, may I continue?"

"Sure."

"Proper English?"

"Yes, please continue."

"At 3 p.m., retrieve Mr. Byron and deposit him at his indoor golf lesson at Hudson Yards. You will remain parked at the curb because at four, Mr. Byron must be transferred to his Mandarin lesson. At five, you will deliver Miss Carolyn to her daily cocktails with her girlfriends; at six, retrieve Mr. Byron from Mandarin; at seven, deliver Miss Carolyn safely home; and, with any bit of luck, since Mr. Irving is currently abroad, that will be the end of this beautiful, intriguing, hopeful, and inspirational day." He saluted the sky and quickly recalled something. "On Saturdays and Sundays, the schedule will constantly change and evolve according to appointments and needs."

"Sounds simple enough."

Mr. Perez peered at Kelly from below a pair of invisible eyeglasses. "We shall see." He gave her the schedule and a mobile phone. "Connect this phone to the Bluetooth. Leave it operable at all times in the event I need to contact you with a change in the *sheddule*." He dangled a set of keys. "The Rolls is the car of the month. Aaaaand...you're off!" Mr. Perez waved an invisible flag like he was starting a horse race.

Kelly slid into the driver's seat of a Rolls-Royce Phantom, shut the door, and was instantaneously sealed inside a blissful, luxurious cocoon. It was a mind-numbing sensation of total peace and silence...and something much more. Kelly had entered a purposeful rejection of the rush of life. This was a safe harbor, a sacred place. She allowed herself to sink into the plush, ergonomic seat. She brushed her fingertips along the supple leather steering wheel. She slid her hand across the 24-karat gold rearview mirror. She gently started the ignition. But this engine did not roar. It didn't sound anything like the yellow cabs or Ubers or jitneys on the city streets below. This engine hummed softly, a single musical note resonating from a high-tower church bell far away from this city. Kelly rested her head against the headrest and inhaled.

Dad had tried to tell Kelly and Mom about this luxurious sensation over the years, although she hadn't believed him until now. She always assumed he was exaggerating, trying to bring glamour and significance to his mundane job. And who could blame him? *"This is why these cars are so expensive, Kel."* She could hear Dad's voice. *"It's not their looks. Oh, sex appeal matters, but it's what's on the inside."*

Kelly already knew all about the inside of this auto. Beneath the hood of this Rolls was a 563-horsepower, 6.75-liter, twin-turbocharged V12 engine. This wasn't a sports car. The top speed was only 155 mph because speed was never the engineer's goal. This was an extravagant car. The sensation of floating on a puffy white cloud was more its style.

The dashboard glowed with a heads-up display and a digital instrument cluster designed to mimic the old-school Rolls-Royce of yesteryear. With collision warning, pedestrian warning, and lane departure warning, this car could drive itself. And then there was the elaborate system of cameras—front view, rear view, side view, corner view. This model included a thermal impact night vision camera to alert the driver to annoying paparazzi in hiding.

But the very best accessory, in Kelly's opinion, was The Gallery, of course. A custom three-dimensional art installation behind a wide glass panel on the dashboard. An exhibition space was a better name, wherein the owner was able to commission and curate art. The horizontal setting ran the entire length of the dashboard, framed in 24-karat gold and enclosed in glass. Rolls-Royce promised to collaborate with an artist of the owner's choosing, and if the owner had no real artistic interest to commission, Rolls had several of their own unique offerings.

Mr. Irving had chosen the famous rose display.

Kelly was familiar with the Rolls Gallery because The Met had commissioned this same floral artist during its porcelain exhibit last summer. For the Rolls gallery, a single white rose had been clipped from the English countryside by an award-winning gardener and flown to Bavaria, where it was examined in its various stages of bloom by the famous Nymphenburg porcelain makers. A new porcelain formula was conceived in Munich, Germany, over a period of three months, then utilized to create the perfect poetic reproduction of that same flower.

This pristine single white rose shone before her now, its creamy petals and soft green leaves placed delicately on its side, as if the flower had been freshly cut and was awaiting its crystal bud vase. Kelly lost herself in that rose for a moment. She imagined how the colors might appear when the sunlight struck at the right angle, or the moonlight...

A stern rapping on the driver's window glass. Kelly rolled down the window.

"Kindly familiarize yourself with the driver's manual before proceeding," Mr. Perez said.

"I already know how this car works."

"You did your homework, I see."

"Something like that."

"Very well, then. The automobile does not drive itself. Although it is fully capable, Mr. Irving prefers a driver, so on with it!" Mr. Perez issued a double clap.

Kelly's first stop was the son, Byron. She would pick him up at 6 a.m. sharp and arrive fifteen minutes early for school because Byron only ate the school breakfast, whatever that was all about, and then she must remain parked at the school for another forty-five minutes to ensure Byron did not "escape." *This should be interesting.* He must have been a little rebel, probably never used the name Byron, and who could blame him? Maybe had a few hidden tattoos, some piercings. Could this juvenile delinquent have been the reason so many drivers quit? Anybody can handle a little teen angst.

Or was the real problem Mr. Irving's girlfriend, Carolyn? Wasn't that her name? Kelly could only imagine that one. Entitled, rude, demanding. Manicures and hair salons and facials and Botox. Kelly had grown up in New York City and seen it all, so what else was new?

Or maybe Claire, the dog walker, was the issue. Kelly could manage her easily enough. She'd simply threaten to drop Claire off in Central Park in the middle of a bright, sunny afternoon. Now there was a horror movie for you. Claire could be abducted by a dachshund wearing a Burberry jacket, or far worse, a teacup poodle in a pink Chanel collar.

No, the most likely problem was Marcus Irving himself, but luckily her new boss was currently out of town, which couldn't be more

perfect. His absence provided the perfect opportunity to become acquainted with his family, maybe garner some info on Irving before he
returned. Kelly would be ready for him, whoever he thought he was
and however difficult he must be.

She floated the Rolls around the corner, and there was Jack, the
doorman, just as Mr. Perez had described. Jack was positioned below
a hunter-green awning, where he guarded two wide glass doors ostentatiously etched with *Fifteen Central Park West*. He manned his post
with obvious pride, as if he had architecturally designed the building
himself and constructed it with his own bare hands.

Gusts of icy wind slapped Kelly's face as she left the comfort of
the Rolls. Jack eyed her approach suspiciously, as if she was wearing
a ski mask and carrying a concealed weapon, and when she reached
his awning throne, he blocked her pathway. This was obviously Jack's
territory, but Kelly wanted to assure him she had no intention of
becoming a doorman anytime soon.

Jack spoke first. "Looks like another new driver."

"Kelly O'Sullivan." She offered her hand.

Jack disregarded her handshake and turned his attention to the
Rolls. "I can't wait to see how long this one lasts." He wore a navy-blue
jacket similar to that of an officer in the navy—gold stripes at the
shoulders, red stripes at the biceps, shiny gold buttons depicting an
anchor insignia—and a matching top hat. He was visibly aged. His
neck sagged in horizontal folds that matched the lines on his forehead.
Tufts of red hair poked from beneath his hat, and his ruddy com-
plexion and bloodshot eyes added to his wearied appearance. Kelly
recognized that look from the patrons at her bartending job. But at
this hour of the morning?

"Oh, this driver is here to stay," she answered.

"They all said that. Now this one is saying it, too. What else is new?"

"Well, this one is a little different than the rest."

"They all said that, too."

The wind sifted the falling snow into a foggy mist, and with one swift pivot, Jack retreated to the warm interior of the lobby and peered at Kelly through the glass. Kelly followed his lead, returning to the Rolls and surveying Jack through the car window in much the same manner.

So, this would be their relationship. Not a "good morning," not a "good evening," but a tolerable coexistence. *Fine.* She wasn't looking for friendship. Just a steady paycheck. And it seemed Jack had some problems of his own.

From her warm driver's seat, Kelly still had a clear view of the well-lit lobby. And sure enough, just as promised, at exactly six o'clock, a short figure emerged. It shot from the elevator, moving swiftly toward the door, seemingly unaware of anything or anyone but its singular purpose—get to school.

Jack flung the door open wide just in time to prevent this moving object from crashing into the glass, and Jack issued some sort of routine greeting that was blatantly ignored. The object in motion stayed in motion, spied the Rolls parked at the curb and headed directly toward it, pushing through the whipping wind.

It was purposed. It was determined. She'd give it that much.

It was Byron Irving.

Kelly matched his speed and rushed around the front fender to greet him, but Byron reached his door first. He waited. The snow pelted his open face and the wind pushed his small body back and forth, and he held tight to the side of the Rolls to steady himself.

Kelly reached him. "What's wrong? Is the door locked?"

Byron did not respond. He was a miniature Statue of Liberty, standing erect and tall and proud against the inclement weather, waiting for his driver to open his car door.

"Oh, for heaven's sake." Kelly swung the door wide. "Here you go."

Byron took his own sweet time. First, he methodically shook an oversized backpack from his shoulders and laid it carefully on the center seat, upright, facing forward. He brushed the snow fastidiously off the backpack. Next, he removed his gloves and laid them beside the backpack, upright, facing forward, fingers spread equally and in proportion to one another.

Kelly was freezing. *Get inside the car already.* But she spoke not a word.

And just as Kelly had the sudden desire to give this kid a gentle shove into the Rolls, Byron paused. He very blatantly and almost insultingly observed Kelly from head to toe. The wind tossed his scarf. Even the weighty Rolls seemed to be swaying in the storm. What was he waiting for?

"I'm the new driver," she said.

"I see that."

Byron continued his stare.

What was this kid's problem? Did he want Kelly to lift him up and place him inside the car? Fasten his seatbelt? Tie his shoelaces? She widened her eyes like a question, but he mumbled something beneath his breath and finally—thank the lucky stars—climbed into the back seat. A deadbolt would have come in handy right about then.

Kelly battled the weather to return to her position behind the wheel, and the storm instantly evaporated to the realization that she was driving her very first passenger. She took a moment to brush the snow from her coat. She adjusted the windshield wipers and set the interior thermostat. She started the engine and placed her hands carefully at ten and two, but as she pulled away from the curb, Kelly made one small mistake. Dad had warned her about that. He was right again. She should have listened.

She glanced back in the rearview mirror.

"First thing"—Byron patted his runny nose with a fresh tissue—"don't watch me in that mirror. It's rude and it's creepy."

"I was just making sure you were buckled in."

"I can take care of myself. Second, where were you? When I come out of a building, my door should be open and ready for me and—"

"I was moving as fast as I could."

"I'm not done yet. I want the heated seat warmed up and the massage set to high. The footrest should be up already too, and where's my Diet Coke? I need the Coke poured and in the cup holder, because it's only about a forty-minute drive to school, and I have to study on the way there and don't have time to get my drink ready. It's okay that you didn't do it this time. It's your first day. I get it. You got a learning curve. But from now on, all of that stuff better be ready."

"Of course."

"Oh, and do you know where the umbrellas are? Because nobody ever knows where the umbrellas are, and—"

"In the lobby." Kelly recalled seeing an umbrella stand.

"You didn't let me finish again. Do you always do that? That's rude too. I'm not talking about those umbrellas. Those are for Jack and the other tenants. Our umbrellas are inside the car door. They're heated. I could have used one of those today. Now I have to sit in school all day with a red nose and wet clothes."

"Sorry. I didn't think about an umbrella. It's not raining."

"Snow turns to water when it melts. Anything above zero degrees Celsius or thirty-two degrees Fahrenheit turns icy precipitation to liquid. I think we learned that in about the third grade. I'm soaking wet now." Byron tipped his head down and swept a few droplets from the top of his blond buzz cut. "Let's just hope I don't get sick. That won't go over well. Trust me on this one. Do yourself a favor and just have the umbrella ready from now on, okay? You got any towels?"

"No. Nobody told me to carry towels."

"Does everyone have to tell you every single thing in life? Can't you figure anything out on your own? How about paper towels?"

"I'll get some today."

"It'll be too late by then. Get some cotton towels and paper towels, just in case I need them."

"Sure."

"Sure?" Byron scowled.

"Certainly. I will be happy to have the door open, an umbrella ready and waiting and some one-hundred-percent organic cotton towels."

Who was this five-foot character doling out orders like a king? Byron was short for his age. Kelly had noticed that when she first saw him. He was fourteen, according to the Elite manager, but he dressed more like a fifty-year-old. He wore a camel-hair coat, a glen plaid scarf and leather gloves. His blond hair was cut short and spiked on top, but not purposefully. Kelly had a feeling Byron had flattened that hair into submission before he left the house this morning, but the wind had a different idea. His wire-rimmed glasses were all fogged up, too.

Kelly added, "Water can be very dangerous." It just came out.

Byron wasn't listening. He pressed the button to elevate his footrest, and he must have turned on the massage setting because his head was vibrating and his lips were quivering. He opened the drink station, popped open a can of Diet Coke with a *fizz*, poured the drink into a cup and set the cup in its holder. He lowered his veneer tabletop, unzipped his backpack and withdrew a spiral-bound notebook. He returned the backpack to its exact original position—upright, facing forward—and set the notebook on the table, opened it and began reading.

"Oh, I almost forgot," Byron said without looking up. "Turn the stars on. Always have those on before I get in the car. And the music, too. I like Little Richard."

"Little Richard?" Kelly laughed. "I haven't heard that name in a while. Good stuff."

"Or Chuck Berry." He snapped his fingers. "The stars."

Kelly found the button and ignited the fiber-optic ceiling lights. They twinkled against the black velvet ceiling. "Oh, I do like those." Then she tuned Spotify to 50's music. Kelly checked on Byron and found his head bobbing to the beat.

In return, Byron's response was an expression of stern warning.

"What's wrong now?" Kelly asked.

"Privacy." His lips tightened.

"Fine. I'll pretend I'm not here unless you need a drink or a massage or some stars or an umbrella or something."

"So, you *were* listening. Maybe you'll last an extra day or two. I hate training new drivers all the time."

Kelly bit her lip. At the first red light, she noticed the car beside her. The passengers were staring and pointing. She had almost forgotten she was driving a seven-hundred-thousand-dollar automobile, not unusual for the streets of Manhattan, but still a fascinating sight. She pressed the button to close the back window blinds as traffic resumed. She was thinking ahead now. Byron was not going to chastise her again.

"Stop!" Byron shrieked.

Kelly slammed the brakes, and the Rolls shifted into defense mode, its wheels locked into their anti-skid setting, causing the six-thousand-pound vehicle to slide sideways in the snow, almost sideswiping the car in the next lane.

"Look what you did!" Byron's cup had toppled from its holder. Diet Coke was splattered everywhere, and he was blotting his coat and pants with his scarf.

"Look what *you* did!" Kelly shouted. "You scared me half to death."

"I don't want those blinds closed. Ever."

"You almost caused an accident. Please do not shout out like that from the back seat ever again. I thought it was some kind of emergency."

"It was an emergency. Do not close the blinds."

"You said you wanted privacy. People were staring at you."

"They can't see me. The windows are tinted. Do I have to tell you everything? I hate closed blinds. Don't ever do it again. Do you hear me?"

"I can hear you just fine. You're sitting three feet behind me." Kelly knew she shouldn't have added that last remark, but any desire to remain professional was long gone. She'd been driving the Rolls for less than one full day and almost crashed it. Wouldn't that have been a fantastic first day of work?

"Okay." Byron's voice lowered. "I'm sorry I asked if you could hear me. You're right. Of course, you can hear me. What I should have asked you was..." Byron leaned forward and spoke the next words in deliberate slow motion. "Can. You. Understand. What. I'm. Saying. To. You? How should I know if you have a real low IQ or something? Maybe it takes you a little longer to get stuff. You are just a driver, you know."

"I have a degree from NYU, so don't worry about that one."

"Congratulations. How many years did that take you?"

Kelly fixed her eyes on the road and merged with traffic.

"No answer?" Byron raised his voice.

No more conversation. Wasn't that what Dad had warned? Especially with kids.

But Byron would not relent. "So, what's your name, anyway?"

Just the facts, Kel. You are an extension of the auto. "Kelly O'Sullivan."

"Is that your real name?"

"Yes."

"Short for something?"

"No."

"Middle name?"

"No."

"It's a simple name. Sounds fake."

"It's Irish."

"Hmm."

"Is Byron your real name?" Kelly offered a rebuttal.

"Yeah, and proud of it."

"By for short?"

"Byron for short."

"It's a great name. Very unique."

"Quit lying. Another rule. Don't lie to me. You don't like my name. Everybody I've ever met tries to give me a nickname. I want my real name, Byron Irving, the one my parents gave me. Is something wrong with that?"

"Nothing at all."

"Were you ever a driver before?" Byron launched his questioning again. "Have you ever been to driving school?"

"No, but I come from a long line of drivers."

"I come from a long line of surgeons. Got a knife on you?"

"No, I do not, and you better not be carrying one either."

"Married?"

"No, almost, but I—" Kelly caught herself before she mentioned Damean. Byron had her so wrapped up in banter that she wasn't thinking clearly. "No, I'm not married."

"But what?"

"I never got married. That's all."

"So, you're all alone?"

"I really don't care to discuss it, if you don't mind."

"Why not?"

"Why so many personal questions?"

"I have a right to know what sort of person is driving me around this city all day long, don't I? I'm putting my life in your hands, and I want to be sure you're not some ex-con or child molester or..."

"We both know your father would run a thorough security check before hiring a driver."

"Oh, so you know my father, do you?"

"No, I haven't met him yet, but—"

"Then you don't know what my father would do. Answer the question. Why did it end? You and that person you almost married?"

Kelly thought carefully before responding. "Irreconcilable differences."

"In other words, you aren't going to tell me."

"How about you? Girlfriend?"

"Hello. This is me interviewing you, not the other way around, and I'm done now. I have an algebra test to get ready for. I need some peace and quiet. In fact..." Byron used his rotary knob to lower the privacy screen, separating the front and rear seats.

Kelly called back, "I thought you hate blinds?" She met Byron's glare in the rearview mirror as the privacy screen formed a wall between them, lowering slowly over Byron's forehead, eyes, nose, mouth, chin...until he was gone.

What a nice kid. I bet he has lots of friends at school. A regular class clown. An all-around fun guy. Kelly collected herself. She wouldn't fall for that again. *Professional, Kelly. All business from here on out.*

After a period of blissful silence, they arrived at Madison Academy, a stately brick and stone mansion in the Upper East. It reminded Kelly of a miniature castle. The sides rose into turrets at each end, and most of the building was covered in dark ivy, lending an air of intrigue to the place. A tree-lined walkway led from the curb to the grand entrance—a bright red double door.

As Kelly pulled up to the curb, Byron lowered the privacy screen and said, "Do *not* open my door. I will open my own door whenever I'm at school."

"Fine."

Kelly waited in the driver's seat, but nothing happened. Byron did not budge. His notebook had been tucked safely within his backpack. The tray table had been returned to its upright position. The footrest lowered. The massage setting off.

She had to ask. "What are you waiting for?"

"I am waiting for six forty-five. I always go in at exactly six forty-five."

"Why?"

"Because that is what I always do."

"Well, there's no reason to ruin a good routine." She watched the dashboard digital clock: 6:43, 6:44, 6:45 and *pop!* The back door flew open, and Byron sprang out in one swift movement and slammed the door behind him before Kelly had a chance to say anything more, like "Have a nice day" or "See you later." The object in motion stayed in motion as it moved up the front walkway and through the front doors. Classmates were congregating on the snowy lawn, chatting, laughing, but Byron ignored them all. He was on a mission. Get into the building at precisely the correct time, partake of the breakfast he refused to eat at home (Kelly imagined some type of eggs Benedict or avocado toast with a side of caviar) and be seated in his first classroom by 7 a.m. Prompt perfection.

Good grief.

But Kelly couldn't leave. Not yet. Her instructions had been to remain parked at the curb for one full hour to be sure this kid didn't escape. This made no sense whatsoever. A boy like that who did everything according to a rigid plan did not skip school. There must have been more to this story. She leaned back against the headrest and waited. She watched the morning sunlight strike the porcelain rose at different angles. She played soft spa-like music, then eighties rock, then some disco. She glanced at the vacant school grounds. No sign of a prison break. No five-foot villain propelling from the second-floor window by a bungee cord. No parachute off the rooftop. No wire-rimmed eyeglasses peeping from beneath a manhole cover.

This was ludicrous.

After about forty-five minutes, Kelly decided it was time to go.

Mr. Perez had instructed her to use the next couple of hours to clean the car and eat something. She wasn't really hungry, but it was now or never. Kelly drove the Rolls through a brushless car wash and placed her order at the drive-through window of Tim Hortons—a breakfast fajita and a coffee with two creams and three sugars. She opened the wrapper on her lap, using it as a sort of paper plate, and nibbled the fajita as she made her way back to the garage. She had a mouthful of sausage and eggs when she saw Mr. Perez standing at the top of the ramp, motioning frantically at her.

"Why weren't you answering your phone?" His voice grew louder as she rolled down her window. "Where on earth have you been!"

"I washed the car and grabbed something to eat like you told me."

"You washed the Rolls? Where would you wash a Rolls-Royce in the city of New York? We have our own facility here, specifically designed for these expensive automobiles. I hope you didn't use any of those dirty wire brushes. Please reassure me you did not drive this Rolls into one of those bourgeoise automatic car washes? If there are any scratches, scuffs, even the most minuscule damage, Mr. Irving will take note. I assure you...he...he...What on earth are you stuffing into your mouth?"

"I found a brushless car wash." Kelly covered her food-filled mouth with her hand. "It's a breakfast fajita."

"You are not allowed to eat or drink inside this Rolls-Royce or any other automobile! Never. I don't care if you are starving and lightheaded and ready to faint. I don't care if it is a scorching summer afternoon and the temperature is over a hundred degrees and you are parched and dying of thirst, you are not permitted to consume any food or beverages within this automobile."

"Byron had a Coke on the way to school. I thought it was okay." Kelly stuffed the fajita inside the wrapper, trying to make it disappear.

"The rules for Mr. Byron do not apply to you. He is the son of a billionaire chief executive officer and you are the driver. Your sustenance may be found here in this refrigerator. There is an array of fresh delicatessen sandwiches and soups and a microwave in the office."

"Listen, I'm so sorry, Mr. Perez. I would never do something that you would disapprove of, but you never told me any of this."

"I most certainly did. Now, where is that mobile phone I gave you this morning?"

Kelly had forgotten to link the phone to the Bluetooth. She cringed as she freed it from her coat pocket.

Mr. Perez leaned into the vehicle, snatched the phone from her hand, and slammed it into the Rolls's charging station.

"Park the car." He stretched his arm in the direction of an open spot. "I will clean this mess up myself. Go into the back office. Finish your grotesque and nauseating fast food meal, use the restroom, and wash your hands." Mr. Perez had a crazed look in his eye. "Oh, one more thing I neglected to tell you: Do not relieve yourself inside this automobile."

"How ridiculous." Kelly exited the auto. "I would never do anything like that."

Mr. Perez hovered over two feet above her. "From this point forward, I am going to make absolutely certain to state each and every instruction in the utmost detail. In this way, I can rest assured you are able to clearly comprehend."

"Mr. Perez, honestly, I was trying to follow orders. I found a brushless car wash, and I got a fajita. I wasn't even hungry, but you told me I should clean the car and eat now. There's no mess to clean up. Well, Byron did spill his Coke but I wiped that clean. I promise. And by the way, now that you brought it up, what if I do have to use a bathroom? Am I allowed to stop somewhere for that? And one more thing: I was wondering if I have an expense account of some kind. Because I used my own credit card for the car wash and the food, and—"

"You have no expense account." Mr. Perez clutched his head. "Oh no, no, no...please do not tell me you filled the gas tank."

"I didn't need any gas yet."

"Thank God!" He shook both hands toward the heavens. "This is what we get when we hire an inexperienced driver. Whom did they expect? Dale Earnhardt?"

"With all due respect, I think Dale Earnhardt is dead."

"I am fully aware of that fact. I was speaking metaphorically. Oh, never mind." Mr. Perez pointed to the break room. "You have thirty minutes. Get on with it."

Kelly watched Mr. Perez open a steel cabinet. The shelves were filled with fluffy chamois cloths, glass cleaners, room fresheners and other supplies. He swiped a towel from the shelf and began buffing the Rolls's sides.

The first day of work wasn't going very well. Kelly inched a little closer to Mr. Perez. "Listen, I'm really sorry. It won't happen again. You're right. I've never been a driver before. To tell you the truth, this isn't my dream job. I never wanted this job. But it's good, steady work, and I'm grateful to have it. I need the money and the health benefits. Not just me, but my family. You can be sure of one thing—I'm going to do my very best."

Mr. Perez dropped the towel to his side. He looked at Kelly as if he were seeing her for the very first time.

Kelly knew she had said too much, once again. Would her mouth ever stay shut? Didn't she have any self-control? She backtracked. "What I meant was, I'm really happy now that I'm here. I really like this job. Well, it's only been half a day, but so far, I do like it, in a way. It's better than bartending. Let me say that much. I really believe I belong here; that's what my dad thinks, anyway. My great-grandfather, my grandfather, my dad—they were all drivers, and my dad thinks I—"

"Stop right there." Mr. Perez jutted his chin. "O'Sullivan. As in Seamus O'Sullivan?"

She nodded. "That's my dad. Do you know him?"

"I have had the pleasure of meeting Mr. O'Sullivan on several occasions. We lunched at the Katz Deli counter quite often over the years. I enjoyed a good matzo ball soup, and he a corned beef sandwich."

Mr. Perez fell into a far-off expression. "We would solve the world's problems within the hour. Those were the days." Then back at Kelly. "That gentleman was an excellent driver, a man of integrity; however, his beliefs...Let me simply say, he possessed some very outrageous opinions."

"He still does."

"I'm sorry to say I had to properly educate that man on several current affairs matters."

This, Kelly highly doubted. She offered a surprised expression, and Mr. Perez smirked.

"Give him my regards, and as far as all this..." Mr. Perez waved a hand toward the Rolls. "This disaster never occurred. It was a moment shared between the two of us that, I might add, will never happen again. Go into the break room, pull yourself together, and when you appear a second time, we shall begin again." He raised his hand in triumph. "I am a believer in second chances. Sometimes even third and fourth chances as well." He dropped his hand. "Lucky for you."

"Thank you. It will never happen again. I can promise you that."

As Kelly moved toward the office, Mr. Perez added, "How was your morning with Mr. Byron?"

"Just fine. No problems at all."

"Is that so?" He clicked his tongue. "The fact that you believe it went well is more concerning than your car wash. It appears that lad has you wrapped around his hormonal teenage finger. This means trouble. The day you return to this garage and declare that boy to be an absolute diabolical scoundrel is the day I will rest assured that all is fine."

"Oh, he's not all that bad."

"Hmpf."

Kelly closed the door to the break room, sank into the velvet sofa and pulled the throw over her lap. Okay, so this was going to be a little more challenging than she had imagined, but it truly wasn't all that bad, because those people didn't know what a hard day really was. Mr. Perez was frantic over nothing at all.

A car wash. A fajita.

A kid who only eats the school breakfast.

When your problems were very small, the least little catastrophe could bring you to your knees, but when your problems were big, the worst that could happen only made you stronger.

Kelly knew what a hard day was, and this wasn't even close.

Although she hadn't met the infamous Mr. Irving yet.

4

Chapter Four

At 10 a.m., Kelly pulled the Rolls up to Fifteen Central Park West and took her position beside the passenger door. She offered a half wave to Jack, but he disregarded her. The snow had subsided, and Jack manned his post outdoors again. He seemed to be preoccupied with a small brown paper bag. He lifted the bag to his lips, took a few gulps, then tucked it behind the cast iron urn that flanked the entrance doors. A sturdy evergreen shrub had been planted inside the urn for the holiday season. Kelly had to admit it was a clever hiding spot.

When Jack finished his stealth maneuver, he noted Kelly's attention and offered her an accusatory stare in return. In fact, his expression was almost baiting, but Jack had nothing to worry about. It was none of Kelly's business, and she planned to keep it that way.

She fixed her attention on the lobby, and a soft figure appeared. It was a woman, hourglass shape. She glided from the elevator to the glass doors like a model on a catwalk. Her hips swayed gently, and her feet pounced delicately forward, one foot directly in front of the other. She wore skin-tight black leggings with a matching snug nylon jacket, a fur hat, fur boots, and oversized black designer sunglasses that concealed not only her eyes but most of her face.

Jack held the door open. He offered a little curtsy and mumbled some humdrum morning greeting, but the woman did not respond. In fact, Kelly was certain she was not even aware that someone had opened the door for her. That made two people today who had completely disregarded the doorman. The woman marched onward, purposefully intent on the day ahead.

But something more. Something rushed, almost desperate.

Kelly opened the side door. "Good morning, Miss Carolyn."

Carolyn paused, surveying Kelly through her dark lenses. "*You* are the new driver?"

"Yes. My very first day."

Carolyn lifted her sunglasses. "A woman."

"Yes, again. Kelly O'Sullivan."

"My, oh my." Carolyn slid into the back seat. "Very interesting."

Kelly took her place behind the steering wheel. "Where would you like me to take you on this beautiful morning?"

"Okay, so, Miss Kelly O'Sullivan, I'm going to let you in on a little secret, something just between us two girls. I like to veer from the schedule now and then. I don't like to be so very...predictable, so...boring. I absolutely hate this demand that I present my entire schedule for the upcoming week."

"Yes, that's pretty much what they told me. So, where to?"

"Really? They told you all that? So, they actually noticed." Carolyn mused. "Two surprises in one day. Could change be in the air? I highly doubt it. Marcus Irving hasn't done anything different since he first held a calculator in his hand. No surprises coming there. But me? I am always up for a change in routine. Please take me to Aman."

In yoga pants and a running jacket? "A spa day?" Kelly coaxed a friendly conversation.

"Let's call it coffee with a friend."

"On our way to Aman." Kelly pulled the Rolls gently away from the curb. Traffic remained heavy at this hour, and she wondered how long this supposed "coffee with a friend" might take. Kelly had to be back in time for the dog walker.

Carolyn's voice from the back seat. "So, what was that you were saying? It's a beautiful day? Really? It's New York City in December, for God's sake. It's cold and snowy and windy and downright horrific outside. This is the reason people leave New York in the winter. But not us. Never us. We are far too busy. We go away, the month of July, the exact same house in the Hamptons, the exact same restaurants, the exact same people, year after year. Well, let me rephrase that: for the past three years I've been with him, that's where we've gone. Although I did hear he's gone to that house there every summer since he was a boy. I am not without sentimental nostalgia. But that one house in the Hamptons? Only that house? Year after year after year?"

Although she knew better, Kelly glanced at Carolyn in the rearview mirror. There was no denying the fact that Miss Carolyn was a beautiful woman. High cheekbones, upturned nose, perfect jawline, but something was off. Like Carolyn's rehearsed stride through the lobby earlier, and her expression was startled, desperate. Yes, probably some Botox side effects contributed, but an undeniable tenseness could not be erased.

Carolyn interpreted Kelly's blatant stare as an invitation to vent. "Oh, I know this all sounds very spoiled of me, but it is the very nature of his so-called vacation—predictable, controlling...like him. Everything in Marcus's world must operate exactly according to plan. Including me." She sighed. "What got me on this topic, anyway? Oh, yes, the beautiful weather we're supposedly having. I was hoping you were going to be different from the other drivers. Can we dispense with the small talk and be honest with each other? Girl to girl?"

Kelly was not here to entertain Miss Carolyn with meaningful conversation, but Kelly did need Carolyn to like her. It was obvious that Byron was not a fan. "Okay. You're right." Kelly conceded. "The weather is downright miserable. Cold, windy, cloudy. A typical winter day in the city, and yes, we are both stuck here instead of lying on some beautiful beach, sipping a frozen daiquiri."

Carolyn did nothing to hide her grin.

"But," Kelly added. "You are having a coffee at the fabulous Aman Hotel, and I'll be sitting outside waiting in the car."

Carolyn took the bait. "Why, Kelly, are you implying that sipping a coffee at Aman is better than driving this magnificent Rolls-Royce around all day?" Carolyn flipped open a compact and applied a pink shade of lipstick.

"I would guess that whatever you're really doing at Aman would be better than sitting outside in a car." Oh, Kelly shouldn't have said that. Why did she say that?

Carolyn snapped both her compact and her attention back, and her grin fell into a smirk. "I do like you after all. Go on. So, you think I'm up to something. What made you arrive at that conclusion?"

"I didn't mean that. I don't know why I said it."

"Please. I'm curious. Tell me what you really think."

"Well...Let me first say that I don't care what you're doing in there. It's none of my business. I'm the driver. I'll take you wherever you want to go and bring you back home when you're finished."

"But...go on. This is resourceful information. Exactly what am I unintentionally revealing?"

"I have never even been inside Aman, but I feel pretty certain that there is some sort of a dress code in that restaurant, even if you're only having a coffee, and you're wearing yoga pants."

Miss Carolyn laughed out loud. "I wore this today because I did *not* want anyone to suspect a thing. I'm wearing gym clothes. Just another boring day running errands. It appears I have a driver who is quite cunning. I hope you rub off on me. So, my turn now. How about I offer you a little friendly observation in return?"

"I suppose that's only fair."

"You are a brave girl, Kelly O'Sullivan. Either very brave or very stupid to be talking to me this way on your very first day of work. Nobody, and I mean nobody, has ever dared to say anything but *Good morning, Miss Carolyn. Good night, Miss Carolyn. It's a beautiful day, Miss Carolyn. You look lovely today, Miss Carolyn. Blah, blah, blah.* I was hoping you would be different, but I'm not sure I was prepared for this much honesty. Let's set another ground rule. Your observations and these conversations will remain inside this car and just between the two of us."

"Absolutely. Of course. Just between the two of us."

Carolyn averted her attention to the opposite side of her window glass, seemingly losing herself in deeper thought. "By the way, I am not doing anything I shouldn't at Aman. And I don't know why I suddenly care about what the driver thinks about me. But, for the record, I'm not that kind of a woman."

"No explanation is necessary."

"In fact, I would like to say that I am, quite possibly, the only person in this family who is not doing something they shouldn't be doing."

"Of course." This was an appropriate time for less talking and more listening, like Dad had warned.

Several minutes of quiet contemplation weighed heavily between the front and back seat of the Rolls, until Carolyn abruptly asked, "Are you married, Kelly?"

Why was everyone asking Kelly if she was married today? "No."

"So, you're one of those girls who doesn't care to be tied down, is that it?"

"I'd love to be married...to the right person." Kelly thought of Daemen. His image appeared before her in the form of a man wearing a costume. A beautiful, charming costume, to hide what was truly lurking beneath. "I don't want somebody who is pretending to be the right person. Maybe that's getting a little too honest again, but you asked. Anyway, I don't know why I'm saying all this either."

Carolyn released a huff. "*Everybody* is pretending to be somebody else. Welcome to Manhattan."

Kelly could not argue with that, but she added, "They can pretend all they want, but they can't pretend forever." Damean had offered meaningless words to Kelly once, long ago, lies and secrets that she naively believed for far too long. By the time Kelly removed his mask, it was too late—she had fallen for him...and she was pregnant. He had been gone for three years now, and she did not miss him. Sure, Kelly missed the person Damean had pretended to be, but she did not miss the real man. Daemen was two entirely different people in one body.

Carolyn gauged Kelly. "It sounds like you're talking from personal experience."

"I might be."

"Go on, then. Keep talking. They can't pretend forever? Why not?"

"They can pretend until real life gets too real, and it's impossible to pretend anymore."

"So true...for them...and for us." Carolyn mused for some time. "The takeaway from this conversation: I should just wear my usual designer outfits from now on." She offered a sly wink as she lowered the privacy screen. That made the second passenger today who preferred to be separated from their new driver for the remainder of the trip.

Kelly didn't regret what she had said because she wasn't only saying those words to Carolyn; she was reminding herself to be exactly who she was, to never change for anybody or anything. No matter how tough life got.

And yet, here she was, a driver for a wealthy family. The one person Kelly vowed she would never be.

***

Aman was one of New York's most luxurious hotels. Located inside the old Crown Building, it was known for its pure opulence, garden terrace and spa, private suites and residences. The shining jewel of Fifth Ave. boasted an ostentatiously high price tag.

Kelly opened the Rolls's door and Carolyn stepped out gingerly, still strutting her sleek catwalk. As she swept up the few steps to Aman, Kelly called out, "Have a nice coffee, Miss Carolyn."

Carolyn glanced over her shoulder and gave Kelly another wink.

"One more thing," Kelly added. "There's no rush, but I have to be back uptown to pick up the dog walker by noon."

"The dog walker?" Carolyn sent Kelly a couldn't-care-less wave. "You probably shouldn't have told me that because now I'm taking my own sweet time."

Time at what? Kelly couldn't help but wonder as she waited in the Rolls, staring at that porcelain rose until the petals melted and the dashboard began to shimmer like a mirage. It was none of Kelly's business, just like Dad had warned. It didn't matter what Carolyn was doing with whom. The only thing that mattered was that steady paycheck.

But after thirty minutes, Kelly needed to use the restroom. A predicament had been created, by Kelly's own doing, as usual. Carolyn could not see Kelly roaming around inside that hotel. Carolyn would immediately suspect that Kelly was snooping, and she was *not*. Kelly would not jeopardize this job under any circumstance. She needed this paycheck more than anyone like Carolyn could ever understand. Kelly surveyed the street for alternative restroom possibilities, but finding none, she ventured into the hotel. She had no choice. A quick in-and-out.

The lobby at Aman was minimalist, simplistic elegance, discreet and shadowed, and anyone other than guests was unwelcome. Security guarded the entryway, and after explaining her position as the driver of the Rolls-Royce currently parked at the curb and awaiting its owner, she was given directions to the restroom. *Follow the bar to the end and turn right* seemed simple enough.

The Aman bar unfolded in all its glittering marble and brass and crystal, and Kelly followed instructions. But the security guard did not mention the fact that the bar was open to the restaurant, and Kelly did something that was not included in the directions to the restroom. She paused. Carolyn was seated at the far table by the window—legs crossed, coffee in one hand, pen in the other. She was engrossed in a deep conversation with an older, suited, professional-looking woman. Carolyn was taking notes, lots of them.

A waiter blocked Kelly's view. "Table for one?"

"No, I'm...just using the restroom."

"We get a few drivers during the day, stopping in for a coffee or something a little stronger. You can have a seat at the bar if you like."

"No, no. Just the restroom. The end of the bar?" Kelly jutted her hand in the direction she intended to go, and as she did, she struck the waiter's tray of carefully balanced glassware, and his crystal tower fell to the floor with an expensive crash that jolted the five-star restaurant.

Everyone turned to gawk, including Carolyn, who witnessed the waiter scrambling on all fours to pick up the broken pieces and Kelly hovering above him in a stupefied daze.

Carolyn's face flushed; her lips pursed. She blinked once, very loudly (if blinks had sound), and then she returned to her meeting.

Kelly finished her business and returned to the car, rehearsing her story: she had been using the restroom. Wasn't she allowed to go to the bathroom now and then? She had not known the restroom was adjacent to the restaurant. The hotel gave her permission...

Carolyn slammed the car door. "So, did he hire you to spy on me? Is that what's going on here? Why can't he trust me? He's never home, never, and I'm fine with that, but when he does finally come home, he only pays attention to that dog walker and those dogs of his. But now this?" She wasn't shouting. She was mumbling to herself, trying to sort it all out in her own mind.

"He did not hire me to spy on you," Kelly assured. "I promise. I went in to use the restroom. That's all."

"You did not. You were standing in that restaurant, blatantly staring at me. I suppose you snapped a few pics? Go right ahead. I am *not* having an affair. Although, there have been a few times when the notion has crossed my mind...But I wouldn't. I couldn't. That's not who I have ever been or who I want to be. Who am I, anyway? Who have I become? I am simply trying to—"

"I was on my way to the restroom"—Kelly rubbed her temples with both thumbs—"but then I knocked that tray of glasses over."

"If you are going to be driving me around all day, and I'm going to be seeing you more than I see Marcus, the very least we can do is be truthful with one another." Carolyn sighed.

"Miss Carolyn. I am being totally honest here when I say that I went into Aman to use the bathroom. I couldn't wait another minute, and in case you haven't noticed, it's not easy to find a public restroom with adequate Rolls-Royce parking."

"Ah, the perils of the Rolls-Royce driver." Carolyn considered Kelly. "I suppose that is true."

"I haven't even met Mr. Irving yet. I'm hired to be the driver. Just the driver, nothing more."

"Hmmm." Carolyn's attention drifted toward the window and the hotel beyond. "I don't have a lot of friends; in case you were wondering. Not real friends, anyway. And I must admit, it feels good to talk to another woman."

Kelly remained decidedly quiet.

Carolyn continued. "Well, if you must know, that was an editor I've been working with. I'm writing a few short stories, and I'm trying desperately to get them published." She shot Kelly a stern look. "Do not tell a soul. Promise me."

"What happens in the Rolls stays in the Rolls, and all that sort of thing." Kelly couldn't help but ask, "But why is that such a big secret?"

"They're stories about..." Carolyn twisted her hands. "My life. Marcus's life. Our world. The lifestyle. Our circle. People...friends...business associates...They would not be pleased if these stories were made public, but that editor believes some secrets are meant to be told. She's coaching me, helping me. She says she adores my work, that I have tremendous potential."

"Mr. Irving doesn't know about all this?"

"Marcus, of all people, can never know."

"Well, he's going to find out when those stories get published. So are all the friends and business associates you're referring to."

"*If* they're published. I've been writing for a year." Carolyn huffed. "Marcus doesn't know that either. I have two novels that I couldn't sell. This editor believes my short stories will be my entrée into the publishing world. I'll garner a good following, build a solid platform, and then I can resubmit my novels again."

"I mean no offense by this, but...well...you asked for honesty..."

"What? Please say." Carolyn threw both hands up. "Why stop now?"

"That editor likes your secrets, especially the ones about Mr. Irving. I'm not saying your writing isn't good, but maybe give her something even better."

"What on earth could be better?" Carolyn tilted her head back in laughter. "A murder? It's not that I haven't contemplated that scenario on many occasions, but really?"

Stopped in traffic, Kelly turned back to face Carolyn, eye-to-eye, girl to girl. "Nobody wants to hear about your parties or your designer clothes or your problems that aren't problems for the rest of us. Oh, they're fun for a while, maybe entertaining, but they don't really matter. I'm not trying to offend you here."

Carolyn's chin dropped. "No offense taken. Keep talking."

Kelly hesitated, unsure how to steer this conversation. Carolyn was like a storm—unpredictable and mysterious and stirring beneath the surface. And although Kelly didn't really know Carolyn yet, she couldn't shake the feeling that Carolyn defied those stereotypical assumptions. There was something unexpected about this woman. "Tell them something about you. The real you. How you feel, how you think, what you want, what you long for. Maybe show them you're not so different from the rest of us. We've heard all that other gossip. Sure, it sells in the tabloids, *The Real Housewives of Wherever*, but it doesn't last because it doesn't resonate. It's not important. What we want, what everybody really wants, is to hear something we can all relate to, learn from. Tell us your hopes, your dreams, your heartaches, your joys. Your sad and your happy. They go together, hand in hand."

Kelly felt a lump in her throat. Daemen again. Would Kelly's scars never heal? "Tell us the truth," she said.

Traffic moved again, and Carolyn began taking notes, writing fervently on that same pad of paper she had used with her editor.

"I mean, what do *you* want to be known for?" Kelly watched for Carolyn's reaction in the rearview mirror. "Give the editor all the stuff she never knew she needed. The treasures. Not the garbage."

Carolyn gnawed at her nail. "What if she rejects it?"

"Don't worry about that. Worry about what she prints. Who do you want to be? Someone who breached the confidence of your friends and family? Or someone who said the things they always wished they could say?"

Silence the remainder of the way back to the penthouse. Kelly opened the door for Carolyn, but this time their interaction was different.

Carolyn cocked her head, as if seeing Kelly anew. "Thank you for so much more than a car ride, Kelly O'Sullivan."

"My pleasure, Miss Carolyn."

Carolyn, quite suddenly, leaned in and grabbed Kelly in a warm embrace. Not only did the hug astonish her, but so did the emotion behind it.

With that alarmingly intimate interaction, the expression of Jack, the doorman, turned to sheer horror. Kelly sent him a friendly wave, to which Jack scoffed. The fact that Jack—the longest-standing member, but also the most unwelcoming member, of this cast—was suddenly demoted to least favorite was sort of satisfying.

Now onto the dog walker—the most highly esteemed servant on the pay list, according to Mr. Perez and Carolyn. And on to the two labradoodles, Peter and Nicholas. Who didn't love a dog? These passengers should be a snap.

Within minutes, Miss Claire appeared, wearing head-to-toe skin-tight Lululemon workout gear and an expensive-looking down puffer jacket. She gripped the reins of two very well-behaved, perfectly coiffed strawberry-blond labradoodles. Each dog looked to weigh about a hundred pounds, and Miss Claire appeared much the same. The dogs did not tug on their leashes. Their movement was synchronized with Claire's. When Claire moved, the dogs moved. When Claire stopped, the dogs stopped, awaiting instruction.

Kelly opened the door for all three. "Good morning, Miss Claire."

"Hi there." Claire did not try to hide her flat Midwest accent. She approached the Rolls, raised her tone to alto and clapped once. "Dogs. Inside." The dogs obeyed. One after another, they leaped into the back seat and took their places on the floor. Claire leaped in beside them, and with that, she was buckled in and ready to go, looking out the front window expectantly. Kelly honestly suspected she heard three mouths panting instead of two.

Back behind the wheel, Kelly eyed Claire in the rearview mirror. She wore a shoulder-length bob hairstyle, the same shade as the dogs. Her eyes were soft, her features petite. She had a clean-cut sort of look, like a Midwestern farm girl—little makeup, freckles, naturally pretty, naturally fit.

But something was different, something off. Claire was the first passenger of the day who did not care to know the new driver's name. Kelly should have introduced herself, but somehow it seemed senseless now. Claire was disinterested in her surroundings. The Rolls was obviously nothing more than a mode of transportation, not much different from a train or bus or bicycle, and the Rolls' driver, much the same.

Kelly headed toward Central Park. "What path will you take to walk the dogs?" she asked. "I'll circle the park and try to keep you in sight."

"Oh, you don't have to do all that. Drop us off at the entrance at 59th and 5th, and we'll meet you back there in two hours."

"But I was told to follow you from the street. It's no trouble at all."

"No thanks. I'm just fine walking the dogs alone. I like it better that way. You can tell them you followed me and give yourself a break. John used to go to some corner bar. Don went to the gym. Scott went back home and took a nap or whatever. It'll be our little secret."

More secrets, but this one could be a gift. Two full hours every day, in the middle of the afternoon, to go back home? Claire had no idea what she had just offered Kelly. The park was minutes from Kelly's apartment, maybe twenty if Kelly cut through the center and took the side streets. This was, well, this was everything. "Thank you" was all Kelly could muster.

"Keep this just between us."

Kelly swallowed a lump in her throat. "These two hours mean more to me than you could ever know." She tried to catch Claire's attention in the mirror. "I need to be home as much as I can."

"I didn't ask."

"I can't thank you enough."

"Listen, I really don't care." Claire snapped her attention from the dogs to Kelly, and her bob sprang back and forth. "I need these two hours more than you do. Believe me. Anything to get out of that house, those cameras watching us everywhere inside that place except the bathrooms. I'm just assuming there's no cameras in the bathrooms. That would be illegal, wouldn't it? Oh, never mind. We'll never find out, anyway." Claire smoothed a few unruly wisps of her hair. "Nobody wants to talk about it. I'm not talking about it, but I am getting out of that house every single day for as long as I can. So, whatever it is you have to do, go for it. Freedom never felt so good."

Cameras? So, Marcus Irving had to be the reason all those drivers quit. It had to be him, because although these three passengers had problems, they were not *the* problem. Cameras and microphones—that was the problem. Kelly began scanning the Rolls. If inside the house, then why not the car, too? What sort of crazed, paranoid man was she working for?

Claire read Kelly's mind. "There's no cameras in here. I made sure of that. New York State law says you can videotape somebody without consent except in cases where"—Claire hooked her fingers like quote signs—"persons have a reasonable expectation of privacy, in which case it becomes trespassing." She dropped her hands. "I told Marcus this car is my reasonable expectation of privacy and do *not* go there. So, welcome to the family. You're the only one who's safe around here."

Kelly was speechless, and yet she couldn't help but wonder if any of this was true. Byron would never tolerate something like that, from what she knew of him. And Carolyn? No possible way.

Claire's door swung open before the Rolls came to a full stop. "Meet me back here in two hours," she ordered. "I don't like to stand around on the sidewalk. It isn't safe around here, so be on time." Claire leaped out with the dogs following. She marched into the park entrance, tugging the leashes far too harshly. The larger golden decided to sit, and Miss Claire gave him a swift boot in the hindquarter, which made Kelly shudder. That act caused the smaller golden to pull his leash in the opposite direction. Those dogs did not want to walk with Claire inside that park. Kelly watched the dogs resist, as best they could, until they finally surrendered, ears down, tails hanging low.

Kelly had been making a lot of promises that day. *Don't tell anybody anything. Don't complain about anything. Don't share any secrets.* But this was different. Kelly didn't approve of the way Claire treated those sweet pups. She planned to tell Mr. Perez about this one. Kelly also planned to ask Mr. Perez about those cameras. If there were any hidden surveillance inside this automobile, he would be fully aware, and Kelly would have the right to know, legal or not.

She put the entire matter from her mind for now. Kelly had been gifted two beautiful, precious hours at home. She couldn't wait to tell Dad. He was the only one who would understand, the only one who knew what Kelly's life had been like. Dad would nod, and then he would say something like, "The job always had its perks. I tried to tell you that, Kel. It's the best job in America—that's what it is. The best job in the whole wide world."

***

Kelly headed across town, and since traffic was light, she made it in record time. Her apartment was serene when she stepped inside, soft music playing, some laughter. A palpable peace filled the one-room basement apartment that had never been felt there before.

Mrs. Andrews welcomed the surprise visit. It was good for everyone, she said. She worked around Kelly's presence, maintaining their routine without upsetting the focus.

Kelly sat on the floor cross-legged for two solid hours, doing nothing but being present and inhaling the sight of her beautiful daughter, Rose, engaged in learning and the world around her. Everything was already so much better with Mrs. Andrews. Kelly memorized Rose's every new expression—the delight, the curiosity, the joy. Each word spoken, every giggle, every awestruck sigh. Mrs. Andrews welcomed Kelly to participate in the learning and in the therapy. In this short time, Kelly learned alongside Rose.

Kelly learned that soft noises were better than no noises. "Sometimes, in order to ease the pain of a child with chronic migraines,"

Mrs. Andrews explained, "we focus on treating the child and not only the migraine. We offer a soothing, calm environment. A space that comforts and relaxes. Games and lessons that shift the focus from the pain and onto something different."

As Kelly watched her precious three-year-old daughter, a new fear simmered within Kelly's heart. How long would Kelly be able to sneak home like this? It sounded as if Claire had been giving her drivers time off for quite a while, but circumstances could change. What if Claire changed her mind? What if Mr. Irving fired Claire and hired a new dog walker? What if the dogs got sick? And what about the weather? Would it be too cold or too rainy to walk the dogs?

And once again, happy and sad joined together as the innumerable possibilities of everything that could go wrong consumed everything that had already gone right until the room shrank. The air was sucked into places where air disappeared when you needed it most. Kelly's palms began to sweat. She felt light-headed.

She dropped her head between her knees and pretended she was resting, closing her eyes for a minute or two. The noises on the city street above—car horns, barking dogs, people shouting—fueled her anxiety. The echoes of a city that rushed on, despite the despair and sorrow within it. Kelly withdrew inside the peaceful place created by Mrs. Andrews. Not only was her apartment now a safe haven for little Rose, but maybe for Kelly as well.

Tears of sadness and tears of joy dropped from Kelly's eyes onto the rough concrete floor. She watched them pitter-patter. Little circles darkened the gray cement. One tear slid across the floor and rolled into that stubborn puddle of city water that pooled after any rainfall or snowfall. Kelly had tried to mop it up over the years, but it persisted and returned, over and over again. It wanted to stay, and Kelly had finally given up. Her little tear seemed to be attracted to that puddle like a magnet, and the two liquids combined until one water could not be differentiated from the other. Kelly wondered: if she were able to gather her past three years of tears, how much larger would that puddle be? Would it cover the entire floor? Seep out the windows and flood the sidewalk? It was very possible.

Oh, there had been smiles over the years, too; Mom had made absolutely certain of that. She had shown Kelly that the joy of life was found in relationships—the good, the difficult, the challenging. The wonder of family and friends. That was everything to Kelly's mom, who came from nothing. Mom had no lofty goals or prestigious purpose. But she was always looking on the bright side and showing everyone else the way.

And there had been so much love over these past three years that could not be extinguished by anything or anyone. Despite the circumstances—Damean leaving without even a note. The only thing Damean left behind was more pain and heartache, and that had been quite purposeful. Despite his desire to harm his family in return for the trouble they had supposedly caused him, there was a lot of love after Damean left. Maybe even stronger than ever before because of his cruelty? Because of Rose's illness? Sometimes, you had to believe that.

Kelly stood. Claire and the dogs would be waiting shortly, and she couldn't be late. She wiped her wet eyes with her forearm and said the goodbye she'd been dreading.

Just stay on schedule the rest of the day, follow the rules, keep their secrets, don't complain, and you'll be back home soon, Kelly promised herself this time.

5

CHAPTER FIVE

A t the end of the school day, Kelly found herself the third car in
a long line of limos and Rolls-Royces and town cars, all parked
at the curb of Madison Academy, awaiting their clients' children. She
spotted Byron tucked amid the hurried crowd streaming out of the
school doors—the same crowd that had entered with anticipation and
excitement this morning. The kids were still chatting and joking and
poking each other.

But not Byron. He was hunched over and downtrodden as he
studied the sidewalk and his mobile phone simultaneously. The boy
must have had eyes on the top of his head because he was walking without looking where he was going. Kelly remembered Byron's
specific instructions this morning—do *not* open the door for him at
school—and then she recalled the rest: the heated seat, the Coke, the
footrest.

She had forgotten them all.

Kelly jumped out and hurriedly adjusted Byron's settings, and just
as she was about to lower the tray table, a voice came from behind.

"What do you think you're doing?" Byron's forehead wrinkled like
an old man's.

Kelly forced a smile. "I'm fixing everything the way you like it."

"Not here. You're supposed to do that before you come and get me." His voice was trembling. "It's supposed to be ready by the time I get in. You are not supposed to get out of the car."

"I know. I know. I'm so sorry. I forgot the drink."

"I gave you one chance this morning. One. Because you were new. But now this is two chances. Three chances, and you're fired."

"I do have other passengers," Kelly said. "I'm trying to please everybody here, not just you, Byron, so if it takes me a day or two to get it straight, can you cut me a break?"

"Oh. So, I was right about the IQ thing."

That was downright rude, and Kelly couldn't do a thing about it. She watched Byron set his backpack on the seat beside him in the exact same position as this morning: upright, forward-facing. Then he removed his gloves and placed them in the exact same manner: right side up, fingers forward, spread equally apart.

Byron cut Kelly a look. "Well? What are you waiting for? Get in the driver's seat."

Kelly returned to her post and inhaled a few deep, calming breaths. The truth was, she had let the kid down. High school was not Byron's happy place. That was obvious. She was not trying to worsen his already anxious mental state.

"I'll have everything ready from now on." She pulled into traffic.

No response. Byron had removed a spiral binder and lost himself in study.

Kelly tried again. "You'll see tomorrow morning. Heat, massage, Coke, tray. I got it. Even the umbrella."

Nothing.

Kelly needed this kid to like her, even a little, before his dad returned home. She studied his bent head and tried a different approach. "What are you studying? How was that algebra test?"

A look of appalling disgust met her in the mirror. "You are not supposed to be talking to me, and get your eyes on the road."

"Why not? I talk to Carolyn and Claire."

"Well, no surprise with Carolyn, but Claire? Really? She doesn't even talk to Peter and Nicholas, and she spends the whole day with our dogs. Claire speaks a different language."

"Yeah, I noticed her accent. Midwest or something."

"I'm not talking about *that* language."

"Oh, okay, whatever that means."

"You wouldn't understand." Byron focused on his notebook again.

"For what it's worth, nobody understands algebra. Is that what you're studying? Don't tell your teacher I said this, but it's a big waste of time because you'll memorize all those formulas and never use them again as long as you live. Unless you plan on becoming a rocket scientist. I guess you might use a little algebra there. No place else in the whole world but rocket scientry. Is that even a word? Scientry?"

Byron scrunched his lips to hide a grin.

"Let me think." Kelly fought to keep that smile alive. "I know—you want to be an Engineer. Mechanical engineer, computer engineer. I'm not talking about the railroad kind."

"If you have to know, I'm studying my water polo plays. That's where you're taking me next." He avoided her gaze. "The Athletic Club, Central Park South."

Kelly reached for the itinerary sheet and held it up for Byron to view. "Not according to this. This says 'indoor golf, Hudson Yards.'"

"Two hands on the wheel. I quit golf a long time ago. Everybody seems to forget that, but it doesn't matter. Just take me to polo."

"What was wrong with golf?"

"Have you ever seen a golf course in this city? No, you have not, because there is no real golf here. It's all pretend. You stand on fake grass, you whack a ball onto a fake green, it hits a big net so it doesn't land in the river, and you go home. It's useless. Golf was Dad's idea. He secretly wishes I'd play football, like he did. But I hate football. All that chasing each other around and beating each other up. I don't have the heart for it."

"Could have fooled me."

"What?"

"Nothing."

Byron had heard Kelly's comment but was obviously ignoring it.

"So, what's water polo all about?" Kelly asked.

"You don't know?" His eyes brightened.

"No, and before you say it, it has nothing to do with my IQ."

Byron's shoulders shook with silent laughter. "So, there's two teams and you score goals by throwing the ball into the opposing net. There's a lot of skill involved." He measured Kelly's reaction in the mirror. "It's in the Olympics, you know. Plus, the swimsuits are cool. We wear the Speedo jammers with the blue stripe down the side."

"Very cool. What's your position?"

"Goalie."

"I've never seen a polo game."

"Match. It's called a match." Byron squinted at Kelly. "And do *not* come inside and watch. Stay in the car like you're supposed to."

"I wouldn't think of going inside. Why would I? I'll be too busy sitting out here in this beautiful Rolls-Royce." Kelly gestured toward the car's plush interior.

"That's what drivers do. They stay in the car. Focus on your driving. You can barely handle that."

"Excuse me. I happen to be a great driver."

"Yeah, right." Byron took a swig of Coke.

"I come from a long line of drivers."

"So you said. What a legacy." Byron pressed the button to lower the privacy screen, and as it slid downward, he added, "Goodbye." They drove the remainder of the way in silence while Byron reviewed his plays. Dad's warning came to mind: *"Don't do what kids tell you to do. They're leprechauns."* Was Kelly O'Sullivan actually driving a leprechaun through the streets of New York City? She chuckled. This mischievous trickster wasn't even wearing a green hat. And water polo seemed harmless enough. How much trouble could a leprechaun get into at water polo?

Kelly stopped at the front entrance of the Athletic Club and parked the Rolls in a no-parking zone. A perk of driving a Rolls-Royce was that it seemed like the laws and regulations of New York State's Department of Motor Vehicles no longer applied. She sat behind the wheel and waited for Byron to get out, but there was no motion from the rear doors.

He finally opened the privacy screen. "Well?" His eyes widened.

"Well, what? Did you forget something?"

"You need to open my door."

Kelly sprang to her feet, a little too lively, for added effect. She rounded the front fender at top speed, swung the door open and offered Byron a little curtsy. "Have a wonderful polo match, Mr. Byron."

"It's just a practice, and do *not* come inside."

"I wouldn't think of it. That's your dad's job, not mine," Kelly tested.

"You're right. My dad doesn't miss a game…when he's in town. He likes the sport now. He didn't know anything about it before. Like you. But I explained it all to him, and he likes it a lot now."

Kelly watched Byron's bent back as he sauntered toward the club. He was slouched, shuffling his feet again, and he was too skinny. She wondered if he had brought a snack, a protein bar or something. His Diet Coke was emptied from its cup, but a kid can't live on Coke. She called after him. "Did you get a snack?"

He frowned over his shoulder. "I don't need one." Then he disappeared inside the building.

No snack? How can a kid go to school all day long and then to water polo without some kind of nutrition bar or cookie or something? Kelly drove the Rolls to the bodega she'd seen on the way and picked up a couple of protein bars and a banana. She returned to the Athletic Club, parked the car, and did exactly what she should not do for the second time today.

She went inside.

The Athletic Club was a cavernous structure that smelled like chlorine and echoed with every step on the tile floor. There were two locker rooms, boys' and girls', and a set of stairs that led to the bleachers above the pool. Kelly tapped on the boys' locker room door for some time, then cracked the door open and called inside, "Byron?"

No response.

"Hello?"

She had no other choice but to climb the stairs. The bleachers overlooked an Olympic-size swimming pool, and Kelly found a spot on the aluminum bench. The splashing and sloshing of the water below proved the scrimmage had already begun. Two teams were in place. They wore different colored swim caps, fastened below the chin, and goggles. Byron was already in position as goalie. Kelly recognized him immediately. He appeared a little smaller than the other players, but he kept perfect pace with his teammates. He was using two hands to block the attacks. His arms shot out, left and right, tapping balls away from the net, then diving into the water to retrieve them.

Kelly was impressed, both with the game and with Byron.

But then something very odd occurred.

Byron raised his hand and motioned to the coach, the coach nodded, and Byron abandoned his post and took a seat on the bench with the extra players who were waiting their turn to join the game. The coach quickly replaced Byron with another teammate, who floundered about in the water and let in two goals. The new kid wasn't any good at all. Not like Byron.

About fifteen minutes later, Byron raised his hand again, and the coach put him back in. These periods of time-out continued throughout the entire scrimmage. Byron would play for about fifteen minutes, take a break, then re-enter.

In all sports, players were occasionally switched in and out of the game, but this was different. The coach was not pulling Byron from the game. Byron was pulling himself. But why?

The winning point occurred when Byron was still on the bench. The opposing team swam swiftly to the net and drove the ball with a hard downward serve. Byron's less-than-adequate replacement didn't have the skill for defense, and the ball hit the net dead center.

The crowd roared and Byron's eyes lifted to the bleachers. He scanned the benches as if he were searching for someone. He saw Kelly. He held to her, and his expression froze. A blank stare fixed on Kelly and held firm. The protein bars felt damp in her hand. She thought to wave them, show Byron why she had come, but at this point that would only agitate him. Byron clearly did not want to acknowledge

Kelly's presence in any way whatsoever. She was wearing the chauffeur uniform, after all. She couldn't blame him.

Kelly snuck away from the crowd, returned to the Rolls and waited by the side door.

After about thirty minutes, Byron appeared. He was wearing his school uniform again, his camel-hair coat, his leather gloves. But no hat. Even with his short buzz cut, Kelly could see his hair was still wet.

"You should dry your hair before coming out in this cold weather." She held the door open.

"Just tell me one thing." Byron slid into the back. "Why'd you do it? Why?"

Kelly tossed the protein bars onto the seat beside him. "I brought you a snack. You can't go from school to polo without some sort of snack."

When Kelly was behind the wheel, Byron continued ranting. "It. Is. None. Of. Your. Business." He pronounced each word purposefully and distinctly. "Do you understand English?"

"Yes, I understand, but I can't sit here and do nothing." She found the banana and tossed that into the back, too.

Byron swatted it away. "You are just the driver. Why can't you get that?"

"I'm a parent too, and I would never send my child to an after-school sport without a snack." Kelly didn't know that for certain, but she assumed it. She dreamed of it. She hoped for it. *Rose going to school? Rose playing an after-school sport?* It was a miraculously wonderful image.

A pause from the back seat. "You have a kid?" He did it again. Byron had a way of making Kelly confess more than she ever intended.

"Stop changing the subject," Kelly said softly. "Bring a snack from now on, and I won't come inside anymore."

"A son or a daughter?"

"Just eat your protein bar."

"So, you're not saying?"

"No."

"Okay, well, don't ever come in that pool again. Do you hear me?"

"Yes, I can hear you. We've been through all that before. I can hear you. You can hear me. I am smart enough. You are still learning." Kelly bit her lip.

Byron recoiled in disgust over that last remark, but before he had the opportunity at rebuttal, Kelly added, "By the way, it's a cool sport. I really like it. And you're good at it. You're the best goalie on the team. And you're right, those swimsuits are pretty cool. But why did you keep taking a break? Your team would have won if you stayed in, you know. That other kid gave that goal away."

Byron hesitated. "Coach wants everybody to have a chance to play, that's all." Then he changed the subject. "I'm late for Mandarin. Are you coming in there, too? It's not as exciting. Trust me on this one. I wanted to play the harp, but Dad thinks the harp is extinct. Like I said before, good music never dies." Byron combed his fingers through his hair. "Never mind all that. Just stay in the car. Actually, I have an idea. You go into Mandarin, and I'll stay in the car."

Kelly met Byron in the mirror, and they exchanged a smile through Byron's chewing and chomping lips. He had found the protein bars.

"How's that snack?" she asked.

"Tastes a little like cardboard, but the chocolate chips make up for it."

Byron popped another Coke and slurped, and they drove the remainder of the way to Mandarin with a mutual understanding...of some sort.

The last few hours of Kelly's first day of work progressed smoothly.

She picked up Carolyn and drove her to her happy hour or cocktail hour or whatever it was called. This evening's outfit was tight leather pants, a cropped top covered by a fur vest, and five-inch heeled over-the-knee boots. Carolyn looked more like a hooker, but it was not for Kelly to say. What did Kelly know about expensive designer fashion? She was suddenly grateful for the convenience and ease of her driver's uniform.

By eight o'clock that evening, the Irving Family was tucked snuggly within their penthouse, having enjoyed a day about town, thanks to their new driver, Kelly O'Sullivan, with perhaps some lighthearted conversation and good old common-sense advice. This job wasn't so bad after all. What was so tough about this?

But there was one family member Kelly hadn't met yet. Mr. Marcus Irving, CEO of CyberScape and, Kelly had a feeling, the self-proclaimed CEO of the Irving Family unit. But he wouldn't be home again for weeks.

In the meantime, the same daily schedule continued and became an easy routine. Carolyn, of course, changed her morning appointments, just as Mr. Perez had warned, like the shifting zephyr off the Hudson River, but her timing remained punctual. The miserable Claire walked two miserable dogs through the park every afternoon. Byron was attending school with no obvious prison breaks.

Kelly continued to bring Byron a protein bar, and she continued to sit in on his practices. She was discreet. She always took the very back row, corner seat. Byron noticed her right away, almost as if he had been looking for her, but they never spoke of it again.

There were times in life when no meant yes and yes meant no. Especially with a teenage leprechaun.

But the very best part of every day: Kelly's most precious two hours, every afternoon, at home with Rose.

***

On Thursday evening, Kelly returned to the penthouse garage, where she found Mr. Perez waiting with a stern expression—no, strike that, a very hostile look. She parked the car and handed him the keys.

Kelly had been obeying all the rules, or so she thought. She had been washing the car and refilling the drink station daily. Everyone had been delivered to their assigned locations, timely and safely. Nevertheless, a sudden dryness coated her tongue.

"Well, Ms. O'Sullivan, however was your very first week as a driver?"

"I'd say it's going fairly well," she stammered. "Everybody got where they needed to be on time...and we all seemed to get along fine."

"Is that so? Splendid. Simply maaaaaarvelous." Mr. Perez pressed his hands together, as if in prayer. "Would you care for some feedback, or do you prefer to carry on as if the world were the most pleasant place you've ever been and meanwhile your head is stuck inside a deep pile of quicksand? It's quite dark and warm and quite cozy down there, isn't it?"

"What are you talking about?"

"I am talking about feedback. Would you care for some? Although I must warn you, it could be unpleasant. You may have to see the light."

"Sure." Kelly's arms slackened.

"Sure?"

"Yes, thank you, I would appreciate your feedback."

"Mr. Byron has not reported for school all week."

"What? That can't be. I dropped him off. I saw that kid walk through the front door of the building. He never came out. I waited at the curb, like you told me to. He went through that door every morning, and he came out that same door every afternoon. He's been studying algebra and taking tests. He told me so."

"An intriguing dilemma, indeed. We have ourselves a mystery to solve, do we not? Or, better yet, perhaps a ghost story. Mr. Byron is able to pass through walls. Or is he, in reality, Superboy? Faster than a speeding bullet? More powerful than a locomotive? These are all entertaining theories. But then, I am afraid, we are left with the basic facts. Byron Irving did not report for school today. Not Monday, Tuesday, Wednesday, or this day, which we refer to as Thursday. In fact."

Mr. Perez removed his top hat, flipped it upside down and pretended to pull something from within. "Look what we have here. A fluffy white rabbit, and he's grinning ear to ear! It appears Mr. Byron has outwitted you. I warned you that that diabolical, hormone-raging teenager was up to something." Mr. Perez returned his hat to his head. "I suppose I must add *savvy* to my list of adjectives because the boy has clearly outwitted every driver we have ever hired, including the honorable Kelly O'Sullivan, a fourth-generation royal chauffeur."

Kelly accepted that last comment as a compliment, whether Mr. Perez intended it or not.

Mr. Perez continued. "Tomorrow is Friday, the final day of the school week. I have an excellent idea! It just struck me! Let's make absolutely certain Byron Irving attends school tomorrow. Wouldn't it be lovely if I could report to Mr. Irving that his son was actually delivered to school *one* day this week?"

"Mr. Perez. I promise you. I took that kid to school. I saw him walk inside that building. I did my job. I'm not his bodyguard."

"Actually..." Mr. Perez scratched his chin. "Yes, actually, you are his bodyguard. And you are now also a private investigator as well."

Dad and his mystery novels came to mind. Kelly would ask Dad's advice. He had been a driver most of his life. But then again, no. She didn't want Dad to think she was failing at the job, not this soon anyway.

"I'm not quite finished. Oh, how I wish I was, but I am not." Mr. Perez pulled a starched handkerchief from his breast pocket and wiped his moist brow. "Miss Claire never walked Peter and Nicholas through Central Park but rather was seen at The Plaza Hotel leisurely lunching with a friend. She enjoyed a chicken salad on croissant and a nicely chilled Chardonnay. No, strike that—she drank two nicely chilled Chardonnays in the middle of the afternoon, which even I find very inappropriate. And even worse, the canines were nowhere to be seen."

"Wait a minute here. Claire didn't walk those dogs?"

"Am I failing to speak proper English? What portion did you not comprehend? I didn't use any big words there, did I?"

"I can't believe this."

"Did you follow Miss Claire around the circumference of the park, as instructed?"

"Well...no. I offered, but...she said she didn't need me."

"Well, there you have it. One mysterious code quickly cracked. However, we remain uncertain as to exactly where Miss Claire was storing those dogs while she luncheoned." Mr. Perez feigned a shiver. "Now onto Byron, and why do I have the feeling his solution will be similarly obvious."

"I'm not surprised about Byron. I get it. He has some issues." Kelly shoved her hands in her pockets. "But Claire? We had a deal. I needed those two hours. I needed that time at—" Kelly caught herself.

"You need two hours? For what desperate purpose or secret agenda might this be? You do recall the rules previously set forth regarding the utilization of the Rolls-Royce for private purposes, such as drug dealing and marketing illegal paraphernalia and sexual relations?"

"I would never do anything like that. You know my family."

"I *thought* I knew your family. Please do not fall into the same category as every other driver who has stumbled into this garage. I have uncovered secret side trips to every local drinking establishment as well as inappropriate behavior with women in the back seat, to which I later discovered two pairs of black lace panties and some sort of paraphernalia I do not wish to describe any further and, to this very day, regret ever having touched. I've had drivers jitneying friends and family and downright strangers all about town in exchange for cold hard cash, and the list goes on and on. If you are planning to fail at this career, would you be so kind as to do something...unique?"

Kelly began pacing. "Claire made me a bargain. She said if I didn't follow her around that park, I could have a couple hours to myself, that's all."

"Where did you go?"

"Home."

Mr. Perez gauged Kelly for some time before replying, "And do you work for Miss Claire?"

"No."

"Correct."

"There's something more about her. Something's not right." Kelly stopped pacing. "I only saw it once, but now that we're speaking honestly..."

"Have we not been speaking honestly all this time? My error. Certainly, let's embark upon the truth. Whatever might this be? Do tell."

"I saw her kick one of the dogs." She met Mr. Perez squarely in the eye. "It was only once, but it was very upsetting."

"You must be imagining things. Miss Claire would never do such a thing."

"How long has she been working here?"

"Almost nine months now. And I will be the only one posing questions in this conversation."

Kelly persisted. "Mr. Irving loves his pets. You said so yourself. I saw the dogs' reaction to Claire. They cower to her."

Mr. Perez rolled his shoulders. "I will mention this in my weekly report. As a suspicion. Nothing more." He became lost in thought. "The canines are healthy. They undergo monthly checkups. Although...their absence from Claire for two hours every afternoon is most certainly disconcerting." He shook his head awake. "Rest assured, the incident will be well reported. In the meantime, we have the dilemma regarding Mr. Irving's absent son. It is Byron you should be fretting over. You will return to work tomorrow and refrain from setting up any so-called 'deals.' You will make absolutely certain Mr. Byron gets to class, that Miss Claire gives the dogs a proper walking. Let's give it another college try, shall we?" Mr. Perez crooked his arm into an upward punch.

Kelly hated to ask. "What about Carolyn?"

"Thank you for broaching my next topic. On the contrary, it appears Miss Carolyn is quite thrilled with her new driver, with whom she has developed a special friendship and from whom she is taking advice and mentoring and counseling and herbal medications—"

"I have never given Carolyn any meds!"

"No? What a shame. In any event, Mr. Irving is very concerned, and when he returns, earlier than scheduled, he would like you to retrieve him from the airport so the two of you can become thoroughly acquainted and have a little chat. In summary, you have one more week to get the job right."

"Carolyn and I are friends. Is that a problem?"

"Yes, actually it is a very big problem. She claims you are best of friends and that you are enlightening her to the very meaning of life and love and happiness. My, I had no idea you were an intellectual philosopher, Ms. O'Sullivan. You certainly hide it well."

"So, Carolyn is not allowed to have any friends?"

"Miss Carolyn has a plethora of girlfriends, all dim-witted and shallow. She also has a therapist—several, in fact. Her driver, however, was not hired for either of these purposes. News flash: Your resume was not properly vetted for counseling and therapy, and there is no telling what dangerous advice you might be rendering. You are the driver. Just the driver. Period."

Mr. Perez straightened his spine. "Nonetheless, tomorrow is a new day, and if at first we don't succeed, we shall try, try again. I'm not quite ready to give up on you yet." He wagged his finger in Kelly's direction. "There's something about you...something...and it's not the fact that your father was a friend. It's something more. I can't put my finger on it, but when I do..."

"Am I allowed a question? I have a concern of my own."

"Certainly. Whatever more could possibly be troubling you? Your necktie is too tight?"

"Does Mr. Irving have cameras in that Rolls?"

"What on earth...? Whatever would give you that ludicrous notion?"

"Claire, that's what. She said he has cameras inside that penthouse. That's why she has to get out of there every day. So why not the cars, too?"

"I can assure you, neither Mr. Irving's home nor his automobile has hidden surveillance mechanisms. Miss Claire is suspicious of her own shadow. Do not believe a word she utters. And as for that Rolls-Royce

Phantom, I inspect that car myself. Ms. O'Sullivan, save yourself a world of unsubstantiated concern and just be the driver."

Kelly shrugged. "I don't know why I care so much. The guy is obviously having his family followed all around the city. And probably me too."

"That guy you are referring to is properly known as Mr. Irving, and his personal life is not our concern. If he is making himself aware of his driver's whereabouts, or the dog walker's, it is for one reason only—he wants to ensure that his family is being transported safely and timely."

"Mr. Perez, with all due respect, you don't follow your dog walker into The Plaza Hotel and watch everything she's eating and drinking just so you can be sure she's safe and the new driver is doing her job."

"You are missing the point. Miss Claire is not fulfilling her side of the contract. She is being paid for a service which she is not performing. And by the way, do find out where she's depositing those dogs all day long while she gallivants around town."

"There is another point here. Mr. Irving is having everybody followed. If there's cameras inside that house, it's weird, just plain weird, where I come from anyway."

"There are no cameras. I can assure you."

"What about in this garage? Have you ever thought of that?"

Mr. Perez's gaze drifted across the ceiling.

"See?" Kelly raised her voice. "You're wondering now, too." She withdrew. "Oh, it doesn't matter. Let him watch me all he wants. I'm not doing anything wrong. I have two weeks left before Mr. Irving returns. I'll figure it out. I promise you. I'll fix everything."

Mr. Perez raised a brow.

Kelly retreated into the back office to change into her street clothes. How could she have been so gullible? Didn't anyone tell the truth anymore? Didn't anyone care about trust, honesty, friendship?

Well, it would be all business from here on out. Kelly needed this
job more than any of those people could ever understand. And nothing, absolutely nothing, was going to stop her from affording Mrs.
Andrews.

***

By the time Kelly made it up to her apartment in Harlem, the
snow was falling again—light, soft flakes rocking gently to the ground,
whitewashing the dirty streets and soot-stained buildings. It was dark
and quiet on 134th Street, and Kelly entered her basement apartment
in the same manner. She did not want to disrupt the serene peace.
Rose had been tucked into bed for the night, and while Mrs. Andrews
gathered up her belongings, preparing to leave, Kelly knelt beside
Rose's little bed.

The concrete floor pained Kelly's knees, but she ignored the discomfort. She leaned against the mattress and traced soothing fingers
across her daughter's precious forehead and through her baby-fine
hair, softly, gently, lovingly. The simplest touch sometimes meant so
much more than words ever could. As Rose slept peacefully, Kelly
outlined Rose's turned-up nose and heart-shaped lips. Gentle breaths
moved in and out of this precious little form. This one life that had
changed Kelly's world in the past three years in ways she never expected.

Often, late at night, when a hard day was finally finished, Kelly
would feel a sense of relief, although small. One more day had come
and gone, and they had gotten through it without too much pain,
without too much suffering. Kelly and her daughter, Rose, were still
there, together, fighting. They would never have to live through that
exact same day ever again. It was over and done.

There was something to be said for that.

And yet, with all the hardship and pain, Kelly could never imagine a life without sweet Rose. The joy far outweighed the sorrow. The happy outweighed the sad. It always did. It had to.

Damean had not felt the same. At the first sign of trouble and maybe some inconvenience, he abandoned them both. Kelly never heard from him again. She wasn't even sure where he was living, or if he was living. But life was different now. Especially without Damean. Life was getting better, day by day.

Kelly spoke to Mrs. Andrews without turning. "Thank you so very much. I can't thank you enough...for everything."

"Rose had a really good day today. Her migraines were managed with the medications. We read three books. We colored. We learned new letters, some numbers. We sang. We even danced a little today."

"That is so wonderful." Kelly rubbed the back of her neck and stood to face Mrs. Andrews. "You will never know."

"Oh, I do know."

"I'll be able to pay you the full amount soon. I'll have my first paycheck in a couple days."

"That's fine."

"We never had anything like this before. I never could afford it. A real teacher. These lessons, the classes. Real therapy. It's all so amazing."

"We have a long road ahead." Mrs. Andrews braced a firm hand on Kelly's shoulder. "I'm not going to lie—we're off to a great start. She has so much potential."

"I kept telling everybody that, but they wouldn't listen. They said nothing more could be done. But I knew there must be something..."

"I'm here now. I'm listening." Mrs. Andrews opened the door. "I'll see you in the morning."

"See you in the morning."

Kelly's three-year-old daughter, Rose, had had a good day. That was all that mattered.

One good day.

The Irving family's petty problems and Mr. Perez's anger floated away, softly and gently, like the flakes outside, like the winter breeze, gone now in this warm, sleepy apartment with little Rose by her side.

Kelly knelt beside her daughter again and continued to sweep the soft hair from Rose's peaceful forehead. Just like Kelly's mother had once done for Kelly as a child. A cool, soothing hand. A loving, gentle touch meant so very much. There were times when Kelly had pretended that she was still sleeping while her mother stroked Kelly's head. She had not wanted the tender moment to end.

Kelly imagined Mom's hand in place of her own just now. She remembered Mom's wrinkled skin, her bent knuckles from her years as a seamstress. Kelly swept her mother's fingers through Rose's baby-fine hair.

"You taught me this, Mom. Now, I'm teaching Rose."

6

CHAPTER SIX

On Friday morning, Kelly parked at the curb of Fifteen Central Park West and nodded a greeting to the doorman, Jack. She adjusted Byron's heated seat, turned on the massage setting, lowered his tray table, raised the footrest, poured his Diet Coke, and ignited the ceiling stars. On second thought, she lowered the footrest and turned off the stars. She was ready for him...that little green goblin without the beard and hat but full of mischief. In fact, she couldn't wait.

Byron made his way through the lobby and out the door, dressed in his usual camouflage attire—camel-hair coat, leather gloves, tweed cap. He ignored Jack's greeting and held firmly to his pathway toward the Rolls.

"Good morning, Byron," Kelly said.

"Hi." He carefully placed his backpack in exactly the same position on the seat—upright, forward-facing—and his gloves in the same manner before sliding into the back. Byron's sulking scowl revealed something wasn't quite right.

"Something wrong?" Kelly asked.

"You forgot the footrest."

"I did? Sorry about that."

"And the stars! You've been here for a week now. You'd think you could remember something like that. It's not a big deal, but still, how did you forget?"

"You're right. It's not a big deal. Go ahead and set it up yourself." She rounded the front fender and took her position behind the wheel. "Did you bring your snack?" Kelly had purchased a box of protein bars after that first day of work to be sure Byron ate something before polo, and this exchange was now part of their morning routine. Kelly would ask Byron if he remembered his snack, Byron would reply that he forgot, and she would toss him a protein bar.

Byron liked routines.

"I forgot," Byron said.

"How could you forget something like that? I've been reminding you all week to bring a snack."

"Who cares? What, am I on trial here?" Byron reached inside his backpack and pulled out his spiral notebook. "Toss me a bar. I need to study."

"Another exam today? That school sure gives a lot of exams."

"Global History."

"Okay, study away." Kelly used a little extra force to throw the protein bar at Byron, and it struck his chest with a smack.

"Hey," he shouted.

"Oops."

Byron stuffed the bar into his backpack and returned to his notes, and Kelly observed him in the mirror. What could that kid possibly have been studying? He had no intention of going to class.

She drove in silence, parked the Rolls at the curb of Madison Academy and remained seated. Byron did not like Kelly to open his door at school. Kelly watched the other students congregating on the sidewalk, walking two by two or in groups of three or more through the front door. Packs of kids huddling together, talking and laughing, like it should be.

And then there was Byron. He waited until the exact appropriate time and then *pop*, out of the car and into the building in a flash of lightning speed. He acknowledged no one, entered the double doors, and disappeared.

So, Kelly thought, if he wasn't escaping through that front door, he must have been using some other exit, probably the back of the building. She abandoned the Rolls and tromped across the snowy school grounds, following the brick wall to the rear of the building. There were only two doors in the back. One appeared to be the entrance and exit for teachers and staff. The other was a very wide double door for loading and unloading supplies, food, and equipment.

Kelly hid behind a wide oak and monitored both doors intently for over an hour.

Nothing.

No one entered or exited those doors. No one was seen trespassing on the school grounds. The building was quiet, with classes having begun. Maybe Byron decided to actually attend class today. Maybe the ever-absent Mr. Irving had figured out a way to deal with the matter himself and have a word with his son instead of Kelly solving all of Mr. Irving's problems while he was gone. *Now, there's an idea.*

Just as Kelly was preparing to surrender, a sudden movement caught the corner of her eye. At the far end of the brick wall, a basement window, a shifting object. Short, wily, and agile. Gangly, skinny arms, hoisting himself up and through that small open window, headfirst...like a polo player diving into the water to block a goal.

Kelly wove between trees and shrubbery until she was hidden between that basement window and the parking lot beyond.

She waited.

The polo player sprang up from his goalie position and brushed off his clothes. He was still wearing that long camel coat, the hat, the gloves, the wire-rimmed glasses. He didn't even bother to look around. He had made this offensive move many times before, and he was quite certain of the outcome. That's where Byron made his biggest mistake.

In every attempt to escape from an educational institution and enjoy a day of freedom, one must always be on guard, apprehensive and prepared for anything. Although this was not a convictable crime, there were those persons of authority in the school system, particularly the superintendent, who would take great pride and joy in the capture and conviction of such a criminal. Kelly knew all about that from personal experience.

As the goalie marched steadfastly toward the parking lot, he drew closer to Kelly. A few yards away...now several feet...now inches. She stuck her leg out, blocking Byron's path, and he tripped. He fell to the ground, headfirst into the snow, squirming and fighting to free himself from the slick surface, much like treading water.

"Hey there. Whatcha doin'?" Kelly stood above him.

Byron scrambled out of his icy trap and stood. "None of your business. You're the driver. Just a driver." He adjusted his hat. "A nobody, really. Some misfit who couldn't land a decent job, so you got to drive successful people and their kids around all day and be their servant. I'm a fourteen-year-old kid, and I get to boss you around. What kind of a life is that? I'll tell you what kind. It's the kind of life for somebody who has no real goals, no intelligence other than to take orders and follow through, that's what. So, get back in the car and mind your own business."

Kelly grabbed Byron by the jacket sleeve and proceeded to drag him back to the Rolls.

He twisted, fighting to break free. "Let me go. I'll have you fired. You stupid driver. You got an IQ of about three, and you're trying to tell me what to do? You're a nothing. A nobody. If it wasn't for my family, you'd probably be dead broke and lying on some park bench somewhere or digging food out of a garbage can."

Kelly opened the car door and placed Byron firmly within, and then she came around to the opposite side of the Rolls, but rather than taking her usual position behind the wheel, she slid into the back seat beside Byron.

"What do you think you're doing?" he shrieked. "Get in the front seat where you belong. I'm gonna tell my dad you hurt me. My arm hurts." Byron rubbed the wrong arm. "It's probably bruised. I'll have you fired so fast you won't know what hit you."

"Keep talking." Kelly folded her arms. "Get it all out, and when you're done, I'll take a turn."

"You're stupid."

"Yes, sometimes I am." She shrugged.

"And you're a nobody."

"That's probably true too."

"You got no goals."

"Wait a minute now. There's where you're wrong. I actually do have goals, but I can't afford them. Not yet anyway. But someday."

"You're...you're..." Byron's mouth twisted.

"Are you about finished?" Kelly asked.

He gritted his teeth. She could see the muscles in his jaw pulsing.

"First of all, I can't be that stupid," she said. "I caught you, didn't I?"

No response.

"Second. You're right. I'm not somebody famous or important, but I am a somebody. There are people out there who care about me and would be very upset if I was gone. I do matter. Even in this job, I matter. We all do. Every person matters. Even those people you were talking about who have to find their food in a garbage can. They matter."

Still nothing.

"Third, I have goals and dreams, a lot of them, but I also have a daughter who needs special help. She needs a certain kind of teacher and therapist who can come to my apartment every day. I can't afford that teacher while pursuing my dreams, so my dreams don't matter that much anymore. That's what happens when you love somebody. You care more about them than you care about yourself. So, you're right, I had to take this stupid driver job, a job I promised myself I'd never take because my dad and my grandfather and even my great-grandfather were all drivers, and I wanted something more out of life, but it didn't turn out that way. Life isn't always fair, but you make it work. You take what you're given, and you try to make it better. Sometimes you do, and sometimes you don't. But I'm here to tell you—and trust me, I know about this—there's something good in every single day. There's happy beside the sad. Always. If you stop feeling sorry for yourself long enough to look for it. Even those homeless people you were comparing me to matter. They have a story. We all have a story. Some turn out good and some not so much."

Byron's expression softened.

"No response?" Kelly asked.

"So, what's your daughter's name?"

"Rose."

Byron scrunched his lips.

Kelly continued. "And you're not really the boss of me, are you? Because I dragged you into this car and tossed you in the back seat. You might be smarter than me, Byron Irving. I'll give you that. But you're not stronger. Not for a good two or three years, anyway. In a couple years, you will toss me over your shoulder and deposit me in the driver's seat, and there'll be nothing I can do about it. But for now, I will be the one carrying you around."

With that comment, the corners of Byron's lips curled. Kelly had stumbled upon Byron's every dream and hope and wish with that one statement. He was too small, too skinny, and he must have been worrying if he would ever get any bigger.

"Let me ask you something." Kelly angled toward him. "No lies. Remember you asked me that once? No lies?"

Byron nodded.

"Where on earth have you been going every day?"

Byron turned away, focusing on something outside the window. Not the school, but somewhere farther beyond. "I go down to the courthouse."

"The courthouse?"

"The New York Supreme Court, 60 Centre Street, New York, New York, 10017."

"I know what it is and where it is, but why?"

"I want to be a lawyer. I'm not learning anything in that place." He thumbed at Madison Academy. "But I'm learning all kinds of amazing things at the courthouse." He snapped his attention to Kelly. "So why do I have to waste my time in that dumb school? Why can't I skip it all and go to law school or be a paralegal to some attorney until I'm old enough or something? Anything but that place." He offered a new finger to Madison Academy, and it was not the pointer finger.

Good question. Excellent question, actually. "Because," Kelly began, "you wouldn't be a good lawyer if you only knew about law. Do you know what my grandpa used to say? He said, 'Too soon old and too late smart.' Wisdom comes with age, but it also comes with education and experience. All sorts of different classes in all sorts of subjects make us who we are today. Every experience we've ever had stir up together. The things we've seen; the words spoken to us by our family, friends, even strangers; our mistakes, our triumphs, the good and the bad; all blend together like a beautiful watercolor painting that becomes who we are." She paused. "You're smart enough to know it takes more than medical school to be a good doctor, more than art class to be a great artist. It takes all of you, every single ounce of who you are. So, tell me the truth: what's your real reason for skipping school?"

Byron blinked back a few tears. "I don't want to go in there any-more. I don't fit in." He widened his eyes. "In case you haven't noticed, I'm not like the other boys, and they hate me for it. I'm tired of it all."

Kelly should have known. "Exactly what's going on in there?"

Byron's lips flattened.

"Who is they?"

"You promise you won't tell?" Byron's voice fell into a whisper.

"Not a soul. I promise."

"Okay, well, there's a few guys in there. Bullies. I'm their...pet."

"What do you mean by 'pet'?"

"They call me Bingo. I'm their dog. They pet my hair. They put a leash and collar on me. Some days they make me eat from a dog dish. They tell me to—" He stopped. Tears filled his eyes. He didn't want to say any more.

Kelly took a shaky breath. Horrible images she didn't wish to see clawed at her mind. She anchored her hand to the corner of her seat and fought to stay composed. Her voice joined Byron's whisper. "You're not alone. You're not the only one. I guarantee they're doing this to other kids in there, too. Did you report this to the principal?"

Terror shocked Byron's features. "Never!"

"Okay, okay, we'll handle this one ourselves."

With that comment, Byron's shoulders relaxed. He held Kelly's gaze, obviously eager for her to utter some profound wisdom, some miraculous solution.

"Did you tell your dad?" she asked.

"No. I can't. I don't want Dad to know. He's already disappointed in me."

"Disappointed? No, he is not. He'll figure out a way to help you."

"Here we go again." Byron slapped his knees. "Do you know my dad? No, you do not. Have you ever met my dad? No, you have not. Trust me, he would be very disappointed in me. Do you think he wanted a son like me? I am not going to tell him. Do you understand? Never."

"Okay, I get it. We'll handle it on our own...for now."

Byron added, "Like I've been doing for the past year."

"But now you're not alone anymore. How many bullies are there?"

"Three."

"Can you point them out to me? When school's over?"

"Sure, but I'm not going back in there. Not today. Not on a Friday. They will be all revved up. I can't take it, and they're going to—"

"Hold up. I never said anything about you going back in there now. We'll come back when school is ending." Kelly returned to her post behind the wheel. "Buckle up."

"Where are we going?"

"Where do you think? The courthouse, of course. Isn't that where you said you go every day?"

"Yeah, but..."

"I wouldn't mind seeing that place myself. Then I have to pick up Carolyn and Claire. But I'll be back for you at the end of the day."

Byron's features were a combination of shock and utter delight.

So that was it—the reason Byron didn't want to go to school. That also must have been the reason why Byron didn't have the confidence to play the entire polo match. He'd been beaten down, like the dogs, Peter and Nicholas, until he didn't think he deserved anything more. He consistently forfeited his goalie position to the boy on the bench. Maybe it was empathy for the kid who never got any playtime. That was fine for all the right reasons but not the wrong ones. Not because you've been trained to believe you aren't worthy. Not because you have been brainwashed to believe you don't matter.

"Are you going to be safe in that courthouse, all alone all day?" Kelly couldn't help but ask.

"The courthouse is the safest place in the city, apart from the police station. There's more lawyers and judges in there than spit on the city sidewalk."

Kelly twisted her lips to hide her smirk.

She walked Byron up the 100-foot-wide flight of steps and through the fluted columns into the courthouse, wherein Byron instantly became an eager docent, offering a detailed tour that included the history of each room, its purpose and the current case. Kelly was more mesmerized by Byron's knowledge of the building than the courthouse itself.

Byron spoke without seemingly taking a single breath. "A Boston architect, Guy Lowell, won a competition for his design for a round building, but he changed his mind to this Roman Classical style." Byron beamed as if he'd constructed the building himself. "Did you notice the quote at the front door? 'The true administration of justice is the firmest pillar of good government.' George Washington said that and..."

When Kelly left Byron, she briefly thought she might want to be a lawyer too. His passion for the legal world was contagious. She hoped her little Rose might feel the same way about something someday. Anything.

Kelly had some time before picking up Carolyn. Kelly returned to the parking garage and joined Mr. Perez in the break room. He was seated on the sofa, reading *The Times* and drinking tea from a delicate porcelain cup and saucer covered in blue forget-me-nots.

She plopped down beside him with a bounce, and his tea sloshed over the cup's sides. He grimaced. "Have you come to ruin what brief time I have to enjoy my day? A tea and the newspaper. Is that too much to ask?" He set the teacup down, snapped his paper open and continued reading.

"I caught him. He was climbing out a basement window."

Mr. Perez tried in vain to conceal his surprise. "You reported this to the school, I presume, and this will be the end of the matter. Mr. Irving will be pleased."

"No."

He peered up from his paper.

"It's not that simple." Kelly cast a sideways glance at Mr. Perez.

He threw the paper into his lap. "For a driver, it is exactly that simple. Do not become involved."

"Well, it might be a little too late for that."

"Explain." Mr. Perez wound his hand like a clock.

"I promised Byron I wouldn't tell anyone. But I want you to know I'm handling it."

"You made a deal with a teenage juvenile delinquent?" Mr. Perez stood. "Did this childish contract include any sort of secret handshake or rap lyrics? You are going to sabotage your career by your so-called 'handling things.' That's what you're doing."

"Career? Is that what this is? Because I thought I was just a driver for a rich family. I thought I was supposed to watch the schedule and be sure to drop people off and pick them up on time and have their massage chairs running."

"You are. And that is all you are expected to do."

"I hate to tell you this, but I am not a robot. I'm not some cold, unemotional, unfeeling creature who can watch these people sitting in my back seat, suffering, full of all sorts of problems and issues, and do nothing about it."

"You are not their therapist. And you are certainly not their father or, in Miss Carolyn's case, her strictest confidante."

"I don't want to be any of those things. But there is one thing I already am, and there's no turning back now."

Mr. Perez waited.

"I can be a friend," Kelly said.

"I can honestly say, in all my many years in the service of the Irving family, we have never encountered this predicament before—a driver who declared herself a long-lost friend to all mankind." Mr. Perez waved his pointer finger at Kelly. "There's something different about you. I've said it before, and I'll say it again. But you are not that family's problem-solver. Mr. Irving is the sole proprietor of that title. I must warn you: he will not appreciate you meddling in his affairs, business or personal. He is a very private man, almost to a fault. He is also a very proud man. He would never want to believe that his driver, the lowest person under his employ, would possess the aptitude required to solve all the problems that Mr. Irving could not." Mr. Perez blew air from his nose. "On the other hand, Mr. Irving will gladly offer you advice from time to time, as superficial and worthless as it might be, and you did not hear that from me. But a driver offer Mr. Irving advice? I dare say never."

"I'm helping Byron out with something. Mr. Irving doesn't have to know about it."

"Oh, but that is where you are so very wrong, Ms. O'Sullivan. As you have recently become aware, Mr. Irving knows everything that occurs within his family. He is the one who contacted me yesterday, informing me that Byron did not attend school, that Carolyn had become infatuated with her new driver, that Claire failed to properly walk the dogs. Believe me, he knows."

The supposed hidden cameras came to mind. "I don't care. I have nothing to hide." Kelly stood abruptly. "I can't wait to meet this man. Maybe it's time for my side of this story."

"Watch your words. Unless you, too, wish to be filing for unemployment. You have been granted total autonomy once inside that vehicle because you consistently neglect to connect the mobile phone I gave you, which I am beginning to believe is quite intentional rather than accidental. There is something about the interior of an automobile. It is a world unto itself. We feel safe, protected. We are more prone to road rage, to obscene hand gestures, to applying the horn. We believe we are sheltered, almost like a steel armor of sorts. I must warn you that your armor will melt to the ground when Mr. Irving returns because that automobile, the license plate, the gasoline, the insurance, and even those passengers seated in the second row all belong to him."

"I have to pick up Carolyn now."

"Yes, you certainly do." Mr. Perez smoothed his hair. "I'm not chastising you, Ms. O'Sullivan, although I'm sure it sounds that way. I'm giving you good, solid advice...from one driver to another. The same advice I know for certain your father would give."

"I get it. And I need this job, more than you know. I'm going to do the right thing."

"We can only hope."

"I will. I promise." Now to figure out exactly what that *right thing* was.

7

CHAPTER SEVEN

K elly waited beside the Rolls for Carolyn. They had had a good conversation the night before when Kelly drove Carolyn to her cocktail hour, which ended up being exactly that—Carolyn and friends huddled around a candlelit table at Bemelmans, listening to smooth jazz and chatting simultaneously. Carolyn had claimed she didn't have a friend in the world, but Kelly knew from personal experience that not all friends were the sort you could confide in. Some friends were looking for only happy times, laughter and fun. Carolyn's so-called friends didn't want to get their hands dirty because of their perfectly polished nails.

This morning, a frosty fluttering of icy crystals dropped from the cloudy sky, glittering everything they touched and staying awhile. The temperature had fallen below zero, and Carolyn wasn't wearing her usual workout clothes. She appeared in a white and black chinchilla fur coat that fell to her ankles, black earmuffs, black leather gloves and leather boots. The boots were not sensible, at least five-inch stiletto heels.

Carolyn was not yet aware, but their usual friendly, girl-to-girl morning conversation was about to take a drastic turn from the past week as well. Kelly was happy to listen to Carolyn and offer some common-sense advice. The problem was Kelly needed Mr. Irving to like her more. She hadn't even met the man, and he was already preparing to reprimand her for befriending his wife. Kelly corrected herself—his girlfriend. Kelly was wondering why Carolyn would share their friendship with Mr. Irving in the first place.

Kelly's tone was purposefully flat. "Good morning, Miss Carolyn."

"Good morning, Kelly. We are off to the publishing house today! Wish me luck. How is your morning going?"

"Fine."

"Just fine?"

"Mmhm."

Carolyn sensed the change immediately. *Women know things like that.* One word off, one expression, crooked or missing. Carolyn slid into the back, and Kelly manned her post at the wheel.

"What's wrong?" Carolyn asked.

There was no time for small talk. "Well, I was told last night, after my first week of work at my new job—a job, by the way, that I need very badly—that my boss, who I haven't even met yet, is mad at me because his girlfriend told him I'm counseling her."

"Oh, for heaven's sake." Carolyn fell against the seat. "That man is so controlling. So manipulative. He takes everything I say and twists it all around. He's not even here most of the time. He's got those cameras all over that house, but...oh, this is interesting...there must not be any hidden inside this car, because if that was news to him then..."

"You know about the cameras too?" Kelly asked.

"Of course. We all know. How did you discover the secret curse? It doesn't matter because it seems you're immune, for now. I'm beginning to wish I was the driver instead of the girlfriend. I have an idea—let's trade places. Oh, don't look so surprised. You know I'm kidding."

Kelly's expression had not changed in the least.

Carolyn continued. "I know what you're thinking. My world looks so beautiful from the outside. Like a lovely bouquet of pretty spring flowers, but I can assure you, on the inside it's more like weeds hiding a grave. I suppose we all hide things, now and then—"

"Carolyn, I hate to interrupt you, but this isn't about *you* anymore."

Carolyn released an audible sigh. "Don't worry. You're not going to lose your job. So, you've been talking to me. So what? Everyone talks to me. I have that look—friendly, alluring, whatever. Actually, maybe I look naïve and gullible. I don't know what it is, but that's why Marcus likes me so much. Everyone is attracted to me and that makes Marcus attracted to me too. Am I making any logical sense here whatsoever? Anyway, he was infuriating me on our phone call last night. He wasn't listening, as usual. Would it kill the man to put his work away and listen to me for a minute or two? So, I said a few things that made him stop what he was doing and take notice. Something about the fact that my new driver listens to me and at least I have someone in my life...or something like that. That's all."

"I cannot be the only driver who ever talked to you."

"Talked *to* me, yes, of course, there were many. But talked *with* me, no. You are the very first, and I'm so grateful and—"

"You're grateful? For what? For the chance to make Mr. Irving angry?"

"Nothing in all the world makes Marcus Irving look up from his precious computer like something that hurts his pride. I've learned that the hard way. Marcus isn't most men; he's important; he's busy; he doesn't have time for small talk. I get it. The only thing that catches his attention is something...something...that hurts. There, I said it. I hated to say it, but it's true."

Kelly steadied her breath. "Carolyn, you need to understand something. This isn't a big game to me. This single paycheck has changed my world in ways you could never imagine. I'm more than happy to help you, but I have someone who needs me more. I cannot jeopardize this job."

Kelly could feel Carolyn's stare on the back of Kelly's head.

"You have a child," Carolyn surmised.

"A daughter."

"Okay, I understand. I'm sure he's forgotten all about it by now. Don't worry about a thing."

"Oh, I'm worried, alright. Mr. Irving wants a word with me the second he gets back home. This isn't about you anymore. It's not even about me. This is about protecting my daughter."

"You and your daughter will be fine."

"We are *not* fine. We have not been fine since the day she was born. But we are surviving. We are making it, day by day, looking for something good inside all the heartache."

Silence wafted between them like roaring thunder.

Carolyn twisted in her seat. "I'll call him tonight. I'll straighten it all out. I can fix this."

"One question. Why are you trying so hard to make Mr. Irving mad? You think hurt is strong? Well, I'm here to tell you, it sure is. It's so strong that it'll bring you to your knees, to a point where you think you can't go on, but you do. You go on because you know there's something greater out there, something stronger than the pain." Kelly adjusted the mirror to remove Carolyn from view. "If you can't find any love in your life, then be that love for someone else. The only thing that matters is you have it."

Silence from the back seat for the remainder of the trip. When Kelly opened the door for Carolyn this time, Kelly's heart softened a little. "I wish you the best with your meeting today. You know I do."

Carolyn grabbed Kelly's arm. "What's your daughter's name?"

Kelly held Carolyn's gaze. "Rose."

Carolyn offered a half nod, as if she understood more by hearing the child's name, and maybe she had. Maybe names were meant to be. Maybe they were assigned before birth, whispered into a parent's ear, specifically for this child at this time and this place in history.

Carolyn gave Kelly's arm a good squeeze, then turned to go.

Kelly returned to her post behind the wheel and waited. She watched the white porcelain rose on the dashboard change hues with every passing cloud, with every gust of snow. She thought of Claire, the dog walker. Kelly needed those two hours promised every afternoon, and her mind spun and fretted with ways she could fight to keep them. But, like everything in life, she had learned there was only so much she could do. There were times when circumstances were beyond her control. It was times like those that she did whatever she could and let the rest go, like snowflakes in reverse, floating back up into the clouds. Sometimes she sent back the stuff she wished had never fallen to the earth to begin with: the sickness, the disappointments, the lost love, the lost dreams—all of it. She sent them back up to the sky, to the past, to the place they had come from, out of sight and out of mind.

Within the hour, a tapping on the rear window jostled Kelly from her thoughts.

"Unlock the door," Carolyn said frantically. "I can't wait to tell you. Hurry up."

Carolyn jumped into the back seat, and Kelly spun to face her.

"They loved my book!" Carolyn's eyes glistened. "They absolutely adored it! They said it's fresh and new and different. They've never seen anything like it. The book will reveal the important things in my life. You were right. I'm a person, just like everyone else, and it's time I told my story. All of it. I'm starting with my childhood and going from there. How I got here, why I got here and why I stayed."

She took a deep breath and slowed down, speaking softer, choosing her words carefully. "People always see me with this diamond bracelet." Carolyn jiggled the pavés encircling her wrist. "But at the end of the day, I take it off and put it inside my jewelry cabinet. At night, I wear this bracelet instead. It's a charm bracelet. Remember those?" Carolyn held each tarnished silver charm between her thumb and forefinger. "A heart, an ice skate, a telephone, a key, a coffee cup, a peace sign... I wore this every single day when I was a kid. I never threw it out. I wear this every single night, but I've never worn it in public, during the day. Not for many, many years." Carolyn held the charm bracelet up high for viewing. "Until today." She jiggled the silver trinkets.

Kelly's smile spoke everything words could not.

"That's not all," Carolyn continued. "I gave her a few chapters, and guess what? She liked my writing."

"Of course she did," Kelly said. "Because you are the very best writer on the island of Manhattan, and we both know that, and you are about to change the world of tabloid nonsense. That's what you're going to do."

Carolyn paused, turning her attention to somewhere beyond her windowpane. "I haven't told Marcus yet."

"Well, maybe it's time."

Carolyn leaned forward. "I realize I have a few things I need to straighten out with Marcus. Beginning with you."

"I would appreciate that." Kelly started the engine. "In the meantime, I'm going to have a word or two with that dog walker."

"Ha!" Carolyn clasped both hands together. "I do hope you're going to rip off her pretty little mask and expose the evil witch for all to see?"

"Something like that."

"Who knew your driver could be the most influential person in your life?"

Kelly realized she was purposefully continuing to disregard both Dad and Mr. Perez's advice, but it was too late to turn back now, wasn't it?

Just a little while longer, she promised herself, like everyone does now and then.

8

CHAPTER EIGHT

Miss Claire pranced through the lobby of Fifteen Central Park West, the two labradoodles tightly reined in beside her. All three—golden-haired, trim and fit—moved in unison toward the Rolls.

"Good morning, Miss Claire." Kelly waited beside the car.

"Dogs. Inside." Claire slapped their behinds into the back seat and jumped nimbly in behind them. "Well, what are you waiting for?" Claire ordered Kelly now, too. "Let's get going. Snap. Snap. We have two beautiful hours ahead of us."

Kelly stood firm. "Let me ask you a question. Do those dogs have names? I've never heard you call them anything but 'dog.'"

"Yes, I suppose they do. Now ask me if I care."

"So why did you take this job anyway, if you hate those dogs so much?"

"The same reason you took your job." Claire blew air through her nose. "Now, shut up and shut the door. It's cold out."

Kelly did not budge. "Where are you going?"

"Where do you think?"

"Considering that I was just told you didn't walk the dogs all week, I really don't know where you're going. Wait a second. I remember now. You were lunching at The Plaza."

Claire seethed. "How do you know that, driver?"

Kelly matched her tone. "My boss told me that, dog walker."

"That snake in the grass. Does he have spies all over the place? I'm with his dumb mutts twenty-four seven. Did you know that? They sleep on my bedroom floor. I even have to eat with them!" Claire gave a backhanded slap to the air. "Look at them, sitting there drooling at me like I'm their mother. Stupid animals."

"Careful," Kelly said. "They're listening."

"Oh, those dogs don't understand a word I'm saying. It's the inflection, you idiot. It's the voice pitch."

Peter and Nicholas were cowering. "Are you so sure about that?" Kelly pointed. "They look pretty upset to me."

"Of course, they are. I'm yelling at you! No wonder you're just a driver. Take me to the park and get lost. Go drinking with your friend or meet up with your boyfriend or whatever you do for two hours. Do it! Go! Now!" Claire gave a single clap.

Kelly stood firmly. "I'm not going anywhere. You got me in some trouble. We had a deal. So, now the deal's off. Yes, I need those two hours more than you could ever imagine. But I need this job more."

"I am going to the park!" Claire was outright screaming. "Take me to the park right now!"

Kelly opened Claire's door wider. "Get out."

Claire sat firm, arms crossed, jaw clenched. "I'm waiting. To the park. You work for me."

"No, that's where you're wrong. I work for Mr. Irving. Get out of the car, or I'm pulling you out." Kelly motioned to the entrance to the penthouse. A small crowd had gathered. Jack among them, of course, mouth gaping wide. He hovered beside a couple of older women who had been heading out to a luncheon of some sort, wearing matching fur coats and hats. The wind had picked up and the group was hugging their sides and shivering, but the spectacle was apparently well worth it.

"Are you going to get out?" Kelly asked one last time.

"No."

"Okay, then. My pleasure to assist."

Luckily, Claire weighed less than a hundred pounds, the same as each dog, and Kelly yanked her out of the back seat with ease. Claire squirmed and twisted a little, trying to free herself from Kelly's grasp, but even Claire knew it was futile. Kelly was stronger and more determined.

Claire reached for the dogs' leashes. "Dogs. Come!"

"Not them," Kelly said. "Peter and Nicholas are going for a walk in the park today."

"I'll have your job!" Claire threatened.

"You will? Okay, fair trade. I'll be the dog walker, and you can be the driver. I'll walk these two adorable guys around the park all day, and you can be stuck inside this car listening to everybody's problems."

"I will have Marcus fire you the second he gets home."

"That's not going to be as easy as you think. He loves his dogs. That's what I've heard. I wonder how he will feel when he finds out those dogs have been mistreated. No, not mistreated—abused is a better word."

"The driver speaks the truth," Jack, the doorman, called out. Unexpected, but nonetheless, he apparently had witnessed a few atrocities too.

A sudden realization struck Kelly: if nobody liked the dog walker, then why was the dog walker still employed by Mr. Irving? Oh, why hadn't she seen it sooner? Or at the very least suspected it? Of course, this woman, petite and pretty, who hated dogs, was clearly not a dog walker at all, but something so much more.

Kelly took a chance. She leaned in close to Claire and whispered. "You're having an affair with Mr. Irving. That's the only reason you're still here, and I'm going to blow it all out of the water."

Claire's face turned stone cold. She was listening now for the first time. "Marcus knows about the affair, you fool."

"But does he want everyone else to know? He's going to be very angry with you. I have an announcement to take to the entire Irving household and maybe even the tabloids, unless..."

"Unless what?" Claire hissed through clenched teeth.

"Unless you want to really walk Peter and Nicholas around the park for a couple hours every day. You can go into the boathouse and warm up. Have a cocktail at the Tavern on the Green. They will allow three well-behaved dogs on the bar side. I don't care what you do, but you will be inside that park for two solid hours, mostly walking those beloved pets around so I can have the two hours you promised me. How does that sound?"

Claire's hands fisted at her sides. "Whatever." She flopped back inside the Rolls.

"One more thing." Kelly was on a roll. "If I ever see you mistreating them, even speaking to them without a loving, kind, gentle inflection, the deal is off. You can start by calling them by their proper names."

They had a new deal, Kelly and Claire, and Kelly felt absolutely certain Claire would not deviate from this one. Kelly transported the three to the park as planned and deposited them at the front entrance. "Have a lovely walk, Miss Claire. It's good for you, the fresh air, the exercise. I think you will come to really enjoy it, over time."

"Why don't you shut up and go and—"

"Hold on now," Kelly interrupted. "I warned you. We don't want those pups hearing any foul language."

Claire spun on her heels and kept a brisk pace all the way into the park. The snow was falling heavier now and the wind had picked up. It was a miserable day for a walk. Kelly was sure Claire would duck into a few buildings to warm up, but that didn't matter. The dogs could use some warming up too.

The only question that remained was exactly how Mr. Irving had uncovered Claire's whereabouts in the first place. How had he discovered she had left the park and gone into The Plaza? Did Irving have a friend in The Plaza who had seen Claire? Was it nothing more than a coincidence? Or maybe Mr. Irving had been having Claire followed. Kelly had not yet met this man, but she wouldn't put it past him. The home surveillance cameras did not point to a person who extended very much trust.

Kelly really didn't mind if Mr. Irving was watching her. In fact, she thought, all the better, because this man's family was a mess. There were problems behind every turn, literally, and Mr. Irving needed to get home and address them.

***

Kelly left Claire in Central Park and headed to 134th Street. Two precious hours with Rose. A gift above any other gift, other than this job itself.

But first, one quick stop along the way.

She had seen the pop-up Christmas tree shop for a month, walked past it without giving it a second thought, until today. With this paycheck coming, Kelly could afford a tree, and she chose one very carefully. A blue spruce, like her dad always had. In fact, she chose two.

One for her apartment and one for Dad's. Each tree was about four feet high and fit nicely inside the Rolls's trunk, but the lid wouldn't close. The shop owner gave her some twine, and she tied the lid down as best she could. When Kelly pulled away, she couldn't help but laugh. A Rolls-Royce winding through the Upper West with a couple of Christmas trees sticking out the back was an unusual sight indeed. Somebody who owned a Rolls could easily order Christmas trees, probably from some expensive tree farm up in Connecticut or Maine, and have them shipped directly to their home. The movers would set up the trees and the designers would decorate them.

Since her mom passed away, Kelly's dad had never asked for a Christmas tree or any happy thing that reminded him of Mom. "It's a new time now," he'd say. "Not worse, not better, just different."

Yes, Dad, Kelly thought, *it is a new time again, and it's time for a tree.* And yet, a pit formed in her stomach at the thought of Dad's reaction. There were times in life when happiness seemed an insult to the sorrow; everyone deserved time to grieve; there was no right or wrong length. But maybe, just maybe, a nudge in a happy direction would be good for all of them.

Kelly pulled the Rolls up to 134th and parked. She yanked one of the trees from the trunk and hoisted it into her apartment building, down one flight of stairs to her garden apartment, and opened the door with a kick.

Mrs. Andrews and Rose were seated on the bed, reading a book. Rose was propped up against her pillows, as usual, with Mrs. Andrews seated beside her. They both looked up in great astonishment as Kelly lumbered inside the tiny space with the live evergreen. The tree seemed much larger in here than in the parking lot. "Look what I bought."

Mrs. Andrews smiled, but Rose was immediately confused, as Kelly predicted she would be. Rose's sweet face contorted with fear of the unknown, and Kelly abandoned the tree to the floor, coming to Rose's side and stroking her hair.

"It's a Christmas tree, Rose," Kelly explained. "We are going to keep it inside the apartment and dress it all up. We're going to string colored lights on it and hang some pretty decorations and it's going to brighten up the whole place...and..." Kelly placed Rose's chubby palm against her heart. "Inside here, too."

Rose looked from the tree to her mother and back again, longing to understand, but it was clear that her day hadn't been going well. "Not a good day?" Kelly addressed Mrs. Andrews.

"The headaches seem to be worse. I gave her the medication. We've been sitting quietly and reading, napping now and then. We'll tackle the alphabet again tomorrow."

Setbacks were expected in their weekly routine, but they were minimized because there was always tomorrow. Rose did not have a definitive diagnosis other than chronic migraines. She was developmentally delayed in speech and cognizant reasoning and problem-solving. She had crawled and walked at the proper times but lagged in certain milestones compared to her age group. As Rose grew older, she was able to point to her head, use the word "hurt," but the doctors could find no biological or scientific reason for the pain. Blood counts had been done dozens of times, along with MRIs, CT scans, and X-ray upon X-ray. She'd had Botox injections, acupuncture, hormone therapy, vitamins, minerals, physical therapy, and homeopathic remedies of all kinds, but nothing worked.

The headaches prevented Rose from attending any sort of preschool or childcare center. She needed to rest during the day, lie down in a dark, quiet place. Rose had been confined to the apartment for most of her three years on earth. She had grown to fear the outdoors because everything that waited for Rose beyond the protection of these four walls—the sunshine, the traffic noise, the strong odors of car fumes and fried food and stagnant sewer grates—made her head pain intolerable.

Kelly had worked with Rose as best she could, between Kelly's bartending job and the babysitters, but Rose needed a real teacher, and finally, after three years, Kelly could afford one. Mrs. Andrews was certified in special ed and elementary ed and physical therapy, and together they would fight to get Rose ready for the hope of elementary school.

This was Kelly's dream—her daughter attending a real school. Something most parents took for granted.

Rose watched intently while Kelly set the blue spruce up at the far corner of the room. She put the tree inside her old tree stand and tightened the bolts, and then she brought out two strands of Christmas tree lights. They were multicolored, her favorite kind, and she wrapped them loosely around the tree.

Kelly owned no ornaments, but she had an idea. She used a spool of red paper ribbon she had been saving for Christmas gifts and looped it around the little tree from top to bottom.

"That box of candy canes," Mrs. Andrews suggested, and Kelly hung miniature hooks of red and white stripes on the tree.

Now for the treetop. Kelly rummaged through a drawer to find that old Christmas card, sent from her mother years ago. It was a photo of an angel, blue and white and glittering gloriously. Kelly had saved it, not because of the photo on the front, but because of the words inside. Mom had written *Miracles are found in the most unlikely places. Never stop looking.*

Kelly wedged the paper card atop the tree. Then Kelly plugged in the lights.

Rose's eyes glowed in the reflection of red and green and yellow and purple. She climbed out from beneath her bedcovers. She was still wearing her nightgown. That was not a good sign. Rose had been feeling far worse than Mrs. Andrews revealed. Kelly would have to speak to Mrs. Andrews about that. Kelly had witnessed every sort of hard day, and she wanted to know the truth. She needed the truth.

Rose approached the tree and knelt in front of it. She reached out and gingerly touched the tips of the piney branches. A needle pricked her finger, and she pulled back suddenly, held her finger tight to her chest, and tried again. She traced her hand down a single evergreen branch, from back to front, over and over again. She examined the lights, held the little gleaming bulbs in her palm and watched them for some time.

"A tree," Rose said over and over. "A tree."

"A Christmas tree," Kelly corrected.

"I love." Rose tried to hug the tree and Kelly laughed.

"I'd say this tree is a hit," Kelly said to Mrs. Andrews, who had come up alongside her.

"This was a great idea," Mrs. Andrews replied. "But I had better warn you, you might never get that tree out of this house."

Kelly turned to face Mrs. Andrews. "Would that be such a bad thing?"

"It would be very special. Oh, and something wonderful did happen this morning. Rose is putting three words together. She looked out the window, saw the snow falling, and said, 'More snow outside.'"

"One more hurdle added to the list. Every single one helps."

"It's not just the words." Mrs. Andrews's eyes lit up like the tree before them. "It's the processing. She remembered the words. She used them properly and logically, and she recited them correctly. This is more proof, one more piece of the puzzle that shows she is capable of learning and will never stop."

Kelly's eyes clung to her daughter, who was still mesmerized by the tree. "Never stop," Kelly repeated.

On her way out, Kelly noticed that annoying puddle of water forming again in the middle of the room. "Just mop that thing up now and then," she instructed Mrs. Andrews. "These puddles come and go. Don't worry, it's fairly clean water. There must be a leaking pipe somewhere. We are in the basement, you know, but the rent is cheap, and that's all that matters for now."

"I mopped it, three times. It keeps coming back, but it doesn't get any bigger than that. Very odd."

The puddle was about twelve inches round, as usual. It formed a perfect circle in the center of the room. "They've always cleaned up before." Kelly worried. "At least temporarily." Apartments at this price did not exist in the city without a catch. And this catch was never a problem before.

"This one must be more stubborn than the others," Mrs. Andrews joked. "I'll set a pot over it, and we'll ignore it."

"I'll take a look when I get back home tonight. Please don't report it to the superintendent. I've lived with that water for years now. It'll be fine." Kelly put the matter out of her head. It was easy to do. After years of disappointments and heartaches, she had learned that placing them out of thought was a wonderful way to gain peace. *Don't worry about something that hasn't happened yet.* That puddle wasn't a real problem. Yet.

Kelly slipped into her chauffeur coat and double-checked the keys in her pocket. "I have to run. I have a couple of dogs waiting. Actually three."

Mrs. Andrews overemphasized her surprise.

"I'm not kidding." Kelly kissed Rose atop her head. "I love you, Rose." Kelly always said those words coming and going, and she couldn't help but wonder if Mr. Irving ever bothered to say those words to his family.

When Kelly returned to the park's front entrance, she found Claire slipping and sliding up the icy sidewalk with both dogs in tow. The snow was still falling, whipped sideways by the wind, and ruffling Claire's coat and the dogs' fur, but Claire appeared no more frozen than when Kelly had dropped her off. Not on the outside, anyway.

Kelly opened the door and ushered the three inside. "Did you have a nice walk?"

"Hmpf."

"It looks like you found someplace to warm up a bit."

"So now you're going to try to tell me where I can go *inside* the park?"

"Just making an observation."

"Yeah, well, keep your driver's observations to yourself. Take me home." Claire leaned forward, craning for a better view out the front windshield. "Take the shortcut."

Kelly made a sharp turn through the park. She was familiar with the pathway Claire had requested. The road was shorter in distance but longer in time at this hour, but Kelly didn't argue. And when she dropped all three back at the penthouse, Kelly breathed a sigh of relief.

Jack observed the drop-off with renewed interest, seemingly expecting something out of the ordinary to occur, but he wasn't going to witness an entertaining scene this time. Or maybe he was. Kelly followed his line of sight. The evergreen tree was peeping from the trunk of the Rolls. Claire had not even noticed that tree. If eyes could pop from within a head, then Jack's were dangling waist level and bouncing up and down on coil springs. He raised a limp arm and pointed at the trunk.

"It's a Christmas tree," Kelly said matter-of-factly.

He blinked hard and looked again. "The doorman has now officially seen it all."

***

It was finally time to pick up Byron at the courthouse.

Kelly found him waiting out front, blowing puffs of warm air into his cupped hands to keep warm. He spotted the Rolls and stuck his thumb out to hitch for a ride.

Kelly pulled up to the curb and rolled down the rear window. "Can you hop in by yourself this time? It's freezing out."

Byron peered inside the backseat. "Sorry. I can't."

"Why not?"

"There's a reindeer back there."

"Very funny."

"I figure the chance of a Rolls-Royce driving around the city with a Christmas tree sticking out the back is as good as the chance of a reindeer riding in the back seat drinking my Coke."

"Just get in. And not a word about that tree. I'm dropping it off later today."

"My lips are sealed." Byron slid into the back. Kelly had preadjusted Byron's heated and massaged seat and set up the tray table, the footrest, the stars, and the cup. She was an employee of the Irving family and was trying to remember that. As always, Byron laid his backpack in the upright, forward-facing position and his gloves in the same manner. He sat down and pulled out his spiral notebook and began to scan the pages.

"I have a strategy started." The future counselor in Byron emerged. He had spent the entire day plotting and scheming. "Students have rights, you know. Every kid has a right. Isn't that what every legal case is about to begin with? First, you need some proof. Second, you need somebody to tell the story. It's like this case I oversaw this afternoon where this girl—"

"Oversaw?" Kelly willed her face serious. "So that's what you're doing down there now?"

"Stop interrupting. You have a bad habit of interrupting. You know that? It's rude, and you're never going to learn anything if you don't stop to listen now and then."

"Okay. Sorry. I'm listening."

"The case I saw today had a lot of evidence, but they needed the victim to tell her story, in her own words, to make it stick. I realized it's my word against these bullies, and some of the stuff they've done to me is so hard to believe that sometimes I wonder if it all really happened, and stop looking at me like that—yes, it really happened. It's a figure of speech. So, anyway, we need to get some good, solid proof, and I know exactly how to get it."

"But what are you going to do with proof? You don't want to tell the school. You don't want to tell your dad. Who else is there?"

"I've been thinking about that all day. Sometimes, you have to do something you don't want to do in order to get justice. This is why a lot of crimes never get reported...or solved. The victim just wants to put the whole thing out of their head. The very reason the crime is so terrible is the same reason the victim wants to forget about it. It's too painful to go back there, and you really don't want the world to know what happened to you. You feel weak...ashamed." Melancholy crossed Byron's face. "Secretly you wonder if it might be your fault in some way, like you should have known better, or you should have seen it coming or...you...maybe you...deserved it somehow."

"Byron, *nobody* deserves abuse. Nobody."

"I know that. I'm just trying to show you how twisted your thinking gets when you're being abused. It's like you can't think straight anymore."

Kelly deflated. This was the very reason why she never shared her own story with anyone. She felt like a fool for ever having fallen for Damean. He used her, manipulated her, gaslighted her, and he left her. Strike that. He left them both—Kelly and little Rose. The whole story made her look and feel like a complete failure. She didn't want anyone's pity. She didn't want anyone to think she had been that naïve. And she didn't want anyone to see her as used, wounded...even dirtied somehow. So, she had kept it to herself.

Until now.

"I know all about that," Kelly confessed.

"You know?" Byron shot back.

"Yes. I'm not proud to admit it, but I know how it feels."

"Did you tell anybody?"

"It's over now."

"You didn't answer the question. Did you tell?"

"It wasn't illegal." She looked down. "It was pure evil. But it wasn't illegal."

"Doesn't matter." Byron threw his hands up. "You still have to tell somebody."

Kelly's mouth tightened.

Byron leaned forward. "If you want justice—not just for you but for the other people coming after you, the next victim—you have to tell somebody."

Kelly felt her eyes tearing. "You weren't telling anyone either."

Byron's eyes teared, too. "No, I wasn't." He placed a hand on her shoulder. "Until I met you."

"Do you know something, Byron Irving?" Kelly sniffled. "You are one smart kid. Smarter than a typical kid your age."

"That's because I'm not typical." He wiped his wet eyes with his sleeve. "I'm different. That's the reason they hate me so much." He sank into his seat. "I didn't tell you the second part of my plan. I made a decision. I'm going to show the evidence to the jury. I'm going to tell my story."

"You're taking them to court?"

"No. I'm taking it to the only jury that really matters. Like they said in the Magna Carta in 1215, I'm taking this case to a jury of their peers, the other kids at school."

Kelly was speechless.

"It's not going to be easy," Byron reasoned. "It'll be the hardest thing I ever do, but if I've been hurt and you've been hurt, then how many others? It looks like I don't have a choice."

"I'm really proud of you."

"Yeah, well, don't be too proud of me yet. I've got a lot of work to do." Byron focused on his notebook. "First, I need evidence. Videos are super popular right now. You have YouTube, Instagram, Facebook, Snapchat, TikTok, Vlogs. People like them because videos don't tell you what to believe; they show you something and let you decide. We don't need surveillance cameras when we got the next best thing. We carry it with us everywhere we go." Byron pulled out his smartphone. "Take me back up to school. This is their preferred assault time. Every Friday afternoon at this hour. Well, the days I show up anyway, and there haven't been very many of those lately."

"I don't know. I'm worried about this. I don't want you to get hurt. I can't let you go in there alone."

"I'm not alone anymore. I did a little discovery work during my lunch break. I called a couple of video production geeks. They work the cameras and lighting for the high school musicals. I told them I need help filming something. I gave them a few clues and, well, it turns out I'm not the only kid getting treated like a dog. They're going to help me film this thing, cut, edit, that sort of thing."

"They might be filming, but you're the only one being bullied. I can't even think about what you said they've been doing to you. So, I'm supposed to sit outside and wait while you are being abused? If anything happens to you, it's my fault now. I would never let Rose do something like that."

"You would never let Rose stand up for herself? You don't mean that."

"Not if it puts her in danger. No, I would not."

Byron shook two fists toward the sky. "Don't you get it? I'm already in danger. I've been in danger all my life! Haters are never gonna stop hating. I have to do something about it. I have to defend myself. It's time."

A rush of tears made Kelly turn away.

Byron continued. "Nothing is going to happen to me that hasn't already happened. I promise. And now, I've got two witnesses. I'm not going in there alone."

She bit her bottom lip.

"I'm doing it, whether you approve or not. If I don't do it today, I'll do it another day."

Kelly had no rebuttal. She dropped Byron off and watched him take the same pathway he took every morning, up the stone sidewalk to the bright red double doors, but he seemed a little taller today, a little straighter, a little stronger. He wasn't ambling with his head bent low, shuffling and avoiding all eye contact. He wasn't in a big hurry anymore. Byron took his own sweet time, purposefully marching up those school steps and through that front door.

"Byron, be safe," Kelly rolled down the window and called out.

Byron offered a wave without turning back.

Byron wasn't alone. It was three against three now. His friends would be right there with him, filming. Byron was right. They had to find a way to fight back.

Kelly felt nauseous as she waited in the limo. But sometimes the right thing was the hard thing, wasn't it?

9

CHAPTER NINE

A t the end of a very long Friday, Byron climbed out of the Rolls, and Jack, the doorman, clutched his chest as if he were seeing a ghost. But a ghost would have been much more pleasant than the boy who emerged from the back seat with two black eyes, a bloody lip, torn clothing, and a crumpled hat in hand.

Byron had been wrong. The bullies did not merely humiliate him this time. When they sensed that he was fighting back, they became more aggressive than ever before. Kelly had nearly vomited when she first saw Byron emerging from that school, but he reassured her. "I'm fine. All that matters is we got them. We filmed the whole thing, and they don't even know it. We hid the camera crew."

"Your friends weren't by your side? You were all alone?"

"It doesn't matter. It's over."

Jack clutched his hat over his heart while the winter wind tossed his red hair wild. "What the..."

"Don't ask," Kelly said. "But I should add that Byron is the bravest kid I know."

Jack gave Byron a little pat on the back as he passed by, and when Byron was safely inside, Jack grimaced at Kelly.

"It's not what it looks like," she said. "They started it; Byron ended it."

"It doesn't matter. The driver brought the son home like that, and there'll be hell to pay." Jack's eyes shifted to the Rolls's trunk, where Dad's evergreen was still sprouting from beneath the lid. "And she's still got that tree in the trunk," Jack muttered. "The doorman always had something to say but kept his mouth shut, like all good doormen. That's why he kept this job so long. But now, all of a sudden, in the past few days, the doorman's got nothing to say. A million-dollar car with a dead tree sticking out the back, and not a single word comes to mind." He slapped his hat onto his head.

"You're wrong," Kelly said. "That Rolls is only worth about half a million and that tree isn't dead yet." She slid behind the wheel and left Jack standing at the curb, mouth gaping.

Kelly had two hours remaining before picking up Carolyn for her cocktails. Just then, the mobile phone rang.

"How ever is your day progressing thus far, Ms. O'Sullivan?" It was Mr. Perez.

He couldn't possibly have heard already. Could he? "Fine," she mumbled.

"Miss Carolyn called. She would prefer to stay home this evening, so you are finished for the day. Return to the garage for cleanup."

A wave of relief. "Is it alright if I make one quick stop? I need to drop something off on the way."

"As long as it isn't drugs or stolen paraphernalia or friends who need free transport, and, oh, I suppose I should add dead bodies."

"None of the above."

"You have one hour."

"Thank you. See you soon."

Kelly parked a block away from Dad's apartment because if he saw her traipsing up the sidewalk with this tree, he'd be standing on the front step warding her off like she was a sketchy used car salesman. This was a delicate matter—the notion of bringing back Christmas with Mom gone. It had to be handled gently.

Kelly pushed open Dad's door with her shoulder, dragged the tree inside and dropped it on the floor. "Now hear me out. I don't care what you say. You're keeping it. You didn't have a tree last year, and it's time we all celebrated again. Mom would want that for us. I know it's hard to celebrate things without her, but we've been grieving long enough. We are still here, still trying to live this life, and this year, we are both having a tree, and—"

"I...I..." Dad flipped the lever on his recliner to sit up straight. "Hey, would you let me get a word in edgewise?"

"Be quiet and let me finish." Kelly flailed her arms like a traffic cop. "You always interrupt. That's probably where I get it from. I bought a tree for my apartment, and I got one for you, too. I'm going to set it up in the stand for you. That's all I have time for. You are going to string the lights on this thing, hang a few balls. We're going to put it right over there in front of that window so all the neighbors can see it's Christmastime and the O'Sullivans are living again."

Dad folded his hands. "Okay."

"Okay?" Kelly was dumbfounded. "What is this? Some sort of trick?"

His mouth split into a grin. "I always wanted a tree. But you didn't have one, and I didn't want to be over here celebrating with everything you and Rosie were going through, so I sat tight and did whatever you did. But I'm real happy to see that tree in here again. I'll tell you that much. Real happy." Sudden disappointment shadowed his features.

"Although that thing is scrawny and missing a few branches. Is that the best you could do?"

Kelly sat on the footstool. It had been quite a day. A very big, very difficult, but very good day, and sometimes tears came for reasons other than sadness.

Dad leaned forward. "What on earth are you crying about? I said I'd take that dang tree, didn't I?"

"Yes, but you wanted one all along, and I was too busy with Rose to see it."

"Oh, that old tree didn't matter to me all that much. Sure, I'd like a Christmas tree, but that didn't crush me, not having one. What's going on with you, Kel? You're acting a little more crazy than usual."

"I don't know." She hugged her sides. "I'm feeling some guilt...maybe some regrets. To be honest, I haven't been the best daughter since Mom's been gone. I'm trying. But I'm not her. I can't be her as hard as I try."

"Nobody's asking you to."

"You're lonely. You're sad. I get it. There's an emptiness in this old house and I guess I'm just trying to help."

"No. You're trying to fill something that can't be filled. That's what you're trying to do. We can't fill Mom's place. Not you. Not me. Nobody. It's going to feel different now that she's gone. But that's okay."

"How? How is it okay?"

"Because we still got you and we still got me, and we still got our little Rosie, and maybe, just maybe, that's gonna be enough."

The space fell quiet and still. There was so much truth to what Dad just said.

"So, quit your crying, and let's get down to some real important business." Like always, Dad found a way to bring back the happy. "You got that big, fancy Rolls with you?"

"It's parked down the street because I was afraid if you saw that tree coming..." Kelly stopped short. Dad had risen from his chair and was sliding into his boots.

"Where are you going?" she asked.

"Where do you think? For a ride in that Rolls. You're going to drive me all around town and right past Elite Drivers just like I used to do for you and Mom when you were a kid, and I'm going to sit in that back seat waving at everybody because old Seamus O'Sullivan is in the passenger seat now. Remember how you'd slip on those cheap sunglasses from the drugstore and give everybody in town some kind of royal wave?"

"You saw that?"

"Of course I saw that. Drivers don't miss a trick."

"You're right about that one." Kelly stood and brushed off her pant legs. "Okay, Dad. I'd be happy to take you for a drive."

Dad found his coat. "That thing got those heated seats you were telling me about?"

"Yes, it does."

"How about that massage? I read all about that."

"Yes, that, too. Oh, and there's stars on the ceiling, a footrest and a drink station. I'm sure they wouldn't mind if you helped yourself to a Diet Coke."

"Don't mind if I do. Let's get this party started. Oh, and crank up the music. Frank Sinatra will do."

"What about the tree?" Kelly paused. "I was going to put it in the stand for you."

"I'd like to do that myself. I'll spend the night putting that thing together, like your mother and I used to do. I'll get all those tangled lights out that I used to hate putting up over the years, and I'll probably curse a little just for fun and maybe even enjoy it for the first time in my life." Dad pulled Kelly into a big bear hug. "Sometimes we wait too long to enjoy stuff," he whispered in her ear. "We wait for everything to be perfect, but we'll be waiting forever because life is never going to be perfect, and we need to sit back and find something good and celebrate it and enjoy it every single lousy day of our lives. Before it's too late. With the sad comes the happy, like I always told you. It's there. When we're ready to see it."

Dad grabbed his hat and aimed straight for the automobile. He found it a block down and waited by the back. "If you don't mind." He pointed to the door, and Kelly opened it wide.

"Good afternoon, Mr. O'Sullivan." She bowed. "My, you look handsome today."

"That's laying it on a little thick." He slid into the back. "Just a 'good afternoon' will do."

Kelly drove Dad all around the Lower East, and she could feel him smiling behind her. He played the radio, opened the sunroof and all the windows despite the frigid temperatures, and waved at the people on the sidewalk. He even leaned into the front seat and honked the horn a few times.

This was exactly what Mr. Perez had asked Kelly *not* to do, but if Mr. Perez knew it was Seamus O'Sullivan in the back, she suspected he might turn a blind eye.

"Oh," Kelly said. "I almost forgot. Someone wanted me to tell you hello."

"Who's that?"

"Mr. Perez. He manages my garage, if you want to call it that. It's actually a penthouse for automobiles."

"Perez? That old guy? I used to meet him at the diner every afternoon. I'd get the hot corned beef, he'd get the matzo ball, and we'd argue about everything from politics to the weather. He's still working? Well, you tell him I said cars are a thing of the past. They're on their way out. Pretty soon, nobody will own one. Sure, collectors maybe, for touching and looking, but nobody will drive anymore. We'll order car service ahead of time, just like they do with those Ubers, and the cars will hover over the road, no wheels and no more drivers. No more car payments, no insurance. You tell him I said that day's coming. He's a thing of history. Like that little side vent window. Or the floor button for the high beams. He's over and done with." Dad had a good laugh at that private joke. "He never was much good at driving, anyway. You can add that, too."

"I hate to ask, but what does that mean for my career?"

"Aww, don't you worry about a thing. You're not working that job forever. Just until you get on your feet, and then, back to your art thing."

Those were the very best words a dad could say to his daughter, especially this one.

***

Kelly returned to the parking garage nearly an hour later than she'd promised. Mr. Perez had been waiting for her again, hands on his hips.

She parked the car. "I know, I know. I'm a little late. Sorry."

"We have another situation. Mr. Irving is now returning earlier than the previous early. Next Saturday morning. He wants you to pick him up at 9 a.m., JFK, private terminal."

"Saturday? At nine in the morning?"

"I would recommend you stop fixating on the time of Mr. Irving's arrival and become greatly concerned with the *reason* for his arrival. He wants a word with you."

"Is it that issue with Carolyn? She promised to resolve that. It was a big misunderstanding."

"It's *Miss* Carolyn."

"Okay, so Miss Carolyn and I sorted that all out."

"That is exactly what she informed Mr. Irving. That she's happier than ever before." Mr. Perez tapped his fingers through the air as if he were playing an invisible piano. "Ms. O'Sullivan has been helping her with some things, and her life is back on track." Now an invisible violin was being played. "Some sort of nonsensical female rationalization, and the two of you have become the very best of friends. Imagine that! The driver and the CEO's girlfriend—the very best of friends!"

Kelly felt a surge of defense. "Why is that nonsense? Women are not allowed to have friends? Women cannot ask for help, especially Carolyn? Or maybe this is the very problem—that Mr. Irving thinks only *he* can help Carolyn get her life back on track, and maybe, just maybe, he doesn't really want that for her. Maybe he wants her to stay dependent on him...for everything."

"Do not go there."

Kelly twisted her mouth. "I'm sorry. I didn't mean any of that. It's been a long day, that's all."

"Well, you have one week left to repair any remaining damage and prepare yourself for Mr. Irving's performance review. You've done fine thus far, but I am warning you, Mr. Irving is different from the rest of the family. He will not tolerate any intrusion. You are his driver. Period. He is probably planning on reprimanding you. He probably wants to meet this dubious pundit who has graced his family's presence." Mr. Perez's eyes trailed Kelly, top to bottom. "To determine if you present any sort of real threat, but when he finally meets you, I am certain he will rest assured there is nothing to worry about."

"Gee, thanks."

Mr. Perez raised his pointer finger. "You cannot be an expert in all things, Ms. O'Sullivan. A driver, yes. A therapist and counselor and very best friend of all time, no."

"Let me set the record straight here. Carolyn needed help and I helped her. And as for Claire..."

"Who said anything about Miss Claire? That woman absolutely loathes you but is being very tight-lipped about the matter, which is unlike her. She is the reason every driver was either fired or quit, but not you. Not yet anyway." Mr. Perez stroked his chin. "A very curious matter indeed."

"Well, the feeling is mutual. I can't stand her for a lot of good reasons."

Mr. Perez worked his jaw from left to right, choosing his next words carefully. "As a driver, you will be privy to some very personal information, some secrets perhaps, some comings and goings that no one is aware of except yourself, and it should remain that way. You are not entitled to feelings of any sort."

"I have no intention of telling anybody anything about Claire. But the proof is there. All that surveillance, that could backfire on Irving someday."

"It's *Mr.* Irving." Mr. Perez threw up his hands. "Not your paranoid hidden camera conspiracy theory again."

"It's not a theory. It's a fact. I've heard it from a few reliable sources. Not just Claire. But even with those cameras, Mr. Irving doesn't know everything," Kelly continued. "That's the problem. He knows the superficial stuff—where they are physically at all times—but he hasn't made any effort to get to know what's happening on the inside, where it really matters."

"Even if that is true"—Mr. Perez raised his pointer so high Kelly thought he might be preparing to soar through the air—"and I emphasize the word 'if,' then this may very well be a problem, but you, the driver, will never be the one to advise him of such."

"Believe me, I understand completely. I need this job, and I am not going to sabotage it." Kelly started toward the break room. "I can promise you that."

Mr. Perez called out, "You have a family lineage to uphold. What would your father say about all this? Oh, I can hear him now. He would not be pleased. Not pleased at all."

Kelly stopped short. She turned back, studying Mr. Perez before responding. "My dad sent you a message. He said to tell you something about cars going extinct. Nobody is going to own any. You will have to order a ride and there won't be a driver behind the wheel. The car is going to hover above the ground, and nobody will—"

"Stop right there. Now I see the root of your delusional theories. It appears to be hidden within your DNA, much like the skill of driving itself." Mr. Perez feigned anger. "I will not acquiesce to such absolute fantastical nonsense. You tell Mr. O'Sullivan that it appears I am still employed in a parking garage, wherein the owner proudly drives hundreds of automobiles all across this beautiful city."

"It could be true—cars going extinct. Look at all the Ubers out there."

With this, Mr. Perez could not contain his grin. "Ahhhh, and as always with Seamus O'Sullivan, a sliver of truth is embedded within his tall tale. Just enough to render the impossible possible."

"My dad always tells the truth."

"Of course. That was never held in question. But the truth that you believe is not the truth that someone else believes. *Seeing is believing*, as they say. I am still employed, caring for the most expensive and luxurious automobiles in the city, and your father is not. You may tell him I said that."

"Okay. I'll tell him. But it might be easier if the two of you met for coffee rather than me serving as your message courier."

Mr. Perez stroked his chin again. "Yes, I do believe your father needs some sense spoken into him. It appears he has lost all semblance of reality since I tutored him last. Tell him that I invite him to a lively in-person debate. Next Friday afternoon, the usual place, the usual time. Be prepared for some dressing-down."

***

Kelly replayed her conversation with Mr. Perez the entire subway ride home, down the cracked, uneven sidewalk to 134th; down the steps; and even into the garden apartment. Mr. Irving was coming home early and he wanted to speak with Kelly. She was confident that she had done nothing wrong. Was it possible to care too much about someone? Was it possible *not* to care? What kind of a person would she be if she watched someone suffer and did nothing about it? But this was different. She wasn't sure what she was going to say to Mr. Irving, but she could not risk losing her job. Rose came first.

"Welcome home." Mrs. Andrews also had a life separate from teaching and babysitting Rose, and she was pleased to be returning home to her husband.

"How did it go today?" Kelly found Rose seated beside the Christmas tree, scanning the pages of a book.

"She seems to feel a little perkier since that tree arrived. Or maybe she feels the same, but the tree brightened this room enough for her to *try* to feel better. Things have a way of doing that. People, places, objects..."

Kelly knew what Mrs. Andrews was implying. Even on our worst days, one bright ray of sunshine can help us to keep moving forward. Or a holiday you've never allowed yourself to enjoy before.

"But that puddle." Mrs. Andrews mused. "I've mopped it up about a dozen times, and it keeps coming back. The odd thing is, I don't see any water trickling in from anywhere."

"It must be coming from the corners of the walls or cracks in the floor. Maybe a broken pipe." But Kelly knew a formal complaint might result in the basement being claimed uninhabitable. Kelly pushed the intrusive thought from her mind and found the puddle, now covered by the old cooking pot. "It's not getting any bigger, is it?"

"That's the strangest thing, too. It doesn't get any bigger or smaller. It stays about a foot around, a perfect circle. After I mop it up, when I look again, there it is, exactly the same shape and size."

"Very strange." Kelly lightened the mood. "Maybe that little puddle likes it here and wants to stay." It felt like the least of her issues right now as she studied Rose, who kept her eyes on the pages of her book. "Rose looks a little better now."

"Oh, yes. She is doing remarkably well. I am actually quite pleased. Today she counted to nineteen. She spoke several new sentences. I lowered the dosage of the medication slightly so she could concentrate on her studies, and she massaged her temples from time to time, but she didn't complain." Mrs. Andrews gazed lovingly at Rose. "She loves her books. She can't get enough of them."

Kelly gently reached for Mrs. Andrews's hand. "I can't thank you enough. Before you came, I had a long list of babysitters, and that was exactly what they did. Sit and watch and complain. They thought Rose was incapable of learning anything. They were so fixated on her temperament, her mood changes, that they couldn't see anything more. I felt like people either wanted to medicate her or say it wasn't really happening. That she was just a finicky child. Nobody listened to me. Nobody believed me, until you."

"We all do that sometimes. We see what's on the outside—the miserable face, the cruel words—and we never look any deeper. We never ask ourselves why someone behaves a certain way; we only want them to stop. Oh, what this world would be like if we took the time to understand each other."

"You understand," Kelly said.

"I understand because I lived it." Mrs. Andrews inclined her head toward Rose. "I was that little girl, so very long ago. Someone helped me, and now I'm doing the same."

The hope of those words wrapped around Kelly like a warm blanket, soothing the tension that never seemed to release. "Rose someday too," she whispered.

After Mrs. Andrews left, Kelly gave Rose a soothing bath and readied her for sleep. But Rose refused her bed. She retrieved her blanket and insisted on snuggling on the floor beside the Christmas tree lights. Kelly prodded and begged, but Rose wouldn't budge. Kelly reasoned that today had been a day for breaking routines, so why not? She shifted the mattress onto the floor and slid it very close to the tree. Rose hunkered down beneath the shelter of the piney branches and twinkling lights, and Kelly lay beside her until Rose was sound asleep.

Now, time to investigate that stubborn puddle. Kelly removed the pot, and sure enough, there it was, as Mrs. Andrews had described: perfectly round, about a foot in circumference. But this water appeared different from the previous puddles Kelly had seen in the apartment before. It was bluer somehow. Clearer, cleaner, if that was even possible. Kelly dipped her finger into the wetness, and it felt cool, almost tingly.

She scanned the corners of the room. No signs of leakage from any direction.

That is odd, she thought. Maybe the puddle wasn't coming from the corners after all. She searched the floor for cracks but found none. They must have been hair-width, so tiny they were invisible, but water always found a way.

Kelly covered the water with the pot again and dismissed it for now. Mrs. Andrews said she didn't mind. There was nothing to worry about.

She tossed bedsheets and a pillow onto the sofa. The studio apartment only had space for a single bed, and that bed had always belonged to Rose. Kelly was unable to give her daughter a real bedroom of her own, but she could certainly give her a special bed, and Kelly had decorated that bed with a princess comforter, fuzzy pink pillows and stuffed animals.

Most nights, Rose would stir, and Kelly would discover Rose watching her. It was a comfort, opening your eyes during a dark and painful night and finding your mother, always a few feet away. Sometimes they would give a little wave to each other, or Kelly would wink, and Rose would try to wink back by squeezing both eyes closed.

Kelly collapsed onto the sofa and rested her head on the pillow. She watched Rose sleeping. Soft breaths swept gently in and out of her lungs. Her eyelashes fluttered. Rose drew her arm up and crooked her elbow around her head. She moaned slightly. Her brows furrowed. A bad dream or pain?

Kelly sat up, waiting, wondering. Should she lay beside Rose? Comfort her in some way? But she didn't want to disturb her. Even restless sleep was better than no sleep at all.

Rose's frown melted. The steady, equal breathing returned. She became still again. Perfectly still and peace-filled, at least for a little while.

Kelly lay her head back down and tried to sleep, too. If Mom were here, she would know just what to do. *But she's not. She's gone.*

Kelly whispered to the dark. "I miss you, Mom. We're doing okay. We got a Christmas tree. You would be proud of us."

10

CHAPTER TEN

T he following week could not have gone better, at least in Kelly's opinion. All passengers remained on a strict schedule. Byron was now attending school with his newfound friends. Apparently, the bullies only attacked loners, and as long as Byron and his friends stuck together, they were relatively safe. Carolyn was absolutely elated and chatted about nothing but her preparations for springboarding into her writing career. Claire was miserable, which gave Kelly a certain assurance that she was, indeed, walking the dogs throughout Central Park.

But Saturday came, whether Kelly agreed or not, and Mr. Irving was on his way home. Early Saturday morning, Kelly transported Byron to water polo. He had missed his practice on Friday and insisted on making it up. He was seated in the back of the Rolls enjoying his heated seat, footrest and Diet Coke, but no massage chair. He had haphazardly tossed his backpack onto the floor and wasn't even wearing his gloves or scarf today.

Kelly discreetly surveyed Byron's healing wounds from a week ago. The bruises were yellowing and the cuts scabbed over. Kelly remembered Mrs. Andrews's words. *We see what's on the outside, and we never look any deeper.* Byron's hidden wounds, his heart, and his soul were healing faster than his physical wounds. He caught Kelly staring, and she looked away.

"I know. I still don't look so good," Byron said, echoing Kelly's thoughts. "But I'm holding my own. Me and my friends have become invisible, like *Stranger Things* and *Harry Potter* all wrapped up into one."

He waited for Kelly's reaction, but his comment did not bring her comfort.

"Anyway," Byron continued, switching to real-world reasoning, "we're editing the tapes today. Wednesday is the school assembly in the aud. We're going to clip our video and splice it into the headmaster's presentation. It's all the proof we need. The school will be forced to take some sort of ethical action against the bullies, probably put them on probation or suspension, but that's not what we're really after because probation is only going to make those guys look tougher than ever before. Oh, they're going to be famous alright, but for a whole different reason."

Kelly swallowed hard. "I'm proud of you. I mean it. You know what my dad always says? He says there's not one single thing on this earth that we are suffering from that someone else isn't suffering from too. We are never the only one. The world is too big. The goal is to go out and find those people who share your hurt and band together, learn from each other, support each other, find a solution." Of course, Dad had been referring to Rose's headaches.

Byron rubbed the back of his neck. "I might say something like that if they ask me to give a speech. I'm not sure they will. They probably won't. I have a feeling the place will go crazy when they see the video. It'll get pretty wild in there. But if somebody wants me to say something, though, I got a couple things I'd like to say."

My, how Byron's world had shifted and changed in a matter of days. Kelly added, "You said you needed two things to win a case: proof and someone to tell the story. You got the proof. Now go ahead and get your speech ready."

But Byron's happiness edged with wariness. He released a long sigh. Kelly knew it was one matter to stand behind a projector and roll a film and quite another to stand at a podium and present an argument. Byron confessed. "What if nobody likes what I have to say? I'm not talking about the headmaster. I'm talking about the students. I've never connected with any of them. Like I said, I'm different."

"We're all different. It's just that some of us try to hide it. Different means you're willing to be who you were meant to be, even if you don't fit in. To stand up for what you believe in, even if it's not popular. Look at it this way: if nobody in all this world ever dared to be any different from the rest, then nothing special would have ever been invented or discovered or sung or written or painted or—"

"Okay, okay, I get it." Byron hesitated, then said, "You're different, Kelly. You know that?"

Kelly blew air through her nose. "I guess I am."

"You're the only driver who ever talked to me. I mean really talked." Byron made an abrupt topic change. "I heard you're meeting Dad today."

"I'm picking him up at the airport." Kelly tested. "Earlier than planned."

"I heard that, too." Byron gave her a look. "I heard Claire talking to Chef, and she told him that you were in some sort of trouble from friending Carolyn. Claire doesn't like you much. If it makes you feel any better, Claire doesn't like anybody. She was really happy that Dad's coming home early and you're in some kind of trouble and that, for once in her life, she had nothing to do with it. Carolyn's to blame for this one."

"I am a friend to Carolyn. That's all. Just like I've been a friend to you."

"We all know that. Everybody but Dad. The problem is really all my dad's fault. It usually is. Carolyn doesn't get attention from him, but Claire sure does. It doesn't matter what Carolyn tries to do, Dad isn't going to treat her the same way he treats Claire. He doesn't see Carolyn that same way. Carolyn is sort of an airhead. You probably noticed that too." Byron held Kelly's gaze in the mirror. "She likes attention...from everybody and anybody. And now she's getting it from you. That's all she wants."

"Oh, I don't know. I think it's more than that."

Byron pointed to the Athletic Club. "Drop me off anywhere."

Kelly offered Byron full disclosure. "Carolyn is going to be a different person when your dad gets back home."

"You're drinking Carolyn's Kool-Aid. She is the exact same person she's always been, now pretending to be somebody different so Dad takes another look at her, and maybe, just maybe, he falls in love with her again and out of love with Claire."

Kelly gripped the wheel tighter. "You're very cynical for a four-teen-year-old."

"I want to know the truth from the start, like I told you the first day I met you." Byron let himself out and added, "You only want to see the good in everybody." He slung his backpack over his shoulder. "I got my own ride home. But in case you have nothing to do, I have a polo match today at two. A real game. Dad can't come because he's just getting into town and everything. But you can come...if you want. Why don't you bring your daughter?"

Kelly's breath caught in her throat. She never took Rose anywhere. Not even to Dad's. Rose didn't like the bright outdoor light; it made her migraines roar, and as a result, she cried at the very notion of venturing outside. Kelly had saved two hundred dollars for a special pair of child-size sunglasses, but Rose would have nothing to do with them. She was only three, after all, and even a hat didn't feel quite right and was quickly discarded.

"She doesn't go out much," Kelly answered.

"So, maybe she should start."

Kelly considered this. Rose's only excursion had been to the doctor's office and back. But Rose was much different than even weeks ago, wasn't she? She was learning and growing and... "Maybe," Kelly said with a hint of excitement. "Two o'clock today, you say?"

"Yep."

"We'll see. I have the afternoon off. I don't know. I'm not sure how she would do."

"You will never know until you give it a try. See you at two. Don't be late. I don't want to cause any commotion up in the stands. We need to focus on this game. It's a big one."

Kelly left Byron at the curb and headed for the airport. Every anxiety she had been feeling about meeting the infamous Mr. Irving melted slightly with the notion of taking Rose on an excursion. She cranked the radio up loud, and the Frank Sinatra music that her dad had requested blasted from the surround sound.

New York City traffic was light this Saturday morning. She took the Kennedy Bridge and merged onto I-278. Mr. Perez had given Kelly strict instructions: "Pull up to the Private Terminal arrivals and wait. Do not leave that car unattended. Not for even one solitary minute. Mr. Irving will find you. He always does. Do you understand?"

"Yes, I understand more than I'm allowed."

Mr. Irving's flight was due to arrive at a quarter past nine, and Kelly had checked the app several times to be sure there were no delays. She pulled the Rolls up to Arrivals at exactly nine, allowing plenty of time for him to exit his private plane. He had only a carry-on, Mr. Perez had said.

And within minutes, there he was, in the flesh, looking exactly as Kelly expected: a tall man, with blond hair cut short and spiked unintentionally, wearing an expensive camel-hair overcoat opened to the wind, leather gloves, and a scarf, with a briefcase in one hand and a roller bag in the other. A grown-up version of Byron.

"Mr. Irving?" Kelly stood beside the Rolls.

"Yes."

"Welcome home." She opened the door, and he slid into the back. She had not considered preheating his seat or preparing the footrest, and what was his beverage of choice again?

She made her way around the front fender, scooted behind the wheel, and started the engine. Frank Sinatra's crooning voice blasted a shock wave throughout the interior, vibrating the entire auto and Mr. Irving with it. Kelly frantically found the volume while Irving folded his arms and tapped his foot (not in beat with the music).

"Sorry," she shouted. "So sorry." She turned off the radio, switched the car into drive and began to pull away from the curb.

"Aren't you forgetting something?" he said.

Kelly slammed the brakes, and Mr. Irving lurched forward, bracing himself against the front seat.

"I know, and I'm so sorry," Kelly fought to explain. "It's so cold out and snowing like crazy, and I forgot to heat your seat up, but I'll never forget again. I made a few mistakes my first day of work, but I corrected all of them. It was only my first day, after all. Actually, I made a couple mistakes the next day, too, but that's over now. I've got the hang of it. Just wait and see." Why, oh why was she admitting all that? *Stop talking, Kelly. Stop.*

"My bag." Mr. Irving pointed to his roller bag sitting forlorn at the curb, teetering back and forth with each icy gust.

"Your bag." Kelly threw the Rolls into park, then quickly retrieved the roller bag, with the initials MBI embossed in leather, and shoved it into the trunk. She inhaled a few deep breaths and made the conscious decision not to speak one more word.

She merged onto the highway. Only about forty-five minutes until Central Park, and Mr. Irving would be deposited safely home. Forty-five minutes of excellent driving skills, no conversation, both hands on the wheel at ten and two. But curiosity got the best of her, and she dared to glance in the mirror, just once, one glimpse of this man she had heard so much about, and there he was, staring back at her.

Glaring might have been a better word.

"So, Ms. O'Sullivan. Let's grab some breakfast, shall we?"

"You mean, you and me? Together?"

"That's exactly what I mean. Head to Bergdorf's. There's a little coffee shop across the street called Viand. I like it in there. It's nice and quiet, and they have a great crumb cake."

"Well, I only have a couple hours." What was Kelly sputtering now? She worked for Mr. Irving twenty-four seven. She knew that; he knew that. He dictated her times, this car...her life and everyone else's. But Byron's polo match...

"Oh, it won't take long," Mr. Irving said.

Did any of this even matter, she wondered? Was she about to get fired, like all the other drivers who'd come before her? And if so, whose fault would that be? Claire's? Carolyn's? Or maybe it was nobody's fault but her own.

They drove the remainder of the way to midtown in silence. Kelly dropped Mr. Irving in front of The Viand diner, found a parking garage several blocks away, and raced back to the restaurant. She fought to catch her breath as she sat across from Mr. Irving in a two-person booth, wedged tightly against the wall. The coffee shop was long and narrow, with tiny booths on one side, the dining counter on the other, and very little walkway to pass between the two. She doubted this was the location Mr. Irving usually chose for breakfast with his business associates. She imagined someplace like the Union League, with thick mahogany walls, velvet chairs, and tuxedoed waitstaff. But this was surely a location he would pick to discreetly fire his driver.

Kelly slipped out of her chauffeur coat but left her driver's cap on. Beneath, she wore the black suit, white shirt, and black tie. The driver's uniform.

Mr. Irving did the same. He removed his camel-hair coat, folded it neatly and set it beside him. Then he pulled his gloves from his fingers, from thumb to little finger, one by one, and laid them neatly atop the coat, upright, forward-facing.

The waiter approached, and Mr. Irving spoke without looking at him. "Two coffees and two crumb cakes." His eyes were fixed on Kelly. "Is that okay with you?"

"That's fine."

When the waiter left, Mr. Irving folded his hands on the table and scrutinized Kelly for a minute or two. She averted his gaze, but in this small space, it was impossible. She fumbled with her hands, watched the waiter taking his other orders.

Finally, Mr. Irving spoke. "So, Ms. O'Sullivan, you've been driving my family now for, what, a couple weeks?"

"Two weeks."

"How would you rate your new position thus far on a scale of one to ten? I'm curious."

"I'd say..." Kelly bit her bottom lip. The normal response would be a ten, of course. The employee simply loves her new job. She's never had a job better than this one. *Oh, thank you so very much for scraping me up off the sidewalk and giving me a life,* or something like that. And some of this was true, but... "Seven," she heard herself say.

Mr. Irving's lips curled. Kelly felt her face redden. He leaned back, crossed one leg at the knee and put his hand on his ankle. "Just a seven? What, the Rolls isn't to your liking?"

That comment irked her. As if her only real responsibility and interaction were with the automobile. "Do I like the car? Is that what you're asking me?"

He shrugged as if he didn't really care if she liked the car or the job. This was all a big game.

Kelly was going to be fired. What did she have to lose? "Is that how you rate *your* job, Mr. Irving? By the comfort of your desk, your ergonomic chair, your desk lamp, all to your liking?"

Irving's expression was sheer entertainment. "I am the CEO of a Fortune 100 company that I built from the ground up. You can hardly compare what I do to what you do."

Her heart raced. "Nope." She said "nope" quite purposefully now. "But I think, and tell me if I'm wrong here, *my* job might also be important?"

Irving shot air through his nose. The waiter brought the coffees, and Irving proceeded to, very precisely, add an exact amount of cream and sugar to his cup. He lifted the cup to his mouth while peering at Kelly from behind the rim. He set the cup down and said, "You are a driver. I'm sure that is a very important job in your world. And a female driver at that. The first we've ever had. Of course, I have no complaints. Equal opportunity and all that jazz is what I'm known for. You have garnered a very important position indeed."

Kelly felt the hair on the back of her neck stand. She steadied her composure. "I sure hope it's important in your world, too. Because I'm responsible for the safety and well-being of your family all day long."

"Speaking of my family." Irving was like a poker player; his expression shiftless and void. "I was going to talk to you about Carolyn, but..." His gaze trailed her uniform, top to bottom. "Not anymore," he added.

There was no turning back now. Kelly heard herself say, "Miss Carolyn is a wonderful person. She's smart. Very smart. And very beautiful. You are a lucky man, Mr. Irving."

Irving smirked. What Kelly had uttered was the most ridiculous thing Irving had ever heard, and he was quite amused.

Well, Kelly thought, *if he thinks that's so funny, I've got more.* "And Claire's smart too," Kelly added. "Not as smart as Carolyn, but there is something about that one."

Irving pursed his lips. He paused, then said, "You are not hired to dissect my family. You are not their psychologist or their confidante. You are the driver. It seems you have some difficulty understanding your job requirements."

Kelly did not back down. "I was told to drive Miss Claire to Central Park, where she would walk the dogs for two hours. I found out she wasn't walking the dogs. She was having lunch over at The Plaza instead. She is a smart one. I take that back. She's unscrupulous, and that falls under my job duties because I can't deliver Miss Claire someplace and pick her up in a timely fashion if she's lying to me."

"Claire was not walking the dogs?" Mr. Irving feigned surprise. "I find that hard to believe. Who discovered that secret?"

"I'm just guessing here, but I think you told Mr. Perez, and Mr. Perez told me? In any case, Claire is walking the dogs now. I'm making sure of that."

Irving pushed back and folded his arms. Kelly O'Sullivan was obviously much more than he had bargained for. Kelly waited for his words. She knew they were coming. Something like *we are no longer in need of your services.*

Instead, Irving said, "I like that."

"What?"

"That you're making absolutely certain that Claire does exactly what she is expected to do."

"It's my job to deliver everyone safely to their designated locations."

"Can we reach an agreement here, then?" Irving steepled his hands and rested them on the table. "That you continue to deliver my family to their predetermined appointments, and should there be any deviation whatsoever, you will notify me immediately?"

A spy. Irving wanted a spy. Kelly needed this job, but Irving wanted her to switch sides.

He made his offer more attractive. "Mr. Perez keeps telling me you're the best driver we've ever had and not to let you go. Because the original purpose of this meeting was to fire you, but I might change my mind. Perhaps a raise is in order?"

Mr. Perez was pleased with Kelly? Or maybe the truth was Mr. Irving's *family* did not want Kelly to go.

He pressed. "Do we have a deal?"

"I, uh, I..." She regrouped. "I will continue to get everyone exactly where they need to be." It wasn't a lie, was it?

"Perfect. I was hoping you would say that. I have your paycheck with me." Irving patted his breast pocket. "There's a little bonus in there. It seems you've had a challenging couple of weeks. I'm not disagreeing that my family can be...how should I say this? They can be...trying."

"You have a wonderful family." Kelly noted his discomfort with her comment. She retracted. "Mr. Irving, I need this job."

Irving's expression shifted to pleasure.

"More than you could know. It's a big job in my world. You're right about that."

Irving pressed further. "One additional small stipulation: You refrain from offering any advice—in fact, any conversation whatsoever—to my family and concentrate on driving and only driving."

Kelly offered a sideways glance, maybe a half nod, maybe a shrug. In any event, she didn't commit to anything. It was too late for that. Irving didn't understand. Strike that. Irving did not want to understand.

Silence between them. They drank their coffees and nibbled on their crumb cakes, avoiding eye contact and glancing about the tight space. A group of boys came rumbling in with their nannies in tow. They leaned over the counter, shouting out orders for fries and shakes. They shoved each other and roughhoused like a pile of puppies.

Kelly smiled.

Irving did not. He seemed perturbed at the intrusion.

One of the boys pushed another, and he fell back against their table, quaking their coffee cups. "Whoa, sorry there." The boy lifted his hands in surrender. Then to his friend, he said, "Toby, you jerk. Look what you made me do."

"No problem." Kelly waved them away.

Irving used a paper napkin to dab the spilled coffee from his saucer. "Look at this mess."

"Well worth it," Kelly said.

Mr. Irving froze in place.

Kelly continued. "To see those kids coming in here, goofing around, having fun. That's what kids should be doing." She was dreaming about her Rose now. "Out on a Saturday morning with their buddies, just being a kid."

But Irving assumed Kelly was referring to Byron. "Byron has a full schedule. He's doing fine without an inappropriate gang like that," Irving corrected. "I would dare to say he is doing even better."

Kelly's voice dropped. She would never demean Byron. Never. She wanted to make that perfectly clear. "I wasn't talking about Byron. Your son is a great kid. One of the nicest kids I've ever met. He's super smart and driven and talented. Savvy—that would be the better word. He has street smarts, intelligence that can't be taught from a book, and he's an absolute pleasure to be around."

Irving reared back and studied Kelly anew.

She continued. "And he's got a nice group of buddies, too."

Irving would not be given any unknown information about his family. He would know it all, and knew it all, and would be the only one with any news whatsoever. "He sure does," Irving said, but Kelly knew Byron had had no real friends until this past week.

"Are we almost done here?" Kelly said. "This is my last stop today, and I'd like to get back to my family." She let that notion hover in the air between them. It was a gift, of sorts, to Irving. Kelly had a family of her own, a life of her own. She was not intent on stealing his.

She drove Irving back to his penthouse in silence, parked the car, removed Irving's bag from the trunk, and opened his door. All the while, Jack, the doorman, watched with great interest, as if he were viewing the next episode in a Netflix series. If Jack could have hauled a Lazy Boy recliner onto that sidewalk, he'd have sat in it, raised the footrest and drank from that paper bag of his with a side of popcorn.

"Have a nice day, Mr. Irving," Kelly said.

"You do the same, Kelly. May I call you that? That's what my family calls you." Mr. Irving did not say this fondly, but Kelly pretended it was a compliment.

"Of course. I'd like that very much."

"Very well then...Kelly." He offered her a firm handshake, too firm, the kind that makes your fingers hurt and you wonder if the person is proving their strength or exerting their superiority. Probably a little of both here.

Irving disappeared inside the foyer and then into the elevator.

Jack gave Kelly a single nod that said something like "Nice work," and she returned the gesture. If Jack only knew.

As Kelly drove around the corner toward the parking garage, she thought that their meeting had gone better than expected. But there were those things that remained unspoken: Carolyn relied upon Kelly as a close friend, Kelly knew all about Mr. Irving's affair with Claire, and bigger and louder than either of those things were Byron's bruises and black eye that Irving would soon witness for himself, if he hadn't seen them already on his camera system. Kelly's mention of Byron's new buddies was meant to calm Irving's bullying fears. Byron took a beating, yes, but something more. He had some friends now, some backup, and things were about to change in his favor.

Everyone needed hope. Even Irving.

Good grief, was Kelly inadvertently advising Irving now, too?

11

CHAPTER ELEVEN

K elly had the remainder of the day off, and Mrs. Andrews was quite pleased to have the remainder of the day off, too. It was a sunny December afternoon, and bright yellow beams made the snow sparkle and the slick streets shimmer like ribbon candy. It was exactly what every New Yorker needed.

Everyone but Rose.

Kelly thanked Mrs. Andrews for her work today and led her to the door.

"She had a great morning." Mrs. Andrews gave her daily report. "We did puzzles by the tree lights. She helped make her own breakfast. She counted to twenty."

"Mrs. Andrews..." Kelly was hesitant to ask. What if Mrs. Andrews did not approve? Kelly knew her daughter, but Kelly did not know everything about education and medicine and therapy. Now that Mrs. Andrews was here, Kelly would not do anything without her advice. "I need to ask you something."

Mrs. Andrews had already donned her coat and boots and waited with one hand on the knob. "Go ahead."

"I want to take Rose out today on a field trip of sorts."

"Oh?"

"I'll bring the dark glasses, if she'll wear them. We're going downtown to a water polo match at the Athletic Club."

"Water polo?" Mrs. Andrews seemed intrigued.

"The boy I've been driving, well, he plays polo. He asked if we'd like to see one of his games today. I think she might..." Kelly glanced back at Rose, still seated on the floor by the tree, working her puzzles. "She might like it."

"Actually, I think it's an excellent idea. Rose has been so fascinated by that puddle that I've been thinking we could build on that curiosity with the next step—a swimming pool. Rose could progress to swimming lessons, of course, but at first, just an hour during the week with the two of you in the water together could be very therapeutic. The zero gravity would soothe her head and neck and be great for her muscles."

"Really?" Kelly had never thought about it, but Mrs. Andrews was right: a pool could be wonderful. "I'm so happy. Really happy. Thank you so much, but..." Kelly glanced back at Rose again. "But...what if she doesn't want to go?"

"Oh, I think she would love to go. Bring the sunglasses and the earplugs."

Mrs. Andrews crossed the floor to Rose and knelt beside her. She didn't coddle her like Kelly always did. She didn't brush her hair back and hug and kiss her constantly like Kelly. She spoke intelligently to Rose, a teacher to a student. "Rose," she said, and Rose immediately turned her attention to Mrs. Andrews. "Today your mother is going to take you to see a real swimming pool. You must wear your sunglasses and your earplugs. You will be going outdoors. You are going to have a very special and very wonderful day."

Rose looked at the window and the bright sunshine and squinted.

Kelly's throat tightened as Mrs. Andrews spoke with such authority, as if she had no doubt Rose would adapt, that Rose could handle it. "It's alright," Mrs. Andrews assured her. "You will wear your sunglasses, and when I return, I cannot wait to hear all about it. You are going to see a real swimming pool, and then, someday soon, you are going to be able to get inside that pool and learn to swim."

"Okay." Rose smiled. So simply. So easily.

When Mrs. Andrews left, Rose was eager to find her coat and gloves. "Go outside," Rose said over and over, much to Kelly's surprise.

"Yes, Rose," Kelly mimicked Mrs. Andrews. "We're going outside and it's going to be a great day." Kelly dressed Rose in a sweatshirt and leggings. She placed the dark glasses on Rose's nose and worked them behind each ear. The wire rims fit snuggly to her face. The glasses must have felt awkward and somewhat uncomfortable, but they were necessary. Kelly knelt before Rose. "Look at you. You are a big girl now. Wearing those glasses and going outside. You got this."

Rose smiled again.

Was life sometimes easier than Kelly had made it? Did she take every situation and focus on the problem? Kelly wished someone would have said to her, "Look at you. You're a mother now. Wearing that driver uniform and driving a Rolls Royce around town. You got this." But there was no one who would say something like that to Kelly. No one but Mom, and she was gone.

She placed Rose in the umbrella stroller. They would be taking a cab today. It was expensive and Kelly rarely hailed one, but this new job was opening up a whole new world. Rose had ridden in a taxi before, when she was a baby. When the crying had been so horrific and had gone on for days, Kelly had taken her to the emergency room. Test after test came back negative, and the doctors dismissed Rose's discomfort as common colic and treated her as such. But nothing pacified her—not filtered water, not non-dairy organic formula, not probiotic drops, not white noise, not rocking or swaying.

When Rose was one year old, it became obvious that she was suffering from head pain. She began hugging her head and rubbing her temples and banging her forehead. Rose was treated with physical therapy, electrical stimulation, a TENS unit, moist heat, massage, and medications like amitriptyline and imipramine in low doses, which occasionally seemed to provide some relief but never lasted.

At three years old, Rose was now taking low doses of triptans, but they were not without side effects—nausea, dizziness, lack of concentration, depression. Mrs. Andrews was implementing relaxation training, biofeedback, and cognitive behavioral therapy, all focused on teaching the child how to control certain body responses that triggered more pain, how to use deep breathing, and how to relax more.

But swimming...It gave Kelly renewed hope, and what a coincidence that Byron played water polo.

They reached the Athletic Club a few minutes late, and the game had already begun. The space was humid, hot, and smelled strongly of chlorine. Voices were magnified by the huge, cavernous walls and the fluorescent lights were annoying, even to Kelly. She straightened Rose's earplugs, adjusted her sunglasses, and tucked Rose safely inside its form-fitting stroller. Rose would be much more comfortable there than on the hard metal bench. She would feel secure, contained. She would feel safe.

But Rose had her own idea. She climbed out of the stroller and scooted onto the bench seat beside Kelly. Rose knew it was a game of sorts in the water below. The people were here to watch the game. Rose wanted to watch too. Not from her own safe place, but from the same place that everyone else was watching.

Byron was at his post as goalie, jumping into the waves with excitement and determination. He blocked the balls, left and right, diving forward with a surge of water engulfing him, then rising above the waves to serve the ball into the opponent's territory with a slap. Nothing got past him. Physical size didn't matter in water polo. Agility and coordination and speed made Byron a driving force at the net.

Kelly found herself constantly stealing glances at Rose, who was craning forward, her gaze fixed on the game. Rose squealed with delight and even clapped occasionally. Kelly had been so preoccupied with Rose's demeanor that she suddenly realized Rose's sunglasses and earplugs had been discarded with the stroller.

Kelly felt tears well. Rose loved it all. Kelly should have exposed Rose to the world much sooner. How long had Rose been missing out on days like this?

Kelly wiped her eyes with the corner of her sweater. The same sweater Damean had left behind, the same tears he had caused for weeks, months on end. She hadn't thrown that sweater out because...because...quite honestly, Kelly needed a warm sweater and couldn't afford a new one.

Oh, how she wished Damean could see the two of them now, sitting there. Kelly and Rose, the two girls he had so easily abandoned. Rose had been a challenging infant, a colicky baby, or so they first thought, and it was all too much for Damean. He had been so happy when Rose was first born because he was getting attention, and the recognition boosted his pride. But babies were a lot of work, and life wasn't about Damean anymore, or for Damean, or centered around Damean, and he disappeared without any explanation.

And Kelly wished Damean could see her wearing his old sweater, not because she longed for him and missed him, but simply because she needed the thing to keep her warm. That was a good sign, wasn't it? It had to be.

Kelly felt a tap on her shoulder and turned to find Carolyn in a red silk dress, stiletto heels, bare legs and an open mink coat. "Byron said I might find you here." Carolyn noticed Rose, sitting beside Kelly. "Is that your sweet daughter?"

"Yes, this is Rose. Rose, can you say hello?"

Rose refused to be distracted from the game. "No." At least she was honest.

Kelly didn't appreciate the interruption either, but that desperate look in Carolyn's eyes... "Go ahead." Kelly patted the bleacher. "Have a seat."

Carolyn did not waste any time. She plopped onto the metal bench, sending a tremor down the row. Rose gave Carolyn a scowl, and Kelly couldn't help but smirk.

They sat for several minutes, watching the game, before Carolyn finally said, "I need to talk to someone. I feel like sometimes...I can be...overly suspicious. Some call it women's intuition, a sixth sense."

"How about a gut feeling that you can't get rid of?"

"That too. I'm not sure how to phrase this. I guess I should just come right out and ask." She turned to face Kelly. "What do you know about Marcus and Claire?"

"I know plenty about Miss Claire, but Mr. Irving just got back home today. I've spoken to him for about twenty minutes, tops."

"That's not what I'm implying."

"I know what you're implying."

Byron blocked a goal and the crowd cheered. Kelly and Rose stood and clapped. Carolyn followed suit.

"So, what do you think?" Carolyn shouted above the crowd.

But Kelly wasn't going to fall for that again. She shrugged. "I don't know any more than you. Probably less, since I don't live there."

The three returned to their seats, and Carolyn said, "I'm sure it's all my imagination. I heard someone say once that most of our problems are of our own making."

Kelly fixed her eyes on the game. "I guess there's some truth in that. But then...there are those problems that are dropped on us. We didn't do anything to cause them. We can't be blamed for them. They just happened."

Carolyn said, "How do you know the difference?"

"Good question. I suppose it doesn't matter."

"But how can I know for sure about Marcus and Claire? I have to know for certain."

"Why don't you ask him?"

"Marcus? I could never do that. He doesn't like to be questioned. What if he told me to leave? What would I do then? I could be over-reacting here. That's what I'm trying to figure out."

Kelly slanted a look at Carolyn. "So, let me get this straight. You're afraid to ask your boyfriend if he's cheating on you because he might kick you out? Something doesn't sound right there."

Carolyn sat perfectly still. She stared at the players below, but unlike Kelly and Rose, she didn't see any of them. "I don't want to be alone."

"Nobody does. But sometimes, you're better off."

"I suppose the truth is, I've been alone for a long while now."

"How long?"

Carolyn whispered. "Since Claire arrived."

Kelly rested an open palm on Carolyn's knee, an invitation, and Carolyn accepted it. She laid her hand in Kelly's. Kelly squeezed.

"I won't get any alimony, of course," Carolyn reasoned. "We're not married. It doesn't matter anyway. I don't know why I'm saying this, but I'm not looking for revenge. I don't want to hurt the man. I just want...I need...a settlement of some kind. A lump sum. I'm sure I could negotiate that with the right lawyer. This could take some time."

Kelly watched Byron lunge through the water and block a great shot. "Go, Byron!" she interjected, then continued. "I'm probably the last person to be saying this right about now, but sometimes money doesn't matter."

Byron waved at the coach. The coach took him out of the game and sent him to his spot on the bench with the other players. But why would Byron voluntarily remove himself when the team needed him most? This was clearly not the coach's decision.

"Marcus is a good man," Carolyn said. "He was a good man when I met him three years ago. He needed me so badly back then. He had just lost his wife. Cancer. He was hurting. I was lonely. We were so strong, the two of us together. I don't know what happened. I don't know who he is anymore."

"People change. Maybe he doesn't know who you are anymore either."

The three sat together on the bench, watching the players soar through the water below. Finally, Carolyn said, "I need to know for absolutely certain."

"Well, I can't help you with that," Kelly said. "But. I might know somebody who can."

"Who?"

Kelly pointed to the goalie.

"Byron?" Carolyn stood, her eyes fixed on the water. She lost herself for a few minutes. Then, without a goodbye to Kelly or even little Rose, Carolyn clomped down the metal bleachers, leaving a clang and shudder in her wake.

Kelly inched closer to Rose, wrapping her arm around her and cinching her in tighter. People loved to say there was a rainbow behind every cloud, something good in every day. Kelly hated those old adages that tried to sprinkle happiness everywhere and minimize pain and suffering. Maybe Dad was wrong. Maybe there wasn't something good in every day. Maybe there wasn't happy beside every sad. Maybe good didn't always win and some wrongs were never righted. What then?

The crowd exploded as Byron's team scored during the final two seconds, winning the game. The hollow space roared with hoots and hollers that ricocheted off the domed ceiling and echoed through the room. Kelly sprang to her feet, clapping and waving to Byron, trying to get his attention.

Then she remembered Rose. The noise level. The earplugs in the stroller.

But the best part of the entire game, the part that would be cherished in Kelly's heart forevermore, was the sight of her precious little Rose standing beside her, clapping too.

They were waiting outside the locker room when Byron emerged—wet hair, damp clothes and wiggling into his camel coat. "You showed." Byron wasn't looking at Kelly when he spoke but rather at Rose, now seated in her stroller, sunglasses on.

"Great game." Kelly's gaze followed Byron's to Rose. "She loved it."

Byron squatted before Rose's stroller. "Hey there. What's your name?"

"Rose." She held up three fingers. "Three."

"Three is the best," Byron said. "Did you have some fun? How do you like water polo?"

Rose nodded eagerly. "Pool."

"She was mesmerized." Kelly laughed. "She never goes anywhere. She doesn't leave the apartment, other than to go to the doctor. I wasn't sure how it would go..."

Byron surveyed Kelly. He was clearly trying to understand what Kelly meant by that statement. *Rose never went anywhere?* Kelly stopped talking.

"Hey, those are some pretty cool sunglasses you got there," Byron said to Rose. She handed her glasses to Byron, he slipped them on, and Rose giggled. Byron took the bait and strutted around the lobby, shuffling and dancing as if that one pair of sunglasses was the coolest thing in all the world. Rose exploded into a deep belly laugh. Then, just as suddenly, she demanded, "Mine."

"Alright, alright. *Typical three-year-old.* Here you go." Byron joked, but he had no idea what those words meant. *Typical three-year-old*—that's what Byron said. The most wonderful words Kelly had ever heard.

Kelly's eyes teared again, and Byron caught it and changed the subject. "So, I saw our infamous Carolyn up on the bleachers."

"You saw her?" Kelly asked.

"She's sort of tough to miss with that blond hair and big fur coat, and anyway, she was looking for you this morning before we left. You still her personal therapist?"

"I'm trying to help her. She's not very happy right now."

"Carolyn hasn't been happy in a long time. Way before Claire showed up." Byron shoved his hands in his pockets, and his attention shifted toward the door. "Well, there's my Uber. I better get going."

"You're taking an Uber?"

"My driver took off today. Can you believe it?"

"What about Mr. Perez?"

"He's busy. No big deal. I don't mind taking an Uber now and then."

"I'll be back on duty tomorrow," Kelly said. "It looks like Sunday is a busy day in your house. I'm driving people around all day long."

Byron's next comment was abrupt and awkward. "Is Sunday busy in your house?"

Kelly had to think about that one. "No. Sunday is more of a quiet day. Family time, Sunday dinner, that sort of thing."

"My family looks for reasons to get away, especially on a quiet day. But...it wasn't always like that. Not when my mom was here." Byron looked at Rose, who had not taken her eyes off him for a split second. "Bye, Rose." He patted her head. "See you later, little buddy."

As Byron walked away, Kelly called out, "Byron."

He turned.

"Thanks for the invite today. It means more than you know."

"Thanks for coming." He stopped. "Fun fact: I've had a driver since I was as big as Rose. They barely talked to me. Most of them wouldn't even look at me. You broke every single rule that first day of work. That's why we like you so much." He took a few steps backward, toward the Uber. "Especially Carolyn. Did you figure her out yet?"

"Figure what out?"

"Why she's using you." Byron walked toward the Uber.

12

CHAPTER TWELVE

K elly arrived at the penthouse on Sunday at 9 a.m. sharp. She had been given a detailed list of pickup and delivery locations for each member of the family. It was going to be a hectic day. She would be driving people downtown, from SoHo to FiDi, from Tribeca to the Upper East, and she wasn't quite sure how she would be able to do it all without running late.

She stood at the Rolls, waiting for Carolyn, the first person listed on the schedule. Kelly never knew where Carolyn was headed until Carolyn sat in the back seat and revealed her plan. Strike that. Her plot.

But today was different. Carolyn came racing out of the building without a coat. She wore a pink jogger and white furry slippers. Her hair was pulled into a ponytail, swinging left and right with every step. "Can you come upstairs a minute? I need some help."

Upstairs? As in, inside the apartment? Was that even allowed? Kelly looked to Jack for any sort of advice, but he was blank-faced, partly from the contents of his brown paper bag and partly from the situation at hand. "Nothing surprises the doorman anymore." Jack took a swig.

Carolyn dismissed him and spoke to Kelly. "Hurry up, would you?" She rubbed her arms. "It's freezing out here."

"The driver better follow orders," Jack said. "The doorman will watch the car."

Kelly followed through the lobby. "Are you sure this is okay?"

"I can't carry all those bags myself."

"Did you ask Mr. Irving if I could come up?"

"Don't tell me you're afraid of him now, too? I was hoping we had a rebel in our midst."

"I'm not afraid of Mr. Irving, but I do want to keep my job."

Carolyn pressed the elevator button for the top floor. "Your daughter is adorable, by the way. You're a good mom. What was her name again? Rita?"

"Rose, and thank you."

"She's amazing. You are amazing. I am amazing. The world is suddenly a very amazing place." Carolyn was oddly jubilant.

"Are you alright?" Kelly asked.

"Alright? No, I am not alright. I am absolutely wonderful! I'm making a big change today. One big change." Carolyn looked through Kelly. "It all starts with one, doesn't it?" But she was not interested in a reply. "That butterfly effect. That one move that sends you on a brand-new trajectory through life?"

Kelly did not want to pop her bubble, but a brand-new trajectory was not always a good thing.

They reached the top floor, the elevator emitted a pleasant *ting*, and the doors glided open to reveal an elaborate foyer of white marble and stained glass and crystal and soft scents of lavender and jasmine. There was a bouquet of fresh flowers on a ten-foot round table in the center of the space. Carolyn tugged at Kelly's sleeve, leading her through the foyer and into the penthouse beyond.

Then Carolyn abandoned her.

Kelly stood in the great room of the penthouse at Fifteen Central Park West. It was like nothing she had ever dreamed or imagined. So, this was where these people lived, these wealthy people she saw on the streets, getting in and out of their limos, going to dinner, coming out of Bergdorf's with arms loaded with shopping bags. High above the rest of Manhattan, above the grimy streets and honking yellow cabs, above the stale air of the subway grates and the push and shove of crowded sidewalks. They lived up here, inside a glittering jewelry box.

White and gray and cream and beige—light colors—and shining glass and plush fabrics. A giant circular sofa, a towering stone fireplace, thick carpets, fur pillows. The only other real color was the crystal chandeliers, if crystal had a color. Kelly supposed that color would be aurora borealis or maybe the color of a rainbow when the sunlight pierced the prisms. The room must have been thirty or forty feet in width. She never imagined a home space of this enormous size existed in the city.

But the very best part was the Christmas tree—a towering twenty-foot evergreen, glittering with glass and crystal ornaments in every color. It didn't seem that a single branch had been left empty. And the lights! There were more lights on that tree than Kelly thought possible. This could be the most wondrous tree Kelly had ever seen (apart from the Rockefeller tree, of course).

Byron strode past on his way from somewhere to somewhere, wearing a plaid robe and neon green fuzzy slippers. He did a double take. "Kelly?" He couldn't hide his delight. More rules were being broken.

"I'm sorry to say, yes." She grimaced.

"What are you doing up here?"

"Carolyn made me. She needs help with some bags or something."

"She's moving out?"

"I don't know. She didn't say. I don't think so. Either way, for the record, I had nothing to do with this. At least I don't think I did..."

Carolyn rushed into the room with two full black plastic garbage bags and flung them at Kelly's feet. "First two of ten. Hold on."

"What's in those things?" Byron asked Carolyn. "Body parts?"

Carolyn rolled her eyes. "Clothes, Byron. All sorts of gloriously expensive treasures that I don't need anymore. I'm donating them all to Goodwill."

"What? Charity?" Byron reared back in exaggerated shock. "Wake me up from the dream, would somebody?"

Carolyn scolded. "Stop that this instant. I've donated before."

"Sure, at some big gala or fancy auction. You and Dad love to hand out lots of money when you're dressed up in a gown and tuxedo and everybody's watching. But bags of designer clothes to Goodwill? Now that's really something. Wait a minute. Are there any shoes in there?"

"Plenty." Carolyn batted her lashes and disappeared.

"Well, there you have it. It's official." Byron turned to Kelly. "She's totally lost it. What's next? Volunteering for a nonprofit? Helping an old lady cross the street?" Byron feigned shock.

Kelly covered her mouth to hide her laughter.

"Well, that's the only explanation I can come up with," Byron said to Kelly. "Unless you're really Mary Poppins or something."

"I don't even own an umbrella."

"There's one in the Rolls's side door, and you haven't used it once yet."

Kelly folded her arms. "Yes, I certainly have."

"When?"

"Well...well...when I floated from the clouds into your parking garage."

As Byron chuckled, Claire rushed past, wearing her usual ensemble: the skin-tight Lululemon workout gear (without the down puffer). At this close view, Kelly could tell no bra or panties had been added to accessorize the outfit. Claire appeared extremely agitated and perturbed, her usual anxious state. From the corner of her vision, Claire spotted Kelly and spun around. "You!"

"Yes, it's me."

"Inside this penthouse? We have never, and I mean never, had a driver in this house before."

The dogs trailed behind Claire, but when they spotted Byron, they shifted allegiance, racing to his side. Byron bent down to pet them while he responded to Claire. "Carolyn asked Kelly to come up." Just then, Peter let out a yelp that shocked the entire room.

"What's the matter, buddy?" Byron pressed Peter's hindquarter. "You got a sore hip? What happened?"

All eyes turned to Claire for an explanation, but she clamped her lips.

"What happened to him?" Byron demanded.

"How should I know?"

"You're the dog walker—that's how. You're with him all day and night, and you don't know what happened to him?"

"No." Claire purposefully softened her voice. "I have no idea whatsoever. Poor little guy. I'll take him to the vet."

Byron checked again. He smoothed his hand across the dog's fur a second time, and Peter winced.

"It could be these frigid temperatures. Arthritis is aggravated by the cold, you know." Claire raised her chin. "It's not fit for beast...or human out there." She addressed Kelly. "By the way, if that temp drops below zero today, I will not be walking the dogs."

"I have some good news for you. It's going to be a balmy five degrees." Kelly smiled wide. "A perfect day for dog walking. Wear your parka."

Byron angled himself toward Kelly. "Kelly, check with Dad before you pick Claire up. I need to talk to him about something first."

Claire seethed at Byron's comment, but she obviously knew her limits.

Carolyn returned with a few more black bags and tossed them at Kelly's feet. "Stay right there." She pointed at Kelly.

Claire brightened. "What's all this, Carolyn? Don't tell me you're moving out?"

Carolyn ignored Claire and disappeared again.

"She's donating some of her things to charity," Byron told Claire. "Do you have anything to donate? Like your favorite broom? Or maybe that black pointy hat you wear on a full moon at midnight?"

Byron laughed too loud, and with that Mr. Irving appeared, wearing a plaid robe and navy-blue slippers and holding a coffee cup. "What's all the commotion?"

The tension in the room instantly spiked and Kelly straightened her jacket. "If you're wondering why I'm up here, Carolyn asked me to help her with something. Of course, I would never come up here uninvited, and even though I was invited—by Carolyn, like I said—I wasn't sure if I should come up here, but then I saw Byron and he said—"

Mr. Irving waved her explanation away. "Oh, I don't care about any of that." The corners of his lips curled. "What was all that noise I just heard?"

"You mean the laughter?" Byron wiped the tears from his eyes, still smiling. "Yeah, we don't get a lot of that around here, do we?"

Claire had a sudden burst of courage with Marcus beside her. "We have plenty of laughter in this house."

"Claire, Claire." Mr. Irving pushed his palm downward. "I can handle this."

But Kelly wondered what *this* was. Byron was making a sarcastic comment, as all teenagers do. Mr. Irving had better get used to it. And once again, Kelly heard the words spewing from her mouth before she had a chance to rethink them.

"Oh, Byron's just being a typical teenager," Kelly said. "Sarcasm, angst, a little rebellion. We all better brace ourselves for the next few years." She winked at Byron.

Claire spat her next words. "We? *You* are not a part of this family, Ms. O'Sullivan. In fact, I still can't figure out why you're standing here in the middle of our salon in those old boots and coat and hat." She shifted closer to Marcus, clearly expecting his support.

"Me either," Marcus said. "Didn't anybody ask Kelly to sit down? Claire, go get Kelly a coffee or something. Maybe a hot tea?"

"I certainly will not!" Claire stomped off, but the dogs remained with Byron.

An awkward pause depressed the room, and Kelly tried to soothe it. "Actually, I had enough coffee this morning. Thanks anyway."

"You want something to eat?" Byron seemed to relish this notion. "I make the best scrambled eggs."

"I think Kelly might prefer a bagel to go." Mr. Irving seemed amused by this idea as well. "She doesn't have a lot of time. She has a tough schedule today, don't you, Kelly?"

"A very busy day," Kelly agreed. "I'll have to take a rain check on that bagel."

"A rain check means you'll be back," Byron said. "I like that idea."

Mr. Irving patted his son's shoulder, and Byron's tone cut serious to his father. "Dad...I need to talk to you about something later. It's about the dogs."

"Of course," Mr. Irving said. "Anything you need."

Carolyn returned with more heaping bags of clothes and tossed them at Kelly's feet.

"How many more?" Kelly longed to get out of there.

"A few. You're doing fine." Carolyn glanced at the small crowd gathered. "Good morning, everyone." Then disappeared again.

Mr. Irving fretted his fingers through his blond crew cut. "What is she up to now?"

"She's taking clothes to Goodwill," Kelly said.

Mr. Irving choked on his coffee, spitting some of the brown liquid onto the white carpet. "Uh oh, I'll get something for that," he said.

Mr. Irving disappeared, and Carolyn returned. "That's it! Let's get this stuff out to the Rolls."

Kelly lifted as many bags as her arms could carry, and Byron heaved two bags over his shoulders.

"Byron, should you be doing that?" Carolyn scolded.

"It's just a couple bags. Give me a break."

"I don't think your dad would like that."

"I'm fine." Byron widened his eyes at Carolyn.

"First the water polo and now this?" Carolyn said.

Byron whispered. "Be quiet. You promised."

"Wait a minute here." Kelly's volume matched Byron's. "Your dad doesn't know about the polo?"

"No, and don't anybody say a word. It's the only good thing I got left."

"Don't you think he already knows, with all his surveillance cameras and everything?" Kelly asked.

The room stopped in time. Carolyn and Byron moved their heads slowly, left to right. "Don't go there," Carolyn whispered.

Apparently, this was one of those things that everyone was fully aware of but rarely spoke about, especially inside this house. "I mean," Kelly backtracked. "All I was saying was—" She stopped short, raised her eyes and surveyed the ceiling. The cameras. Obviously hidden around here someplace. How could anyone live like that?

"Must you always speak absolutely everything that's on your mind?" Carolyn lowered her voice. "It does get old after a while. All that honesty."

"Well, I only meant—"

"We know what you meant," Carolyn spoke on behalf of her and Byron. "What we're asking is please do not ever say it again." She glanced over her shoulder. "Not in here anyway."

Carolyn and Byron loaded the bags onto the elevator, but before Kelly joined them, she took one long look around the penthouse ceilings. *Surveillance. But why?* Irving, wasn't all that bad.

Or was he?

When all the bags had been loaded into the trunk of the Rolls, Byron paused at the curb, still wearing his plaid robe and fuzzy slippers. But something had changed. Byron was bent over, hands on both knees. Overly winded for a fourteen-year-old boy who carried a few bags of clothes down an elevator.

Kelly tenderly rubbed Byron's back. "You okay?"

He shook her off. "I'm fine."

"It doesn't look like you're fine."

"Let it go, would you?" Byron shuffled off.

Kelly stood frozen in place for a moment. With a few logical comments, she had damaged the friendships she had made with Byron and Carolyn. Guilt settled in her chest as she replayed the conversation. It had been lighthearted and fun, until Kelly became too familiar, too honest. She had crossed a line—exactly what Dad had warned her not to do.

Unfamiliar silence hung between Kelly and Carolyn as they drove to the Goodwill drop-off.

"Carolyn." Kelly parked the car. "My turn to get some advice."

"Go ahead."

Kelly waited. She wasn't sure how to approach this delicate matter. She didn't even care about those surveillance cameras anymore. A far greater problem took precedence. She observed the outdoor sidewalk activity through the windshield, hoping to find the right words. The Goodwill store was in Washington Heights, and pedestrians passed the Rolls with wondering eyes, a few tapped on its sides, and one man kicked a wheel. The sidewalk was littered with beer cans. A few storefront windows had been broken and boarded up. A patrol car looped the block.

"It's about Byron," Kelly finally said. "Why was he so tired just now?"

"You will have to ask Byron that question."

"I'm asking you. What's wrong with him?"

"I can't tell you that. It's not my place. I understand everything you've done for me, and I'm very grateful, but I'm sorry, I promised."

"Mr. Irving won't mind. I need to know, especially if I'm driving his son around all day. I'm responsible for him, in a way."

"It's not Marcus that I promised. It's Byron."

Carolyn exited the vehicle and began hauling the black bags into Goodwill. Kelly joined her without a word. When they were finished, they promptly headed back.

Carolyn had a wistful longing as she focused on the images passing by her window. "The truth is sometimes elusive because we allow it," she thought aloud. "I understand that now. I love Marcus. I've always loved him, but that's not enough anymore. The problem is, I don't think he ever really loved me. He needed me. It's not the same thing. I had to understand this for myself. Nobody could tell me what to see, how to see, because I wasn't ready yet." She met Kelly in the mirror. "In this same way, I cannot tell you about Byron. This is something you must be willing to see for yourself. Or...better yet...take your own advice. Why don't you ask him?"

Kelly couldn't ask Byron because he had already made it perfectly clear that he did not want to tell her. *Tell her what?* What was this secret that made Byron so winded and Carolyn so concerned?

Kelly dropped Carolyn off at her apartment and seized her free time to return home. She needed a little time with Rose today more than ever. Something familiar. Somewhere to love and be loved...unconditionally.

***

Kelly found her sweet Rose seated at the kitchen table, workbook open, pencil in hand. But Mrs. Andrews was preoccupied with that stubborn puddle. "It won't go away!" Her bucket was filled with water, the mop dripping wet, her apron saturated.

"It's okay," Kelly reassured her. "Put the pot over it. Stop worrying. It's not getting any worse."

"But where is it coming from? I don't understand."

"It doesn't matter. Just ignore it." Kelly took the mop from Mrs. Andrews and led her by the elbow to the kitchen table. "I'll handle it from now on. Sit down." Then Kelly covered the puddle with the pot.

But something more was bothering Mrs. Andrews. Kelly watched her help Rose with her letters, flipping the pages of the workbook impatiently. "No, Rose, not that way." Mrs. Andrews snatched the pencil from Rose's hand and rewrote the letter A. "This way—do it again."

A bad day for Mrs. Andrews this time? Kelly ventured, "Speaking of water, I never told you—that polo match was a big hit."

"I heard."

"You heard?"

"She keeps saying, 'I love water,' and something about a boy."

Why wasn't Mrs. Andrews more elated by this? "Rose was infatuated with that polo game," Kelly said. "I never saw anything like it. She watched it so intently. She even took her sunglasses and earplugs off."

"That is not a wise idea. You should not have allowed that. Rose needs those. She may seem fine at the time, but later that day or the next day..."

"But, Mrs. Andrews, she took them off herself. I looked over, and she was sitting beside me on the bench, clapping and loving that game. And something else—she had that game figured out. Not all of it, but she knew the goal was to get that ball into the net."

Mrs. Andrews maintained her stiff posture. "Rose is very smart. I already told you that. She is three now, and next year four, and with every year, hurdles will be overcome. You will see progression, sometimes stronger and faster, sometimes slower and more delicate. But there will be hurdles."

Kelly placed a tender hand on Mrs. Andrews's shoulder. "What's wrong? Did something happen here that you're not telling me about? I've seen it all, Mrs. Andrews. Trust me on this one. I can handle anything."

Mrs. Andrews shuffled the loose papers. "Rose is fine."

"I have your paycheck with me if that's the problem. I can give you a little more if you need it. Whatever you want."

"The pay is more than enough." Mrs. Andrews moved to the sofa and rested her head in her hands. "I need to tell you something. It's about my husband." She sighed. "Ed's in the hospital. He's coming home tomorrow. He's going to need extra care. I know I just started this job, but..."

"I'm so sorry." Kelly's heart broke once again. *How many times can a heart break and still continue beating? Is everybody in the world suffering? Different problems. Different causes. Is everyone carrying sorrow of some kind?* Kelly pulled a chair up close to Mrs. Andrews. "I can't imagine how hard this must be for you." Her voice faltered. "I also can't imagine losing you."

"I'm not leaving you. It's just the afternoons I need off. Do you have anybody who can watch Rose? Until Ed is well again? I can teach Rose in the mornings. Someone—anyone, really—can play games and sing and read in the afternoons. Rose naps in the afternoon, so it's only a few hours."

"I want to help you. I wish I could help, but I don't have anybody." Kelly pushed back the tears. "Not since my mom passed."

Mrs. Andrews spoke very low so Rose couldn't hear. "What about Rose's father?"

"He's long gone."

"I see. Alright then, what about your father? I've heard you mention him once or twice. Rose talks about him. Gramp, she calls him."

"My dad." Kelly released a long sigh. "My dad is not capable of watching Rose. He doesn't know anything about babies. He doesn't have the patience. He's too old. He likes his privacy. He lives alone."

"Well, you've given every reason why he can't do it, but what about the reasons he can? It's his granddaughter, you need him, and Rose isn't a baby anymore. She is a very bright three-year-old, she is fully potty-trained, and she can feed herself. It would be good for Rose to have another face around."

Kelly stood beside the Christmas tree. Dad liked his new tree. Kelly had been wrong about that; he said he'd wanted one. "I guess it couldn't hurt to ask."

"Of course not. What's the worst that could happen? He says no? And in that case, I have a friend who might do this for me. She's not a teacher. She's a babysitter. She can play games and read. But she's twice as expensive."

Mrs. Andrews didn't understand Kelly's real dilemma. If Dad said no, then Kelly would be deeply hurt. He had never helped with Rose before. Kelly always wanted to believe that he wasn't good with babies, but she knew Dad couldn't bear to see Rose suffering, so he only stopped by for Sunday dinner.

But Mom was gone, and things were different now. Isn't that what Dad said?

"You're right." Kelly grabbed her coat and headed for the door. "I'm going to ask him."

"I'm sorry to say I need to know today."

"I'm going down there right now. I'll figure something out, Mrs. Andrews. You will have your time off." Kelly turned back. "I know what that feels like, by the way, to need to be home whenever you can. I promise I'll make it happen somehow."

By the time Kelly fought traffic down to the Lower East, she had about twenty minutes to spend with Dad, no longer. She was relieved it would be a short visit. His answer would be either yes or no. More words might cause not only a break in Kelly's heart, but also a wound that might never heal.

But Dad was not in his usual spot—the recliner beside the reading lamp. "Dad." Kelly searched the apartment. He didn't own a car, of course; the parking was too expensive. He had all his groceries delivered. At his age, he had few friends left. Where on earth could he be? She checked the kitchen. Dirty dishes in the sink. Dad never left dirty dishes around like that. His apartment was always dusty, filled to the brim with decaying books, but it was neat. Her heart thrummed, she calmed her breathing, and just as she reached for her phone, the door shut behind her.

"Where were you?" Kelly met Dad and helped him with his coat.

"I went for a little walk around the block." Dad pulled away. "I can get my own coat off, thanks."

"You never go out for a walk like that."

"I do now. The doc says it's good for my circulation. Oh, I'm happy sitting in that chair all day long solving mysteries, but doc says it's not enough." Dad paused. "What's the matter with you, anyway? Something up with Rosie?"

"She's fine. You scared me half to death, that's all. You're always sitting right there in that chair when I stop by."

"Why are you so skittish all the time? And what are you doing over here instead of driving somebody around town?" Dad sank into his chair. He positioned the reading light as if he were deep inside one of his mystery books, unraveling clues. "Go ahead. Tell me what's going on now. Something with that old Mr. Perez?"

Kelly sat on the footstool. "I'm not here about the job this time. But...Mr. Perez did say to tell you: The truth that you believe is not the truth that someone else believes. *Seeing is believing*, or something like that."

Dad threw his hands up. "Perez would say that. I see some things haven't changed. Well, you can tell him I said, the facts are the facts, and you can't see a thing unless you're willing to open your eyes. In fact, you tell him to meet me down at the deli counter any day of the week when he's ready for me to shed some light on that college-edu-cated mind of his."

"He said to meet him next Friday, the usual place, the usual time. He's going to dress you down, or something like that."

"Is that so? Well, it'd be my pleasure." Dad's joy was instantly darkened by Kelly's stern expression. "Awww, enough of that." He shifted in his chair. "Back to the reason why you raced down here. I know you're off doing whatever you want and probably everything I told you not to do because we both know you got a problem keeping your mouth shut."

"I wonder who I got that from?"

"Quit changing the subject. What's going on?"

"I like this job, Dad. I really do. The only problem is my hours are long. I have to be available twenty-four seven, on call, and—"

"Don't I already know it."

"I'm not done. Please stop interrupting. I told you about the new teacher I hired, that therapist for Rose? Mrs. Andrews? Well, you wouldn't believe the progress Rose has made in just a couple of weeks. I'm so grateful I found her. Rose is saying so many more words now. She's working puzzles and numbers. She loves that Christmas tree. You wouldn't believe her face when I turned the lights on. She made me move her bed beside it so she could sleep next to it. And—wait until you hear this—I took her to a polo match."

"Where on earth would you find horses and—"

"It's water polo, and guess what? She loved that too. She sat on that bench beside me, mesmerized by the game, and she followed right along. I'm taking her swimming next, just the two of us. Mrs. Andrews says it will be good for her. Like a therapy of sorts. Rose has been changing every few months. She's not a baby anymore. She's really getting grown up. She can go to the bathroom by herself and—"

"Hold up a second." Dad held both palms out, signaling her to stop. "Don't I see her every Sunday night for dinner? What is this, some kind of lame sales pitch? Good thing you didn't decide to be a car salesman because I'd be walking out the door by now. You're coming on way too strong. You're trying too hard. So, let me guess: Mrs. Andrews can't watch Rosie all day long. Is that it? The woman has a life of her own someplace?"

Kelly shook her head in disbelief.

"I got that wrong?"

"You're right. Her husband is coming home from the hospital. She needs to take care of him."

"Oh, I see where this is headed. It'll start out at two hours, then it will be three, then four, and before you know it, I'll be cooking dinner and sleeping on that couch. Is that what you're really asking me here?"

Kelly stood abruptly, and the stool toppled to its side. "Well, it's not like I'm asking you to drive the Rolls for me, although I suppose you'd like that a lot better. Sure, you'd jump at that chance. I'm asking if you'd watch your one and only granddaughter a few hours a day. Is that so much to ask? This is not about you and everything you know about driving, or cars or those books of yours. This is about a person. Not a thing. There's a big difference."

"Oh, I'd say this time, for once, it is all about a person. Me. Because I think you're asking me to babysit a three-year-old who happens to be my granddaughter, and you're putting up quite a fight here. It's like you don't really want me to watch her, and here, all along, I've been wondering if you were ever going to let me babysit Rosie." Dad jerked his chin toward his tree, all lit up with white lights and old ornaments that Kelly instantly recognized from her childhood. "A lot like that tree you hauled in here, I was hoping this day would come, waiting for it, but you were the one who already had your mind made up."

"So...wait...what? Are you saying you'll do it?"

"Yeah. I'd like to. If you'd quit arguing about it."

"So, you'll take the subway up to my house every afternoon and watch Rose?"

"What do you need, a contract? A secret handshake? That's exactly what I'm saying. I'd be happy to watch her. What time?"

"You're going to have to transfer trains. It could take forty minutes to get up there. I could pay for a cab. Would that help?"

"Kel, I've been riding that train longer than you've been alive. I even know how to transfer. What time do you need me?"

"From one until around dinnertime, sometimes later."

"Okay."

Kelly was speechless.

"What's the kid's name again?"

"That's not funny."

"Maybe it is." Dad eased the mood. "You got any more fights to pick? Because I'm guessing you better get back to work."

"I do."

"So, you do got more fights to pick? Well, go ahead if you have to."

"No...no...I need to get back to work." Kelly stood, buttoned her coat, and paused at the door. She needed to say something more. Anything. She motioned to the tree. "The tree looks good."

"It does, doesn't it? It's got all your mother's old ornaments on it. Every one of those things has a story to go with it— the times in our lives, the good times. I never saw it until now. I had some fun unpacking all those boxes." Dad choked up.

Kelly's eyes latched onto each ornament, one by one, and the memories with them.

He regrouped. "Much like I'm going to enjoy watching over my granddaughter. I might not be a schoolteacher or some fancy therapist like that Mrs. Andrews, but there's one thing we know for sure. I'm old, and with old comes smart. I got a few things I could teach Rosie about cars, for instance. Makes and models, the engines..."

Kelly bit her lip. "She might be a little young for that."

"Too young for cars? You never were too young. Does she have any of those matchbox cars? I'll bring a few of those with me."

"No, she doesn't. That would be fine."

"I can read to her, too. I'll bring some of these books. She's going to love a good mystery. I'll start her off slow, maybe a little Agatha Christie, not a lot of blood and guts in those."

"Whatever you say." Kelly knew Dad was joking, or maybe not. It didn't matter. She had a feeling Rose was going to enjoy another face, especially this one.

"I could teach her how to spit too," Dad added. "I've always been good at that."

"No. You are not going to teach that little girl how to spit. I draw the line there."

"Settle down, settle down." Dad grinned. "I was seeing if you were listening. I don't spit. Have you ever seen me spit?"

Kelly pretended to be aggravated as she huffed out the door and down the sidewalk, and then she let the smile come, and the laughter.

13

Chapter Thirteen

K elly could not wait to give Mrs. Andrews the good news. She found her sitting at the kitchen table helping Rose with a puzzle. "My dad said he'll do it. He will be here every afternoon at one to relieve you. He's fine with it."

"What a relief. I'm so happy to hear this." Mrs. Andrews rubbed her temples with her thumbs. "Thank you for your kind efforts."

"Please don't thank me. You have been a tremendous help to my Rose, and I need to return the favor in any way that I can." Kelly wrote a phone number on a slip of paper and taped it to the fridge. "This is his number, in case of emergency. Seamus O'Sullivan."

Mrs. Andrews knit her hands. "It looks like we are helping each other now, aren't we?"

"I wish I could do more."

"We do what we can," Mrs. Andrews said. "Some people do nothing at all. But we—you and me—are cut from the same cloth, maybe because of our hardships. We do whatever we can."

Kelly clung to those words like a warm breeze on a frigid day.

"By the way, you left here in such a hurry that you forgot your phone." Mrs. Andrews slid Kelly's phone across the table. "You only had one call, and I hope you don't mind but I answered it. It was a Mr. Perez. The nicest gentleman. He said you suddenly have the afternoon off. They all decided to stay home. Come back at dinner hour."

That single message spoke volumes. Claire would not be walking the dogs this afternoon. Byron had spoken to his dad about Peter's injury. Kelly remembered the old adage: "Hurting people hurt people." That truth might shed some light on Claire's inner struggles, but it did *not* give her an excuse.

"That's more good news. The afternoon off." Kelly relaxed in a chair beside Mrs. Andrews and watched Rose fit the puzzle pieces together. "So, how did it go this morning?" she asked.

"Fine." Mrs. Andrews hesitated. "Except...there is one thing you should know. It's about that puddle."

"I told you I would handle it."

"It's not me. It's Rose. Her infatuation has grown into an unhealthy obsession. I'm not sure why, but when I try to distract her from that water, she has quite a tantrum. She refuses to leave the puddle covered up. Finally, I put the pot over it and told her the puddle needed a nap. That sounds absolutely ridiculous, I know, but she believed me. Almost as if that puddle was alive somehow. She's behaving as if that puddle is her new...her new...I don't know..."

"What?"

"Her friend, or something like that."

"Oh, that is ridiculous. A stuffed animal is her friend. A doll is her friend. Not a puddle of water."

"Maybe this is all because of that water polo?" Mrs. Andrews agonized. "Maybe that's the reason for Rose's sudden enthrallment, but I've really never seen anything like it. She stares into that water as if she can see something. Maybe her reflection? You have mirrors in this house and she is not interested in any of them. I can't figure it out."

This gave Kelly concern. "Is this a new side effect, a symptom?" She had read every medical report available online regarding the side effects of constant migraines, patient depression, and withdrawal from reality, and she was always on the lookout for any signs of digression, absent staring, or fantasy progression.

"I don't believe so." Mrs. Andrews knit her hands again. "Rose has extremely high cognitive function. She is very alert and interactive, but we cannot disregard this behavioral change. We should keep an eye on it. Try to distract her. There is some logic involved here. Not every home has a puddle in the middle of the floor that refuses to go away."

That was exactly what that puddle was doing—refusing to go away. "Well," Kelly said, "I'll keep an eye on that."

Kelly certainly had enough things to worry about already, like Rose's legitimate issues with pain and medications and sleeping and eating. Of course, from an educational perspective, Mrs. Andrews would demand Rose's full attention, but really? A puddle? Kelly considered buying Rose a few water toys if that puddle made her so happy. Why not go with it?

***

Kelly parked the Rolls at the curb of Fifteen Central Park West and waited. She was scheduled to drive Mr. Irving and Carolyn to their Sunday night dinner date. Now that Kelly had seen the interior of the penthouse, she imagined how their night was progressing: Mr. Irving and Carolyn in their great room, preparing for their evening out, giving last-minute instructions to Byron and whoever. Mr. Irving donning that expensive camel-hair coat, while Carolyn draped herself in a new sable. Carolyn, apprehensive and anxious about the evening ahead. Mr. Irving, completely and totally clueless.

Kelly also imagined how this night might end: Carolyn finally con-
fronting Irving about his affair and telling him about her book deal.
Two major turning points in each of their lives. Or maybe Carolyn
would say nothing and live with it, like she'd been doing. But the truth
that you believe is not the truth that someone else believes, as Mr.
Perez had said. Kelly would change that adage to *the truth that you are
willing to see is not the truth that someone else is willing to see.*

And there they came. Jack greeted the couple with increased overt
enthusiasm because it was the most honorable Mr. Irving himself this
time. "Good evening. Doesn't Mr. Irving look handsome tonight. It's
a beautiful night for a dinner out." Actually, the snow had picked up
and was sifting sideways, whipping at their open faces and necks. Mr.
Irving tightened his cashmere scarf, Carolyn tucked her chin inside her
fur collar, and the two quickened their pace to the Rolls.

Kelly rolled her eyes at Jack, who had made a fool of himself, working way too hard to win Mr. Irving's approval, and Jack threw both
hands up as if to say, "It's the doorman's job."

"Good evening." Carolyn entered the car first. Kelly had been right.
She was wearing another fur coat, but this one was different from the
past two—snowy white and to the ankles.

"Miss Carolyn, you look beautiful."

"Why, thank you, Kelly. At least somebody noticed."

"I said you looked nice when you walked into the salon," Mr. Irving
growled. "Please tell me this isn't how this evening is going to go, or
I'll go back inside and watch the basketball game with Byron."

"Byron doesn't even like basketball," Carolyn quipped. "He wants
to watch *Dancing with the Stars.* He suffers through those boring
basketball games for you. Why can't you do something for him for a
change?"

Kelly pulled away from the curb and pushed the button to lower the privacy screen. This was one conversation she did not want to hear.

"Do not lower that screen," Carolyn demanded. "You need to hear this."

"Kelly does not need to hear this," Mr. Irving said. "She is the driver."

"She is also our friend. Yes, Marcus, friend. That woman has helped me with more things in these past weeks than you have in the past three years."

Kelly sank into her seat. "Carolyn, I'd rather not get involved in this, if you don't mind."

"Oh, but you are already involved. It's far too late for that." Carolyn then snipped at Mr. Irving. "We're good friends, Kelly and I, and sometimes friendship can be even stronger than romance."

Mr. Irving issued a stinging rebuttal. "Oh, I'm not worried about Kelly superseding me anymore. I gave up on that the first time I met her."

Here we go again. Everyone was constantly insinuating that Kelly was not intelligent just because she was the driver. Was it the uniform? Like a tailored suit or cashmere coat proved wisdom? "Like my application states," Kelly interjected. "I have a college degree, now worthless, but I earned it. And..." She couldn't help herself. "I come from a family of drivers, no fancy degrees, but just as smart as anybody I know." *Please stop talking, Kelly, please.* "Maybe smarter."

"Pardon me." Irving glowered. "Do you happen to have a training in psychology? Psychiatry? Marriage therapy? Relationship counseling?"

Kelly was silent.

"No. You do not. This conversation is between Carolyn and myself. Please stay out of it. This has been the very problem from the start."

"Not the problem, Marcus," Carolyn interjected. "The solution."

"What do you mean by that?" Irving squared his shoulders.

"I don't think the way I used to think, thanks to Kelly."

"Is that so? And why is everybody calling the driver by her first name all of a sudden? We've never done that before."

"You call her Kelly, too."

"I have no choice in the matter!" Irving was shouting.

"Lower your voice, or I'll get out at the next corner," Carolyn said.

"Oh really? And then what, Carolyn? Hail a cab? With what money? You don't have a dime. You don't have a place to live. You wouldn't have all those clothes you donated if it weren't for me. Where do you think you're going without me? Maybe you better ask your great oracle, majestic soothsayer, Gandalf, aka our driver, that question."

"Excuse me," Kelly said. "I never claimed to be anything more than a friend."

"Whatever." Irving swatted the air.

"Before I answer you, Marcus, you must tell me something," Carolyn demanded. "The truth for once in your life. Are you having an affair with Claire?"

Oh no, Kelly thought. *Not here and now. In the Rolls?* She tried to lower the privacy screen again, but Irving jerked his chin toward Kelly. "Leave that screen open. Are you behind this, Kelly? Is that what's going on here?"

"No, I am not. She figured that one out all on her own. I mean, she suspected it, but I haven't said a word. Not that I know anything anyway. We never discussed the matter. I mean, she did ask me about it a couple of times, but I told her I'm not getting involved in that. I have nothing to say." Kelly cringed.

"Stop changing the subject, Marcus." Carolyn's voice cracked. "Answer the question. Are you having an affair?"

He slapped his knees. "No, I am not having an affair."

Something within Kelly boiled. Maybe it was her past experience with Damean? Maybe it was her friendship with Carolyn? Maybe it was Rose, back home, wishing she could gallivant all over the city without an excruciating headache, like these two spoiled brats. Maybe it was the notion of Christmastime, the twinkling lights, the happy music, the storefront windows, trying so hard to cover up all this city's filthy dirt.

Or maybe it was because one of these two full-grown adults, elbowing each other and bickering like children in the back seat, was a liar. He most certainly was. Once again, the words erupted before Kelly could contain them. "Mr. Irving?"

The car fell silent. Absolutely still and silent for more reasons than the shock of truth. Even Carolyn had nothing more to say. She became lost in the starlit buildings slipping past her window, as she often did when she clearly wished she was somewhere else. The only sound was three people breathing, the air moving in and out of their lungs, sometimes shakily, sometimes steadily.

Finally, Carolyn spoke calmly. "I'm moving out."

"It's not an affair." Irving sighed. "Not really. It means nothing to me."

"Marcus, that is even worse. Now it's my turn. I have a secret too. There's something you should know about me. I have a contract with a book publisher. It's a book about my life. Our life, actually."

"What do you mean by *our life*?"

"I've written a book, and they are purchasing it. It's about our life, our friends and—"

"Now, wait a minute here!" Irving stammered. "I have a few big-time lawyers who might have something to say about that one."

"Let me finish." Carolyn opened her window and welcomed the icy breeze to cool her face and ruffle her hair. She spoke with controlled authority as tendrils of her warm breath floated through the Rolls. Even Kelly listened intently. "It's a book about truth. Maybe it's time for truth, and I don't care if you sue me. Everybody is going to want to read this one. The lies, the scandal, the expense accounts, the food, the wine...the women. Not the trips, of course. We never went anywhere but those stupid Hamptons, the same people, the same restaurants. Blah, blah, blah..."

"Carolyn," Kelly heard herself say. "I thought you changed that story to something good, something honest?"

"No. I did not. Sorry, Kelly, but nobody wants to read a boring happy story. They want the truth."

"The truth isn't boring, but it isn't gossip either. I thought we agreed to that."

"You agreed to what?" Irving was shouting now. "You. Are. The. Driver!"

Carolyn interrupted, her voice still stable and calm. "You see, Marcus..." She turned to face him. "I thought I loved you. I thought you loved me too, and I really believe you needed me after your wife passed. The truth was, we had something good, but it wasn't love. That's why you had the affair. Affairs. Whatever they were. I understand that. For some crazy reason, I'm not mad at you, but you lied and you don't even care. You believed your own lie, I suppose, in some insane way, and that scares me more than your indiscretion." Then to Kelly, she said, "Stop the car, please. Right here is fine."

Carolyn gathered her handbag and gloves. "And, Kelly, I believed you for a while. I really wanted to believe you, but you're wrong. Money does matter. All the time. The publisher changed her mind. Her pub board doesn't want some heartfelt romance. Nobody sympathizes with Marcus Irving. Nobody wants to believe he's just a regular guy, because he isn't. Marcus is a snake in the grass, that's what he is, and the whole world is going to find out." Carolyn swung her door open. "Oh, and you're in the book now too, Kelly. They adored the idea of a driver/therapist, imperfect or not."

Carolyn stepped out of the Rolls in her ankle-length white fur in the middle of Chinatown, her white hem slurping across the dirty mush. "I have a room at the Four Seasons. Don't cancel my credit cards. I need the money until I move out. You owe me that much, Marcus. You know you do. I'm not asking for anything more. No lump sum, no alimony, of course, but I suppose you already know that I'm entitled to basically nothing since you never agreed to marry me."

Irving did not respond.

Carolyn paused. "I do not wish you any harm. We had something, you and I, even for a brief moment. It was good, for that little while, and then it was not. You sensed it too. That's why you set up all your surveillance cameras and your private investigators and all your nonsense. It's only those people who are untrustworthy who do not trust others. You can't force someone to love you. And...you can't force yourself to love someone."

The instant surprise on Irving's face caused Kelly's to fall into the same expression. And the crowd of onlookers, who had quickly gathered on the sidewalk, looked much the same—expressions of shock and awe, mixed with sheer entertainment and delight that those inside the car did not possess.

"Did you honestly think we didn't know about those cameras?" Carolyn exclaimed. "For heaven's sake, even Byron knows. Actually, he's the one who told the rest of us. Oh, we all pretended it wasn't going on because that's the only way we could handle it. But we knew." She left the car door open. "Goodbye, Marcus. Good luck with your crazy mixed-up life." She tromped down the sidewalk, then turned back. "Oh, and for the record, I am telling the truth, Kelly O'Sullivan. Not some watered-down, candy-coated version. The real truth, and all the delicious, best-selling, X-rated gossip with it."

Well, this is it, Kelly thought. *I'm fired now.* Her hands froze at ten and two. She eyed Mr. Irving in the mirror, half expecting him to kick her out of the car, too. They remained in that position for about thirty minutes, parked at the curb, Carolyn's door still wide open, her window down, the winter cold invited to slap their faces.

Finally, Irving said, "Oh, it's not your fault. If that's what you're worried about." He was intent on the open window, the direction that Carolyn had gone. "There's nobody to blame here...but me."

Kelly muttered, "Home now?" She longed to get out of that car.

"No. Take a spin around the city." Irving leaned over and closed Carolyn's door and window. "I need some time."

"Yes sir." She pressed the privacy screen a third time and was stopped again.

"A little late for that, isn't it?" he said. "It looks like you know more about my life than I do."

"Not by choice, Mr. Irving. I never intended to grow this close to any of them. You can't sit in a box for hours on end with someone and not grow closer to them or, at the very least, get to know them better." Kelly thought again. "Or worse."

"Well, that's news to me because it seems I've been doing it for years now."

They drove in silence throughout the city streets. Despite the Rolls's gloomy interior, the feeling of Christmas smiled in the air with evergreen trees dressed in twinkling lights and crowds of tourists bundled up in scarves and hats of red and green. Even Central Park, with its bare branches coated in fresh linen snow, seemed to smile tonight. Or maybe it was grinning. A wily, mischievous sort of grin.

After about an hour, Kelly hoped, "Home?"

"How about my coffee spot, Viand?"

"I have a better idea. Luigi's, Lower East."

"Sure, why not."

Kelly wove their way downtown to the Lower East Side, where she had grown up, where Dad lived. Her favorite diner was a little smaller than Mr. Irving's but also a little warmer. There were wooden floors and checkered tablecloths and clay pots brimming with holly and poinsettias. There were candles and balsam boughs, swirled in red ribbon and multicolored lights. The staff was dressed like French waiters: black pants, white shirts and bow ties. But the very best was yet to come—the food. It seemed like a good time for food.

They took a table at the far end. The waiter brought a menu—a yellowed plastic sheet that looked older than the building itself.

"We don't need a menu," Kelly waved it away. "Give us two of the house red wines, and we'll split the cannelloni, chicken parm, a side of meatballs, the pasta Bolognese—oh, and some cheesecake."

"That's a lot of food," Irving said.

"It's been a lot of a day."

They sat in silence, sipping their wine. No words were spoken and none needed for the time being. Irving swirled his wine in his goblet, over and over again. Then, after a long while, he finally said, "How did you find out about Claire?"

"Does it matter? It was sort of obvious. The real question is, do you love her?"

"Who? Claire?"

"If you have to ask, then there's my answer."

"No, I don't love Claire."

"Then why do it?"

"I don't know."

"What about Carolyn? Do you love her?"

"I thought I did."

"Same question. Why do it?"

Irving's eyes narrowed. "I don't have to tell you anything."

"No, you certainly don't. And I have no business asking. But...in case you wanted to talk to someone...I'm curious."

He set his cup down and leaned back in his chair. "I'm not the bad guy you think I am. Those women needed me, for different reasons, and I gave them what I could. I took care of them." He played with his fork. "I do care about them each, in a way, but not the way they want. Not the way I want...Anyway, I didn't hurt them, not really, if that's what you're thinking, because they don't love me either. They needed me. I needed them."

"But you did hurt them."

"You don't know that."

"Oh, I know. Believe me. I know."

Silence from Irving as he studied Kelly. But she wasn't revealing any more clues.

"The truth isn't easy," she said.

"The truth." Irving blew air through his nose. "I don't even know what the truth is anymore."

"I think you do. We all do. We just don't want to see it...or believe it. So, what are you going to do now?" Kelly wasn't sure why she was being so bold with Irving, but she did know this: she cared about this family. Every single one of them, including Carolyn, and even Claire. Including this jerk sitting in front of her. She wasn't sure why she cared. Maybe because of her own hardships.

More silence. When the food arrived, Irving scooped heaping portions onto his plate and ate with a vengeance. He noticed Kelly had not budged. She was waiting for him to answer her question. He wiped his mouth. "There's nothing left for me to do. What's done is done."

Kelly held his gaze.

He threw the napkin onto the table, but the effect wasn't there. It landed softly, one corner in the pasta bowl. "My world is falling apart," he surrendered. "There, you happy now? I said it. The powerful CEO of a Fortune 100 company is ruined."

"You still have Claire."

"I fired her for mistreating my dogs."

"Mr. Irving, with all due respect, you don't know what a world falling apart really feels like. Most of our problems in life are created by us. But the other kind—the problems that are out of our control? Those are what 'a world falling apart' really looks like. We had nothing to do with them, we didn't cause them, and we can't be blamed for them."

"You're an expert on the matter, I see?"

Kelly shrugged. "I wish I wasn't." She scooped some pasta onto her plate and began eating.

"So, tell me, what does 'a world falling apart' really look like?" Irving bore into her. "My girlfriend left me. The dog walker is out. My son doesn't trust me. My private life is about to be leaked in a public scandal. Go ahead, tell me. I'm listening. What am I missing here?"

"You're a strong man, Mr. Irving. You made that company out of nothing. You told me so the first day I met you. You have thousands of employees. You live in one of the most expensive penthouses in the city. You had two women who didn't really love you but devoted their lives to you, but you never really loved them either, so there's that. Hot gossip is about to be leaked about you. So what? It will be the buzz for a couple months, no more than that, and then everybody will move on to the next, latest thing. Your son knows exactly what you've been doing all along, and he'll forgive you. It seems like he already has. That all sounds like nothing more than a speed bump that you built with your own two hands."

He snorted. "You're right about one thing. I've still got Byron. He's all that matters anyway."

"You can't lose him. He's only fourteen. He has nowhere to go. So, why the cameras?"

"They were for his safety and protection. That's how this all began. I needed to know what Byron was doing. At all times."

Kelly took extra time chewing. She knew what she was about to say next would breach Byron's confidence, but sometimes promises had to be broken. This was not for Mr. Irving anymore. This was for Byron. Carolyn was gone. Claire was gone. But Byron had no choice.

Kelly swallowed. Put her fork down. "He's playing water polo."

"He's what?" Mr. Irving shoved his chair back from the table with a squawk. "Who knew about this? I'll fire them all."

Kelly was stoic. "Is this a problem?"

"Yes, it's a problem. He can't play a sport. That's why he's taking Mandarin and violin and whatever else I can think of to keep the kid busy."

"Maybe busy isn't enough. Maybe he wants to be happy."

"Who are you? And who gave you the right to come in here and undermine my authority and stir up all these secrets?"

There was no turning back now. Kelly should have minded her own business, but she did not, she could not, and she was here now. "I saw one of his polo matches."

Irving slammed his fist on the table. "You are not his parent. You have no right to go to that game, as if you're some big supporter of his, some kind of lifelong friend."

"Well, I am a big supporter of his, and we are friends. Is there something wrong with that, too?"

"Yes, there's something wrong with that!" Irving was shouting again. Those in the restaurant turned to watch the production. "You're just the driver!"

Kelly remained poised. "Yeah, so everybody keeps telling me. Anyway, Byron invited me, so I went."

"I am out of here." Irving stood and jammed his arms into his coat.

Kelly looked up at Mr. Irving, wavering like a teetering skyscraper in a snowstorm. "I have one more question," she said.

"I'd say you've asked enough questions. You've caused enough trouble. You know what I'm going to do? I'm going to fire you, too, that's what. I fire everyone eventually. Why not you?"

The words she'd been dreading to hear landed with the finality of a gavel, sending her pulse roaring in her ears. Her thoughts flashed to Rose. Losing this paycheck meant losing the expensive care that kept her daughter's fragile world safe. What had she done? Exactly what Dad had told her not to do.

She fought to keep her voice steady. "Maybe because Byron is happier than he's been in a long time. Maybe because I actually care." Kelly stood to face Irving. "I'm sorry that I went too far. I didn't mean to. But how can someone *not* care? I guess there are people out there who can do that, but it's not me. I'm not wired that way. Just answer one more question. Why can't Byron play a sport?"

"You don't know?" Irving did not hide his pleasure with this news.

"No."

"Well, that is interesting. It appears the two of you are not as close as you assumed."

"Why can't he play? Tell me."

Irving slumped into his chair. "Byron has asthma. EpiPen sort of asthma. He's had it since he was a baby. It's gotten far worse. He's on a lot of medications, and the least little thing can trigger it. Increased activity, extreme temperatures, allergens. If he were to contract, say, bronchitis or pneumonia, he couldn't fight it. The lung X-rays show COPD. That is about impossible for a boy his age who wasn't exposed to a lot of cigarette smoke or chemicals." His voice trembled. "Do you think I don't want my son to play a sport? I would love to see him running around with friends, playing any sport he chooses. But it's far too dangerous."

This Kelly understood, and yet, Byron was playing a sport. He was proving them all wrong. Maybe, like Rose, he was growing stronger year by year. Should Byron be given a chance at life, or should he cower in fear like his father?

"But he is playing a sport." Kelly sat down. "Water polo. He's the goalie. He takes himself out of the game every fifteen minutes or so...now I know why."

Mr. Irving was processing this new information, and his countenance was morphing from anger to pride and back again.

"There's something more." Kelly rested her forearms on the table and leaned forward. "He's really good at it, Mr. Irving. The team wins because of him. When he takes himself out of the game, they start to lose. When Byron's back in the game, they win again. The bottom line is this: he's really, really good."

"That boy will be so good he kills himself," Irving stammered.

"Or maybe not. Maybe he plays water polo and is the best darn water polo player in the city of New York and wins tournaments for his team and collects trophies and makes all kinds of friends. Maybe that happens?"

Irving's eyes darted about, and in any other light, Kelly would never have noticed the tears. He blinked once or twice. Kelly believed she had finally gotten through to the man.

"He's a kid. His brain isn't fully formed," Irving said. "I make all his decisions, and I'm doing the best I know how. I'm not a mother. I'm a single dad, in case you haven't noticed. I got those cameras to keep an eye on him when I'm gone. It's not that I don't trust him. I don't want anybody to push him, make him do things he is not capable of."

"Surveillance." Kelly let the word linger in the air.

"I get it. You made your point." Mr. Irving pushed his food around on the plate. "So, he's playing water polo."

"Yes."

He glanced up. "He's really good at it, you say?"

"Really good."

They sat together, alone in their thoughts while finishing their food, and for this night it was enough. There was nothing more to be said by either of them.

At Fifteen Central Park West, Kelly opened the door for Irving, but he stood beside the car, seemingly waiting for something. Kelly wasn't sure what. The icy wind sifted the soft snow, whitening his hair and coat and shoes. He refused to look directly at Kelly. Instead, he studied his expensive building, the brick structure, the scrolled cornices and elaborate moldings.

Kelly gazed in the opposite direction to the busy city street, the flow of taxis and black cars, the same white snowfall melting into the slushy roadway and disappearing. Finally, Kelly said, "So, am I fired?"

"No."

"I'm not judging you, by the way. Not anymore."

"I appreciate that."

"I have my own issues."

"I caught that."

"I'll see you in the morning, then, Mr. Irving."

"See you tomorrow, Kelly."

When Irving was in the building and out of earshot, Jack spoke his own truth. "So, the driver and the boss speak to each other. They don't look each other in the eye, but she speaks and he answers. The doorman should try that one."

***

When Kelly returned home late that evening, she found Dad instead of Mrs. Andrews.

"We got a problem here," Dad whispered. "Mrs. Andrews called off. Her husband took a turn for the worse. I came right over. Rosie and I had some eggs for dinner, over easy, with toast. She's sleeping now." He motioned to the mattress beside the tree. "So keep it down."

"I am so sorry to hear that. Thanks for coming over, Dad."

"Don't mention it."

Kelly's heart was broken for Mrs. Andrews, but the scene before her stitched it back together. Dad was here, caring for Rose the only way he knew how. This was going to be interesting, to say the least. "Rose has never eaten eggs over easy in all her life," Kelly said.

"Well, she did tonight. She had five."

"Is that even healthy?"

"Sure. Why not? It's protein. Now, if you buy a set of arm weights, I'll have her bulking up in no time. Get a bench, too, while you're at it."

"That is not funny."

"Then why are you smiling? Okay, next topic. Let's talk about that slop of water over there on the floor."

"You've seen it before. It comes and goes. Just ignore it."

"Well, you might be able to ignore it, but Rosie can't. She stares at that thing like it's her long-lost friend."

Not that again. "Mrs. Andrews said Rose was a little obsessive about it. She'll get over it."

"That's an understatement. I couldn't drag the kid away. She doesn't even care about that big tree anymore."

"Listen, I'm too tired to talk about this now. It's a puddle in the middle of the room. It's been here since we moved in. Rose is getting older now, more observant. What child wouldn't be interested? I'll give her some cups and spoons tomorrow and let her play in it. It's clean. Does it really matter?"

"Well, the problem is, it's not a puddle anymore. Before I got here, the thing iced over. It's like a little skating rink now. I can't for the life of me figure out where that cold air is coming from. It must be below the concrete somewhere. Maybe a drain tile from the street. I dunno. Anyway, our Rosie is now standing guard over the thing. She just stares into it and smiles, but no touching allowed."

"Iced over?" Kelly approached the frozen patch. She ran her fingers across the chilled twelve-inch circle and then around its frosted sides. Dad was right; it was solid ice, hard as a rock. "I don't get it."

"Me either. The room is warm. The rest of the floor is warm—well, as warm as concrete can get—but that little puddle is sitting in the middle of its own private winter storm."

Kelly fell onto the sofa, exhausted in body and mind and now spirit too. "I really don't have the time or energy to worry about that now. Keep the pot over it so nobody slips and falls."

"Easier said than done. Rosie won't let me cover it, even with a dish towel. Believe me, I tried. I boiled a pot of water and was about to melt the thing, but she just about had a breakdown. Something's going on with that thing, Kel, and I'm going to find out what, if it kills me. Not for me, but for Rosie. She's acting sort of crazy."

"There's nothing wrong with Rose." Kelly stiffened.

"I'm not saying there's anything wrong with her. Keep your voice down. I'm just telling you what happened here today."

"Okay, okay, Dad. I'm sorry. Thanks for caring. I can't thank you enough for your help here and for actually caring about Rose, not just babysitting her. I'm just tired and cranky. It's been a long day. A long couple weeks, actually. Let's talk about this tomorrow, can we? Why don't you stay overnight and have the sofa? I'll sleep on the mattress with Rose."

"I have not missed a night in my own bed since I married your mother. No thanks. I'm heading back downtown. I'll see you in the morning, and I promise you, I'll solve that ice rink mystery. Don't worry about it."

"Thanks for coming. I mean it."

"Oh, quit thanking me for taking care of my family. You and Rosie are the two most important things in my life. The only important things in my life. You wanna hear a confession? I always wished I could do more for you two. Now, I finally can."

14

CHAPTER FOURTEEN

The following morning when Kelly arrived at the garage, she found Mr. Perez bent over a Lamborghini engine, wrench in hand. He did not look up when he spoke. "It appears your job responsibilities have abruptly altered. You will not be driving Miss Carolyn any longer. She is moving onward."

"I'm sorry to hear that."

"So am I. However, oddly enough, Miss Carolyn left a notecard for you." Mr. Perez pulled a slip of paper from his back pocket and held it behind him. "I must apologize. I read it. It was not sealed, and the temptation overcame me. You've been the best friend she's had in a very long time, blah, blah, blah, and much more nonsensical flattery. Keep in touch." He handed the grease-covered stationery to Kelly.

Kelly studied the note. "I have to admit, she had me fooled."

"I see you found your skepticism. The hard way." Mr. Perez wiped his hands on a towel. "Miss Carolyn is an anomaly. Although, Mr. Irving does possess a knack for purposefully sabotaging any opportunity at happiness, either consciously or subconsciously." Mr. Perez snapped his fingers, not once but twice, as if the first time was not loud enough. "On a brighter note, Miss Claire also departed this morning.

It seems she never possessed the passion to be a dog walker. How or why she arrived at this sudden realization, we may never discover." He issued Kelly a stern expression. "But I do have an inkling. Call it intuition or just good old common sense. In any event, she left absolutely no message for you of any kind. It seems she was not so fond of our new driver. Let's hope we do not find our tires slashed."

Kelly remained silent.

Mr. Perez continued. "Despite the sudden deletion of two family members, your daily *sheddule* remains rigorous. You have gained a most demanding passenger with Mr. Irving's return. You will deliver Mr. Irving to his office on Madison every morning and retrieve him in the evening and transport Mr. Byron in between. Oh, and something we must address immediately. You have not properly cleaned the Rolls in days. I've been filling the beverage trays for you, and I do enjoy tinkering with the engines on occasion." He referred to his grease-stained hands. "But I refuse to become a car washer because it now appears I have the added responsibility of being the dog walker, thank you very much."

Kelly had completely forgotten about the condition of the vehicle because of the more desperate condition of the passengers. "I'm sorry. It's been hectic lately, but I promise I'll take extra care of the car from now on."

She took her position behind the wheel of the Rolls, and as she was about to descend the parking ramp, Mr. Perez signaled for her to roll down her window.

"One final critique, if I may," he said. "To springboard us into this lovely, miraculous, one-of-a-kind, beautiful day." His tone fell flat. "Do you happen to know the whereabouts of that mobile phone I gifted you?"

Kelly patted her coat pocket. "It's right here."

"There is a purpose to that advanced communication device that houses both satellite and computing abilities, and it is not to scroll through Instagram or listen to Spotify or play *Candy Crush*...or leave it behind in one's apartment while traversing the city."

"I'm sorry about that, too, Mr. Perez. I'll have the phone with me at all times from now on. I promise."

"You are making a great deal of promises." Mr. Perez took Kelly's measure. "The question remains: Are you capable of fulfilling them?" He saluted the sky. "Ah, but I have hope in you, Ms. Kelly O'Sullivan. You are your father's daughter. Your father spoke proudly of you quite often, his one and only child."

"All the eggs in one basket, or something like that?" Kelly tried to conceal her self-doubt.

"Exactly," he said. "You've made some inexcusable errors due to rash reasoning and poor decision-making. But. And there is a *but* here somewhere." He shielded his eyes and searched the room. "Ah, there it is." Then he planted a firm look on Kelly. "You've lasted a lot longer than the others. No human being walking upon this earthly planet is perfect. Present company excluded, of course. Quite honestly, a disheveled automobile and a misplaced mobile phone are the least of my concerns."

"Thank you?"

"Not to mention you have somehow singlehandedly thrown a bucket of water upon the wicked witch of the Midwest, for which we are all grateful. So much so, in fact, that I do not mind becoming the temporary dog walker."

Silence was Kelly's best response again.

"Allow me to accentuate the word *temporary*." Mr. Perez waved his invisible flag. "Enough talk. Let's get this party started. Aaaand you're off!"

As Kelly exited the ramp, she noted an abrupt change in the wind today. The snow sparkled with an icy sheen as the cold swept in. The weather station reported a storm brewing off the Atlantic that was due to make landfall on Manhattan Island sometime later that night. A nor'easter, as they called it, was predicted to dump several feet of snow upon a very crowded city that had no place to store it.

Kelly arrived at the penthouse and stood beside the Rolls, waiting for Byron. It was going to be a big day for him. He and his new friends were preparing their evidence for a case that was going to a mock trial at the school assembly in two days.

A shadow appeared in the lobby, too large to be Byron. It hurried to the doorway and bolted outside. It was Carolyn. Her hair was tossed into a messy bun, and she wore a mink coat and a pair of sparkly beach sandals. "I'm packing up the last of my things and I wanted to say goodbye." She rushed at Kelly, and before Kelly knew it, Carolyn had wrapped her arms around Kelly's shoulders and was holding on tight.

"I'm going to be better than fine." Carolyn pulled back to meet Kelly eye-to-eye. "Thanks to you, Kelly O'Sullivan. We are going to be friends, I hope? Did Mr. Perez give you my note? Can we get together? Coffee? I want to keep you updated on my book, and you never know, I might need some dating advice. You're not angry, I hope. I know you always wanted what's best for me. I can't thank you enough."

Carolyn hugged her own sides now. "It's freezing out here. I better get back inside. I'm moving today. The publisher gave me a signing bonus. I found an adorable apartment on the Upper West, 96th and Columbus. Don't you live near there?"

"Not quite."

Carolyn spun on her heels toward the penthouse. She wasn't waiting for a response and probably didn't want one, but Kelly gave her one anyway. "You're wrong about something."

Carolyn looked over her shoulder.

"I want what's best for me, too." Kelly flipped her collar against the wind.

"Well, Miss Kelly O'Sullivan, you're the best thing that ever happened to this family."

"You don't get it. I want the best for *me*. For my family, too." Something within Kelly stirred. She had been fighting to survive, and she'd become pretty darn good at it, or so she had thought. Damean had fooled her, and now Carolyn too. She'd been used and discarded by both, and she should have seen it coming. Maybe not the first time with Damean, but the second time was all Kelly's fault.

"We all matter," Kelly shouted over the wind. "When you hurt Mr. Irving, you're hurting Byron, too. You can forget all about me if you want. I'll get over it. But doesn't Byron matter?"

Carolyn blinked once, but she would have none of it. She waved Kelly off and opened the lobby door.

"And no." Kelly did not back down. "We cannot be friends."

Carolyn paused.

"Friends care about each other. They stand up for each other. Support each other. Put each other first, now and then. That's how friends work. You used me."

But Carolyn retreated to the warmth of the lobby and left Kelly standing outside, swaying in the storm.

Kelly felt a presence beside her. Jack, the doorman. This was the closest Jack had ever ventured to the Rolls. Jack spoke into Kelly's ear. "What makes the driver think Miss Carolyn ever saw her? Miss Carolyn hasn't seen the doorman in three years."

"I guess...I guess I thought I mattered."

"The driver matters because the driver gets Miss Carolyn where she needs to go. That way, Miss Carolyn can't be blamed...by anybody...even herself."

Carolyn studied Jack. He spoke truth, but sometimes the truth didn't make any sense at all.

When you cared, truly cared about someone, you assumed they cared about you too. When your heart broke for a hurting person, you assumed their heart would break for you too. When you placed a person's needs above your own, you believed that person would do that for you too. On occasion? Now and then? In dire circumstances?

But this simply was not the case. Some people care; some people do not. This was why it took so long to learn the hard stuff. Kelly didn't want to believe it.

Just then Byron stumbled into the lobby. He was dressed in his usual wool coat and scarf and hat and gloves.

"What about Byron?" Kelly gestured to Jack. "Can Byron see us?" What Kelly meant to say was, *please tell me that Byron is not playing me too.*

"Byron sees the driver. He needs the driver because he doesn't know where he's going and he's not sure how to get there. He doesn't see the doorman because the doorman isn't going anywhere. He's staying put." Jack took a big gulp from his paper bag.

"The problem is," Kelly said, "the driver isn't sure where she's going either."

"At least the driver is going someplace." Jack retreated as Byron shuffled to the curb, head bent low, shoulders hunched.

"Good morning, Byron." Kelly opened the door and waited for Byron to get adjusted in his seat.

Byron set the backpack in the old upright, forward-facing position. Laid his gloves carefully beside him, pointing forward. "Where is my heated seat?" he demanded. "My Coke?"

"I'm sorry. I was so busy saying goodbye to Carolyn."

Byron scowled, and his expression reminded Kelly of Mr. Irving's. The same piercing blue eyes, the same wrinkled forehead.

She backtracked. "Of course." She leaned across him and fumbled with the drink holder.

"Oh, never mind." He swatted her away. "Are you going to get behind the wheel or what?"

"What's going on?" Kelly stood firm.

"Oh, like you don't already know? Give me a break." Byron pointed at Jack, who was hovering at the edge of the awning, blatantly eavesdropping. Byron spoke loud enough for Jack to hear. "Why does that guy need to know all our business all of a sudden?"

As Jack slunk away, Kelly got behind the wheel. Yes. She did know why Byron was angry. It could only be one thing: Mr. Irving had returned home last night and confronted Byron about his secret sport. It was ridiculous for her to have hoped she had gotten through to Irving, that she had somehow transformed him into a supportive father.

Kelly turned in her seat. "I'm so sorry, Byron. I wanted to—"

"Why did you tell Dad about the polo? Now I can't go ever again. You ruined it. You broke your promise."

"I thought he would be proud of you. I wanted to show him that you can do so much more. Like my Rose. I never thought he'd react like this. He seemed so happy about it..."

"You. Don't. Know. Him. You've met him, like, what—two or three times now? You do not know my dad. He is the boss of the world. He's in charge of thousands of people, and he runs that house like it's his company. Nobody falls out of line, and if they do, they're either fired or punished. My dad expects me to be a certain kind of kid. I'm not that kid. I'm never going to be what he hoped I would be." Byron looked away. "I hate him. That's what I think about my dad. I hate him!"

Byron's anger was warranted, but not for hatred. "Byron, no, do not say that. When I told your dad about the polo and how good you were at it, he was beaming. I thought he would change his mind. I thought you two would have a talk, finally. The truth is, I thought he would understand that you—"

"That I'm not gonna die doing it? Who even cares? What kind of life is it when a kid can't even play a single lousy sport? I can't run. I can't jump. I can't ride a bike. I'm not allowed to go to the park with friends because if they start running around, I might drop dead. That's not living!"

Byron was flailing and spewing pent-up words. Kelly couldn't let him drown like this. "Maybe if we talk to your doctor and get his permission, your dad would agree. We are not giving up on this. I told him you were taking yourself out of the game every fifteen minutes, and I'm so sorry. I didn't mean to hurt you. Honestly, I didn't. I would never do something like that to you."

"I'm not going to that school today," Byron said. "Take me down to the courthouse. Life never gets any better. That courthouse is the only place where you can file a grievance, get people to listen to you. Other than there, life never changes."

"Your life has already changed in just a few days. And your new friends, they're counting on you. You have to show up today. You guys have a plan. Wednesday is the big day. You need to prepare."

"I'm done fighting. What good does it do?"

"I am not taking you down to that courthouse. You're making your own courtroom in that school. It's time to stand up for yourself. You're not alone anymore."

"Fine. Whatever. Take me to that stupid school, and I'll climb out the basement window and take the subway down like I always do. You can't stop me."

Kelly opened her driver's door, exited the Rolls and shut the door behind her. Then she opened the rear passenger door and climbed in beside Byron. He refused to look at her. Arms crossed tight, Byron was intent on his window and Jack, whose curiosity was now soaring.

"Byron," Kelly started. "I'll talk to your dad. I'll ask him to get a doctor's release. I'll do whatever I have to do. I'll fix this thing. I promise."

"You don't have the power. You don't know him."

Byron was right. When Kelly had left Mr. Irving last night after dinner, she felt certain he was going to allow Byron to play polo. She saw his heartfelt reaction to his son's new abilities and new friends. Her power to help this family had its limits, like her power to help her daughter, Rose. Kelly knew how to fight and plead and beg and believe, but in the end, she could only do so much.

It was up to Byron now.

It was time to tell Byron her story. The whole story.

Kelly hadn't told this story in a very long time. She wasn't sure if she could. She started slow, remembering things she had tried so hard to forget, replaying the past three years for Byron, and maybe even for herself:

"When my Rose was an infant, she cried all day long, from morning, noon to night. I didn't know what to do. I was a new mother back then, but I knew it wasn't normal. After hours of fussing, she'd finally fall asleep, and I'd lay her in her crib and go outside and sit on the front step and release my own tears. I would stay out in that cold night air for an hour, no more. Then I would hear her crying again, and I'd go back inside and pick her up and hold her and love her as best I could. The doctors wouldn't believe me. Nobody would listen to me. They said I was being emotional, that I had postpartum depression. I pressed for medical tests, pleaded, demanded and begged. I finally found a doctor who listened to me, who believed me. He thought it could be migraines, and he gave Rose a new medicine that helped a little, not a lot. Nothing helped completely. As Rose got older and she could communicate, she started to hold her head. Bright lights made her squint. Loud sounds made her cover her ears. She hated to go outside. She hated to be around other kids because they were loud. All that stimulation made her sicker. So, I kept her home, alone, with me, in a safe, dark, quiet place.

"Her dad, my boyfriend at the time, well, he couldn't deal with it. He left us a couple months after she was born. I never saw him again. I don't even know where he is today. But I stayed by Rose's side, day in and day out, watching her suffer, and my heart broke so many times, I thought I didn't have a heart left. I pictured that thing inside my chest sort of shredded in pieces, bleeding and bruised. That's how I felt inside. There was nothing I could do but watch my baby girl suffer, and sit beside her, and hold her, and try to make her understand she wasn't alone. When everything was taken from my little Rose, everything was taken from me. That's how it works when you love someone.

"Her sickness stole everything from us. Except one thing, Byron. I had one thing left. Hope. I held out hope that Rose might grow out of it, that as she grew—she was changing every year—new medications might be discovered, that we would find a better doctor, that I could finally afford some kind of homeschooling and home therapy that I heard was doing amazing things for kids like Rose."

Byron didn't move, but Kelly saw his fingers tighten a little around his knee.

"What I'm trying to say is this. There's only so much I can do for my Rose. I've been waiting for her to get big enough to try to learn how to battle the headaches, to work around them, to push herself through. Or at least for her to be able to tell me what helps and what doesn't help, or just to be able to tell me how she's feeling. She's so little. She thinks her pain is normal. That this is life. But this isn't life, and I can't wait to tell her this isn't how it's supposed to be. She deserves more. Whatever ounce of happiness she can get. And I'm going to do everything I can to give her that."

Byron's gaze had shifted to the floor, but Kelly could tell he was still listening. His throat bobbed as he swallowed.

"Let me tell you, there were days I begged God to take my life in exchange for Rose's. I begged him to give Rose a real life. Not a life of pain and hiding in dark shadows and quiet places. A life of sunshine and fresh air and school and friends and jump rope and birthday parties..." Kelly was crying now. "Maybe water polo..." She couldn't stop the tears if she tried. "I would have traded my life for hers in a second, anything to stop her pain.

"I had no real help, other than my mom. She loved Rose and she loved me, and that made it all okay somehow. Mom didn't have all the answers, but she was always there, always holding us and loving us. Some days she just sat with us. Some days she hummed a soft song. Some days she rocked Rose for hours. During the night, I would find Mom beside Rose's bed, brushing her cool hand across Rose's forehead, back and forth, to comfort and soothe her tired body. Just

like my mom had done for me as a little girl. I couldn't imagine life
without my mom.

"And then my mom got very sick. And once again, I didn't know
what to do. I didn't know how to help. So, I would sit beside Mom's
hospital bed into the dark hours of the night. I would brush my cool
hand across her forehead to comfort her, just like she had done for me,
just like she did for Rose.

"And then one day, my mom lost her battle. She was gone, and Rose
and I were left all alone. And I did what my mom had taught me. I held
Rose and loved her. Sometimes that's all you have the power to do."

Byron finally turned to face Kelly.

Kelly wiped her nose on her coat sleeve. "Rose needed medical help
that I couldn't afford. I finally found a steady paying job. My dad was
a driver all his life. My grandfather, too. I promised I would never
go there, those long hours, that meaningless work, but I had to do
it. Because of this one job, I was able to hire a real therapist. Rose is
making progress like I've never seen before. It's so amazing. Every tiny
baby step matters. A new word, a puzzle piece, a number, a letter. She's
smart, my Rose, real smart, but her head pain makes her shrink into a
hidden world of her own. She didn't want to learn until Mrs. Andrews
came."

Kelly looked directly at Byron. "And then there was you," she said.
"You invited us to your polo match. You didn't know Rose never left
the house. You said, so simple, like it was no big deal, 'Why don't you
come to my game Saturday and bring your daughter?' I thought, why
not? What was stopping us? Why can't we try? So, I put her dark
glasses on and stuck the earplugs in her ears, and we made our way
to the Athletic Club. I wasn't sure if the strong smell of chlorine, the
people cheering, the clapping...I wasn't sure if any of it would make
her pain worse and she'd have a breakdown and crawl into a ball.

"I sat on the bench. You were playing goalie. You were crushing it. I forgot all about Rose for a minute or two, and when I turned to check on her, she had climbed out of her stroller and was sitting on that bench beside me. She yanked her sunglasses and earplugs off. She was watching that game. She was loving that game.

"I am here to tell you, after everything we've been through, Rose and I, that day was nothing short of a miracle. Nobody around us in the stands knew, because for all of them, it was just another Saturday. Another polo match, maybe followed by a walk in the park or a pizza or something. But for Rose and me, that day was everything. What I'm trying to tell you, Byron, is..."

Byron wiped his eyes.

"You did that for us. You invited Rose and me to the match, so simple, so easy, and you made me realize that maybe, just maybe, hope was real."

The two sat in silence for a long while. Tears stained their cheeks. Sniffles and an occasional sob could be heard. Kelly finally said, "Why don't you ask your doctor. Tell him about the water polo and ask permission to continue, like a medical release. I don't see how your dad could argue with that. And you need to go back to school today and finish what you started. Are you really going to surrender to those bullies? After everything you've been through? Are you going to give up because you had a bad day? Life is full of bad days. And life is full of good days. I want my Rose to see the good days, to go to school, to make a friend. You have everything I wish Rose could have someday. Don't give it all up because of the bad days. Fight back. For you. For your friends...maybe for Rose."

Byron tried to speak without choking up. "Rose is going to go to school like all the other kids, and she's going to play in the park and make lots of friends. I just know it."

Kelly nodded while the tears trickled down her cheeks. "Yes, she is. I have to hope that for her. But someday, when she's your age, she's going to have hope all her own."

Byron leaned over and buried his face in Kelly's coat, and they held each other for a few minutes.

"So," Kelly finally said. "Where do you want me to take you today?"

"I'm going back to that school." Byron sniffled and returned to his seat. He shoved the backpack on the floor and flipped the gloves upside down. "Hurry up. I can't be late. We got some good hard evidence on a few criminals. We're taking them to a mock trial Wednesday morning at the assembly. The only problem is the school doesn't know it yet."

They drove in silence the remainder of the way. Byron let himself out of the car and leaned in to say, "I'm going to have a talk with Dad tonight, and if that doesn't work, I'll go to the doctor on my own, and if that doesn't work, I'll find some new medical reports to support my cause, maybe some new meds, whatever it takes, but I am not giving up."

Kelly held back tears. Of course, she would never tell Byron to do something that could harm him, but she had witnessed him play polo. He'd been playing for a solid year now. That seemed proof enough. She gave a thumb-up, and Byron marched through the brooding storm and into school, head held high.

15

CHAPTER FIFTEEN

t ten o'clock, the exact time Kelly would normally pick up
Carolyn, Kelly stood beside the Rolls, waiting for her newest
passenger: the head of this household, a supposed intelligent, goal-dri-
ven leader of a Fortune 100 company, who was leading his family
straight into disaster.

The frosty sky was framed by thick gray clouds. A winter storm had
been predicted to arrive later tonight, but the tips of its fingers were
already icing the city. Jack stood inside now, manning his post from
within the shelter of the warm lobby. He cracked the door and shouted
at Kelly. "Big winter storm coming in early. The driver shouldn't be
driving anywhere else today."

"In case you haven't noticed, the driver is not in charge," she called
back.

"Could've fooled the doorman."

Kelly's first reflex was to pick Byron up early. But a bold figure
appeared from the elevator, moving briskly toward the door, failing
to acknowledge the presence of Jack in any way whatsoever. He had
other ideas. He marched through the brewing storm, ignoring the
tempestuous blast that rustled his coat and hat and the daily newspa-

per tucked under one arm. He slid into the back seat, and Kelly shut the door behind him. Neither he nor Kelly acknowledged each other's presence.

Kelly took her position behind the wheel and started the engine but did not pull away.

"Well, what are you waiting for?" Irving peered up from his paper.

"It's a winter storm." Kelly met him firmly in the mirror. "Are you sure you want to go down to the office today? The bridges just closed, the tunnels soon, too."

"This is New York. We live in a snowstorm from December to March. I am going into my office."

"If you're sure."

"The stock market is not interrupted by weather." He issued a wave. "Get moving."

Kelly started downtown via Seventh Avenue just as the snow fell hard and fast. The news had predicted three feet or more, and the weatherman warned of high winds gusting over fifty miles per hour that threatened to transform this storm into a blizzard. There would be electricity blackouts, toppled street signs, and limited visibility. Several schools and businesses were already announcing closures. This one hit hard and fast, and Kelly was worried about Byron being stuck at school.

The winds shifted with gale force, pushing and pulling the Rolls back and forth and swirling the snow ahead. Seventh Avenue was a drifting fog of white, and although Kelly cranked up the wipers, they were worthless.

"Can you speed it up a little? I have an important meeting." Irving glanced up to check their progress. "Why aren't you taking the West Side Highway?"

"I don't trust that highway in this snow, and—"

A flash of red tail lights ahead, and the rear of an automobile suddenly appeared through the blinding white, much too close. Instinctively, Kelly's foot slammed the brake pedal, but the heavy weight of the Rolls could not stop as quickly. The all-wheel-drive car slid on the icy street, and the imported water that Mr. Irving had been leisurely sipping was tossed onto his face and coat. "Slow down!" he demanded.

Even the demands of an infamous CEO were not going to change the current circumstances. "I'm doing the best I can." Kelly's voice was shaky. "Have you even looked out your window? I can't see a thing. You're lucky I didn't hit him."

"I'm lucky? Don't you mean *you're* lucky?" Irving returned to his work, mumbling to himself. "Wonderful. Now I have a driver who gets nervous over a little snow."

"This wasn't supposed to hit until later tonight, and this wind..." Traffic restarted slowly. Kelly fumbled with the radio until she found the weather channel.

"Turn that radio off," Irving shouted. "I'm trying to work back here."

"I'm looking for a weather update."

"I said turn it off."

Kelly threw her hands up. "I am not driving you all the way downtown to get stranded. Who's going to pick up Byron from school?"

"Hands on the wheel!"

"We need to turn this car around and get Byron. Right now. I've never seen a storm come in this fast off the Atlantic. Do you want him stuck at school for days?" She fought to control her temper. "It's just a suggestion, but wouldn't Byron be safer at home during a storm like this?"

Irving considered it for some time. He glanced out every window as if he might discover a change in weather. "Turn this car around.

We need to get Byron." As if it was all his idea. "I'll phone ahead and authorize his early release."

"Great idea." Kelly's comment held some sarcasm, but, of course, Irving did not notice.

It took Kelly hours longer than normal to drive to Byron's school. The Rolls was last in line in a row of expensive, sleek automobiles, none of which were equipped for a snowstorm. Irving commented, "It looks like we're all using the same caution today."

"Yes." But there was a matter Kelly had intended to address on their trip downtown. With the confusion of the storm, she had lost all opportunity.

It was now or never.

"Mr. Irving, I need to talk to you about something." Kelly turned to face him.

"It's a little early to be asking for another raise."

Kelly stayed intent on her mission. "I told you about the water polo because I thought you'd be proud of him. I thought it might give you hope that Byron can do more things than people give him credit for. Maybe as he gets older, his lungs will get stronger. Kids change. Kids grow."

"No, he most certainly will not. Lungs do not heal themselves as other organs do. He has too much damage, too much scar tissue. He will decline as time passes."

"What are you saying? Give up all hope?"

Irving's face reddened. "And how would you know, Ms. O'Sullivan? You don't have any idea what it's like to have a child with medical needs. You act like you have a relationship with my son, but I have news for you: My son already has a parent. That parent is me. I know him better than anyone, and he does not need that sport."

"It's not about the sport. Not really. It's about the chance to be a kid, to be a part of a team, to be good at something. Self-esteem. Confidence."

Irving's tone iced cold. "I do not want to discuss feelings. Byron's issues are far more important than mere feelings. You have gone well beyond your driver responsibilities, and I allowed it for a short period because I can see you are a kind person. Everyone is very fond of you. Except Claire, of course, but she is not fond of anyone." He shook his head. "In any event, I don't believe you intend any harm here, but you are now going too far."

"But Byron has been playing this sport for a year now, and he's no worse off. Couldn't you, at the very least, ask the doctor if he can play?"

Irving slapped the leather seat. "I don't care what the doctor says. I said no!"

Kelly slackened. "So, *that* is the real reason. I wondered."

"What? That I don't want my son to get hurt?"

"You're afraid."

"I am afraid. You're right. I am absolutely terrified."

"You're afraid of Byron failing."

"I am not afraid of Byron failing. I don't care if he fails or succeeds. I want him to be healthy and safe and protected."

Kelly softened. "I know what you're feeling. Believe me. I know. You're afraid of Byron failing because if he fails today, then all hope is lost. It's about the hope, Mr. Irving. It's always about the hope. I understand why you're afraid—believe me, I do. But Byron is changing month by month, year by year, and you have to be willing to change too. All hope will *not* be lost if he fails. He'll find another hurdle to jump, another step to climb, and another and another and another.

Sometimes he will soar over them and overcome them, and sometimes he will fall flat on his face, but he can never stop trying."

Byron appeared in the distance, pushing against the whipping white wind and grinning ear to ear.

"None of us can ever stop trying," Kelly finished.

Byron flung open the back door and dove inside, then tossed his backpack onto the floor and his gloves with it. "This is the first snow day that I didn't want to leave school. I can't wait for Wednesday." He nearly sat on Mr. Irving's lap. "Dad?"

"Yes."

"What are you doing here?"

"It's a snowstorm, son. I decided not to venture downtown today. I'm working from home."

"You never work from home."

"I've never been caught in a snowstorm before."

"Sure, you have. Lots of times. You've been stuck in your office for days. But you've never been stuck at home." Byron eyed Kelly, likely suspecting she had something to do with this.

Kelly decisively said nothing and pulled away from the curb, but Mr. Irving pressed Byron. "You were telling us something. Go ahead. Something about your enjoying school?"

"Aw, nothing."

"It sure didn't sound like nothing." Irving persisted. "Something big happening Wednesday?"

Byron sank into his seat. "We have an assembly Wednesday. Some special speaker. That's all." Byron looked to Kelly.

But Kelly wasn't going to help Byron lie, especially to his dad. She knew why Byron was evading the truth. He didn't want his dad to ruin another good thing. "Speaking of special speakers," Kelly led, "did you know Byron's going to be a brilliant lawyer someday?"

"Oh, so this is the latest career goal?" Irving was humored. "Because the last time I heard, it was a fireman, then a police chief."

"Really, Dad?" Byron said. "That was when I was five."

"Well, you're not going to become a successful lawyer by skipping school."

Good grief, Kelly thought, *can Irving say anything positive? Is the man incapable of abandoning his pride for a minute or two?*

Irving continued. "Apparently, Kelly is not privy to the amount of information she assumes. In any case, Byron and I have had a good long talk about that. Haven't we, son?"

"Sure, whatever." Byron slouched.

"You're missing the point." Kelly couldn't help herself. "Do you know why he skipped school? He has a good reason."

"Stop it, Kelly," Byron said.

"Oh, I am sure there was someplace better he had to be," Irving said. "Like the ice cream shop?"

"Not exactly," Kelly said. "He was—"

"I do not want to talk about it." Byron silenced Kelly.

"Talk about what?" Irving angled himself toward Byron.

"Maybe it's time, Byron," Kelly tried.

"It's not time," Byron mumbled. "It's never time when it comes to him." He thumbed at Mr. Irving. "Look what happened the last time!"

Mr. Irving folded his newspaper and fixed on Kelly. "Oh, so now you're turning my son against me too? Is that it, Ms. O'Sullivan? Your sole purpose in life is to empty my household of my entire family, one by one, until I am left with no one?"

"I haven't committed a single wrongdoing since I got here but tell the truth," Kelly defended.

"The truth?" Irving was fuming again. "Or *your* version of the truth? There's a big difference and—"

"That's enough," Byron shouted. "Alright. If you have to know, the truth is this: I've been going down to the courthouse, Dad. I'm learning trial law. But Kelly convinced me to go back to school, for a lot of reasons." Byron shot Kelly a look.

Irving was visibly stunned. It had been a tough past couple of days for him, Kelly knew, getting to know his family.

"Keep talking," Kelly coaxed Byron. "Tell him the reason you went back to school."

"He'll ruin it."

"He won't ruin it," Kelly reassured. "Not this time. I promise."

"What will I ruin? And may I have a say in this before I ruin everything?" Irving took a swig of filtered water straight from the bottle.

Byron eyed Kelly, who was clearly not backing down. He sighed, then begrudgingly told his story. Byron outlined the bullying, the real reason for the black eye, the bruises, and then he described his grand plan, the evidence, the video scheduled to be shown this Wednesday at the assembly.

The car fell silent. All attention rested on Mr. Irving. Would he sabotage this, too? Would Irving end it all by walking into that school and demanding those three boys be expelled? He had enough prestige and notoriety to do something like that without submitting any proof whatsoever. Byron had always known this, and this was exactly what Byron was trying to avoid.

"So that's how you got that black eye," Irving mumbled. "I never believed that story about you tripping on a curb. Do you know how dangerous that is, Byron? You should have reported this sooner. This is the very thing I am trying to protect you from."

"This is me finally protecting myself."

Silence for several minutes.

Mr. Irving was the first to speak. "So, when did you say this assembly is?"

"Wednesday morning," Byron said. "The last day of school before Christmas break."

"What a coincidence." Mr. Irving flipped through his newspaper. "I have a meeting uptown on Wednesday morning. I think I'll stop by that school. Finally, a perk for sitting on that ridiculous school board this past year. Assemblies have been historically closed to parents, but they're about to make an exception. I wouldn't miss this production for the world."

Byron's countenance lit up, but he didn't reach over and hug his dad. Byron didn't shout for joy. He didn't thank his dad or give a last word.

A quiet satisfaction crossed Byron's face as he turned his attention to his window view.

Mr. Irving had no idea that Byron had just won his first legal case.

Now onto his second.

And then there was the matter of the water polo.

16

Chapter Sixteen

The Rolls fought through thickening accumulations, sliding left and right, slurping and spinning amid the heavy traffic and limited visibility. After several hours, and still several blocks away from the penthouse, the wheels whirred to a standstill.

"We're stuck." Kelly announced the obvious.

"Well." Mr. Irving wrapped his scarf tighter. "At least we're within walking distance."

The three bundled up as best they could and began their march toward the penthouse. They leaned forward into the wind, covering their bare faces with gloved hands to protect themselves from the wind chill that had clearly dropped below zero.

Kelly's driver shoes were not fit for the icy sidewalk, and she slipped and fell. Irving lifted her to her feet and motioned for the group to link elbows the remainder of the way. Two camel-hair coats and one black chauffeur's coat formed a united front line against the pellets of snow and frigid temperatures.

Jack greeted Kelly, Byron and Mr. Irving as he opened the door with a rush of warm air and the latest news: "The governor declared a state of emergency for the city and a ban on all travel. Port Authority bridges and tunnels are closed. All subway stations above and below ground, shutting down within the hour. The ban is in effect until tomorrow at 9 a.m. The Irving family better stay put."

Irving said in front of everyone, including Jack, "That's the most I've heard Jack speak since I met him."

But Kelly had one thought—Rose. Mrs. Andrews could not stay past one, and Dad lived all the way downtown. The subway was closing. "I need to get home," Kelly stammered. "Right away."

"Where do you live?" Irving shook the snow from his coat.

"One Thirty-Fourth."

"All the way up in Harlem? You heard Jack—the subways are closing and you don't want to get stuck. You're more than welcome to stay with us for the night."

"My daughter." Kelly's voice cracked. "She can't be left alone."

"I'd let you take the Rolls, but it's not going anywhere anytime soon."

"I saw a big Hummer in your garage." Kelly was surprised by her bluntness, but when it came to Rose...

"We still own that monstrosity?" Irving said. "Go ahead. Take it. It's the only car that might make it through." Irving cocked his head. "What's your daughter's name?"

"Rose," Byron answered for Kelly. "She's really cute. She's three."

Mr. Irving's expression contorted to shock.

"They came to my polo match," Byron explained. "I didn't think they'd show up. Rose really loved it, didn't she, Kelly? You said it was the first time she'd left the house in forever, and she had the time of her life."

Tenants were flowing into the lobby like the snowflakes outdoors. With every opening of the door, a blast of cold jolted the space. Irving shifted their small group to the far corner, and Jack, the doorman, slyly inserted himself into their pack. Irving shot Jack a look, and he begrudgingly returned to his post at the door.

"That doorman is acting strange lately. Let me rephrase that. Stranger than his usual strange." Irving revived their private conversation. He could not contain his curiosity. "Surely that is an exaggeration, Byron. Kelly's daughter has never left her home?"

Byron realized he had shared too much. "She can't go out. She doesn't feel well." He stuffed both hands in his pockets. "That's all."

But that piqued Mr. Irving's interest all the more. "What's the problem?"

Kelly did not want to go there. This was a personal story that she had shared with Byron because he needed it. Irving was another matter altogether. But Kelly had no choice now. She drew a deep breath. "She's had chronic migraines since she was born. The sunlight hurts her eyes, the loud sounds...it's all too much. She's more comfortable indoors."

Irving's voice dropped like a whispered secret. "So, you do know."

"Yes. I know." But Kelly spoke louder. "Byron invited us to his match, and my first thought was *no possible way*. But then I reconsidered. I tried to think like other parents think, parents who have healthy children with nothing to prevent them from living their dreams, and I thought, 'Why not? What would it hurt to try?' If I stop trying, then what? If I set my own limitations and boundaries because of my fears, who am I really protecting?"

Byron seized the opportunity and blurted, "Dad, you would love polo. Come see a game or two. I take myself out every now and then. If I feel tired, I signal the coach. I'm the goalie. There's not much swimming involved."

"The doctors will never allow it," Irving reasoned.

"I called Dr. Peters," Byron argued. "He said it's okay. Pace myself. I'm old enough to know what I can and can't do."

"You did what?" The veins at Irving's temples pulsed. A tantrum was coming. "You cannot go behind my back like that. I am the one to speak to that doctor. I've been working with that doctor since you were born. You are a minor. I'm in charge of you."

Kelly bit her bottom lip. She had told Byron to ask his doctor, and he did. What was the harm in that?

"You're missing the point." Byron clenched his fists at his sides. "He said yes, and I'm going to do it, and if you fight me on this, I'll...I'll...take you to court."

"Take me to court?" Irving's anger dissolved. "Really, Byron?"

"Really, Dad."

Mr. Irving released a low whistle. "I am finding myself surrendering to everything lately. So why stop now? I suppose I have no choice but to go see one of these polo matches. Unless I want to involve myself in some lengthy trial proceedings." He worked to conceal a grin. "I'm not promising anything here. I'm just coming to have a look. That's all. Just a look."

Kelly followed father and son as they bantered into the elevator. She listened to their heated debate as the car climbed. Yes, those two were exactly the same in many ways, thoroughly enjoying the battle of wits. Especially Irving, who beamed with pride at Byron's every rebuttal.

The elevator reached the garage level and Kelly stepped out.

"Safe travels," Irving said. "Notify us when you get there."

Byron searched his pocket and retrieved what appeared to be a business card. "Here's my direct number. It's not a business card," Byron read Kelly's thoughts. "It's a personal card, in case I meet anyone who might be a potential friend. I can easily exchange numbers. See right here." Byron pointed to the wording. "It lists my hobbies and stuff."

Good grief. Sure enough, this business card, or personal card, or whatever you wanted to call it, listed Byron's home address, his mobile phone, his dogs' names, and every one of his hobbies...all except water polo. Byron added, "It was Dad's idea. Anyway, my number's on there. Send me a text when you get home."

His dad's idea. No wonder the poor kid didn't have any friends until now.

Mr. Perez was absent from the garage due to the storm. Kelly found the Hummer keys in the cabinet and took her position behind the wheel. It wasn't actually a Hummer, as anyone might see on the streets. This was a customized 6x6 Hellcat Humvee. Kelly would definitely be safe inside this mini tank, but before heading into her second battle with this storm, she longed to reassure Mrs. Andrews that she was on her way.

Kelly called several times, but Mrs. Andrews was not answering.

Frantically, she tried Dad, and he picked up immediately. "Kel, I was about to call you," Dad said. "I got it covered up here."

"Rose?"

"She's fine. I'm here with her now."

"Where's Mrs. Andrews?"

"She called me, said a big storm was coming and asked if I could relieve her. I said sure. I caught the express train right before they shut her down. Subway's closed now. You better stay put."

"Mr. Irving lent me his car. I'm on my way."

"You'll never make it up here in that Rolls. That car is for looks only."

"I'm driving a Hellcat Humvee, customized, 6x6."

"No kiddin'? One of those sold at a Barrett-Jackson auction last year for 825 grand."

"Probably one and the same."

"Okay then. You got a shot. Take it slow. Don't get on the highway. No side streets. You can do it."

"I can do it." But the fact that Kelly might not be able to reach her daughter for the first time in each of their lives dropped a rock-sized pit into her stomach. "Dad." She heard her voice tremble. "How's Rose doing?"

"Ah, Rosie and I are just fine. I'm doing everything in my power to keep her away from that puddle. We're keeping busy here. Real busy. In fact, we're having a birthday party."

"Whose birthday?"

"Nobody's. Does it matter? We needed a little party. I found a box of cake mix and some candles. They're the candles you used for your Thanksgiving dinner table, but she doesn't seem to mind. I stuck one in the middle of the cake, and we're on Happy Birthday song number fifty-three. The kid can't get enough of it. I have a feeling I'll be lighting those candles until midnight. We're having cake for dinner." Dad called out, "Light up those candles, Rosie." Then back to Kelly. "Kidding. I'm kidding. I didn't let her hold the lighter. Well, maybe once, just for a second. She wanted to see it. What could I do? Stop worrying. I'll see you soon. Rosie, get over here. Hey Rosie, say hi to your mother." The sound of Dad's feet padding across the concrete floor. "Say hi..."

A meek voice. "Hi, Mommy."

Kelly's anxious rock chipped away with the sound of Rose's sweet voice and Dad's humor. Some silliness. Some laughter. Some ridiculous birthday parties. Some...life.

Dad's voice again. "The problem is, she keeps going over to that little icy patch of ours, checking on it, protecting it. This party is working for now, but I'm not sure how long, and also, Kel, something else weird about that ice. It's—"

Kelly shifted the Hummer into drive and descended the parking ramp. "Dad, I really don't have time for that now. Just ignore it."

"That's what I'm trying to tell you. It's pretty hard to ignore because...well, we got steam coming off that thing now. It's colder than ever before and sitting in the middle of this warm room causing a fog. You gotta see this one for yourself."

"Dad, really? Give Rose some toys and let her play on the ice rink."

"No, that won't work. She won't play on that thing anymore. Maybe it's the fog. I dunno. But she just stares into it."

"Okay, Dad. Honestly, that's the least of my worries right now. Put Rosie by the tree. She loves that Christmas tree. Read her a book. Anything goes on a night like this." Kelly shook her head, reconsidering. "Not anything. I didn't mean that. Almost anything goes."

"There's not much more trouble we can get ourselves into here. It's not like we're going to be out on the front step smoking cigars anytime soon. Although..."

"That is not funny."

"It sort of is."

"Dad, thank you. I mean it. Thank you for everything. I don't know what I'd do without you."

"Those are some words these old ears have been longing to hear for a long time."

17

CHAPTER SEVENTEEN

After hours of plowing through the snow-drifted streets, Kelly arrived back home before dusk and found Rose and Dad making dinner. It was a wonderful scene straight out of a Norman Rockwell painting—Rose with her elbows on the kitchen table, chin resting in both palms, watching as Dad manned the stove, whipping up eggs and bacon.

But Dad wasn't his jovial self. He was hurriedly scraping the skillet and tossing eggs onto Rose's plate. "Something happened here after I talked to you." He cracked two more eggs, and they sizzled in the hot pan.

Kelly collapsed into a chair beside Rose. "What's going on?"

Rose stared at her food but did not reach for her fork.

"Rose, eat the dinner Gramp made for you," Kelly said gently.

But Dad and Rose exchanged an eager look. "She doesn't want to eat right now, Kel. It's okay. I'll save it for later."

"Is she sick?"

"No." Dad ran a hand down his face. "Nothing like that."

"Then what is it?" Kelly's limbs groaned from the long day at work, and now her heart thrummed in accompaniment. "You're making me nervous."

"It's not Rose. It's nothing to be afraid of either."

Kelly waited for an explanation. She glanced from Dad to Rose and back again. The room fell silent. Hot air screeched through the heating vents. A car horn honked outside. A voice shouted across the street. The wall clock ticked.

"Rosie, show your mom what we found," Dad said.

Rose slid from her chair and marched over to the center of the room. She lifted the towel from the patch of ice and placed it carefully to one side. She lowered to her knees, then rested her little elbows on the floor in front of the ice and her chin in her cupped hands. Her form was partially obscured inside a foggy cloud that instantly settled somewhere between the frozen water and the warmth of the tiny apartment. Rose wiggled into a comfortable position and stared into the ice.

"Not this again." Kelly was hoping to relax by the Christmas tree and spend time with Rose. A snowstorm was the perfect excuse for family time.

"Again? Oh, this isn't *again*," Dad said. "This is something you never saw before." He joined Rose on the floor, cross-legged, and waited his turn. Kelly remained at the table, observing their shenanigans. Was this a new game Dad had taught Rose? If so, what harm could it cause? There was not much in the way of entertainment inside these cramped quarters. Kelly sat back and watched them play.

But...something strange was happening here. Something had changed. The ice had turned a shiny blue, almost glowing, and that cloud that lingered above was misty soft and quite beautiful. This was not the same annoying puddle that Kelly had tolerated for a long while. The puddle had transformed into something that had never been here before. The air around the puddle had changed. Even the room around the puddle had changed.

Rose and Dad had changed.

Rose stared into that frozen water for about five minutes. It was as if she and Dad had practiced this routine for hours, as if they had done it many times before, and maybe they had.

When Rose was finished, she moved out of the way.

Dad's turn. He scooted in front of the puddle. He shifted onto his knees, in much the same position as Rose had taken. He braced both palms on the concrete floor, leaned forward and stared into the ice. What was he looking at? His reflection?

But then something very odd occurred.

Something so very different than Kelly had ever felt before. The room rushed in around her. A sense of something coming and of something leaving. All indoor and outdoor noises seemed to vanish. The only thing Kelly could see was Rose and Dad and that ice—that little pool of frozen water, about twelve inches in diameter, that suddenly appeared in a dilapidated basement in Harlem. That puddle that Kelly had tried to clean up, but it refused to budge, and nobody knew exactly where it had come from, how it got there, or why it wanted to stay so badly.

This new sensation permeating the room was not fear. It was not an impending doom or confusion or anxiousness. It was not a feeling of uneasiness or unrest.

This new sensation was a whipping force of peace, rushing into the tiny space, like the blustering storm outside, uncontrollable and unstoppable.

This was the feeling that something new had come, separate from and above this hurting world.

Something wonderful was here, for a very brief time.

Tears pooled in Dad's weary eyes and slid down his weathered cheeks, leaving a trail of wetness, dripping from his chin onto the ice, and he didn't try to stop them.

"What is it?" Kelly leaned forward.

Dad backed away from the puddle. "You're gonna have to see for yourself."

At any other time or place, Kelly would have played the role of the skeptic. She would have shrunk back and refused to participate. She would have claimed it a fraud, a waste of time, a farce. But there was something about the softness in Dad's eyes, the innocent joy on Rose's three-year-old face.

"Do you remember what I told you?" Dad said. "When you first took that job?"

"Yes...I mean, not exactly. You told me a lot of things."

"I said, don't ever underestimate anything that comes your way. Even the not-so-good stuff. If you let it, things have a way of turning themselves upside down and inside out, and all of a sudden, you find a miracle in the most unlikely place."

"Mom used to say that."

"Yes, she does."

Kelly drew closer to the two people she loved more than anyone else in this world. Dad and Rose backed away from the puddle, making room for Kelly, and she sat on the floor between them. She looked from Rose to Dad and back again before sliding closer to the ice. She shifted onto her knees, leaned forward, and rested her palms on the concrete floor, just as they had done.

She paused, searching their faces one last time to be sure, and their eyes seemed to say, "It's okay; go ahead."

Enveloped in the soft fog, Kelly leaned over the coolness and gazed within. She dove deeper, past her reflection, past the shiny surface, into something inside. Time passed. She wasn't sure how long. She could have stayed there forever. She saw what they had seen. She knew what they now knew. Peace filled her, over and through and in and around. Peace flooded the entire one-room apartment on 134th Street until Kelly was certain that if she opened a window or door, peace would flood the sidewalk and street above.

A peace like that could not be contained or demanded or controlled. It existed—apart from her and above her, dependent upon nothing but itself, and yet, somehow, it had come.

She backed away and joined Rose and Dad, still seated cross-legged on the floor. For several minutes, Kelly processed what she had seen in silence.

Finally, Kelly spoke to Dad. "But why? Why here? Why now?"

"Because we need it, and maybe because...it's Christmas."

"I have this feeling...this need to tell somebody...everybody."

"Yeah, me too. I've already shown it to a few of the tenants, and I hope you don't mind, but I asked a couple of my buddies to stop by."

"That's fine." Kelly could not believe what she was saying. *Welcome strangers into this tiny apartment? Invite whoever you can into our home?* But yes, this was the right answer. This was the right thing to do. It was here. It did not belong to Kelly. And yet, sharing it was all she longed to do.

"It won't be here long," Dad said.

Kelly shook her head. "Until Christmas and then it's gone."

"That'd be about right."

"We don't have much time."

Rose climbed onto Kelly's lap and hugged her tight.

***

The light of dawn brought the first knock at the door, despite the storm. Or maybe because of the storm. People had come.

Kelly took a deep breath and pressed her forehead against Rose's. "Looks like it's going to be a busy morning. Are you ready for it?" Rose nodded solemnly. The knocks continued all morning without ceasing. One after another, visitors came—a driver Dad had once worked with, a couple of cousins, a few neighbors. Each one came with the same mix of anticipation and hesitation. Kelly met them at the door, her voice gentle but firm. "We're letting only one person in at a time." There were no arguments. No impatience. No demand.

After removing their shoes, as instructed, each guest would approach the ice and kneel or sit on the floor before it, tentatively. They would look for some sort of confirmation from Dad or Kelly or even little Rose to continue. Dad would offer a nod, and they would lean forward and peer into the foggy reflection. They would remain fixated for several minutes, seemingly unwilling to leave.

Afterward, each visitor's face shone with nearly the same satisfied expression. They spoke not a word, not a question or a comment. What they had seen was enough. There were some tears. There was some laughter. They thanked the O'Sullivan family and made room for the next guest.

At noon, Kelly opened her door to find the line of eager people descending down the sidewalk and around the corner. "How many people did you tell?" she asked Dad.

"About a dozen, but they're telling others. Can you blame them? The news is spreading like wildfire. Nothing I can do to stop it now. Some stories are meant to be told, over and over and over again. This is one of them."

Kelly didn't argue. She could not wait to tell Byron and Carolyn and even Mr. Irving. And Mr. Perez and Mrs. Andrews. And even Claire, if Kelly could find her.

***

By Wednesday morning, the storm had cleared, and the city of New York reopened with an urgent quest to make up for lost time. People rushed about Manhattan in final preparations for the holiday. Friday was Christmas Eve.

Kelly hated to leave her apartment. There would be much to manage today, but Dad promised to man the door. Kelly wasn't sure what to expect, but she imagined hundreds of people forming a line for blocks and blocks. News traveled fast in these Harlem streets, especially some good news for a change.

Mrs. Andrews let herself into the apartment while Kelly helped Rose get dressed. "Good morning," Mrs. Andrews said. "How is everyone today?"

Kelly sat Rose by the tree and met Mrs. Andrews at the door. "There's something I need to talk to you about."

"Oh? Nothing with Rose I hope."

"No, no, nothing like that. It concerns that puddle. We are going to have some visitors here today. I'm not sure how to explain it, but it needs to be seen."

"Yes, I know."

"You know?"

"I saw it, right before I left. We have only a few days remaining, you know. Until Christmas. It will be gone after that."

Kelly felt a dull ache within her heart. This was a temporary sort of thing. Something people needed right here and now, like Dad had said. It would come for a time, and then it would be gone, and they would be left with the memory. Sometimes the memory of something wonderful lingered in such a way that made it even stronger than the thing itself.

Kelly's voice fell to a whisper. "Mrs. Andrews, can I ask you something?"

"Of course."

"Why do you think it's here? In this place? Now?"

"Sometimes instead of trying to make sense of something that is beyond our comprehension and understanding, it is best for us to simply ask, 'Why not?'"

"But here? In one of the poorest apartments in the city?"

"If you must have an answer, I have a theory. I've been wondering this myself since I left here the other day. I believe it has come to this house because the people who live here are willing to believe."

"But everybody who sees it believes."

"Perhaps everyone who is drawn here is first willing to see, and that is why they are also willing to believe. You are assuming one circumstance precedes the other when, in fact, they may be joined as one. When people need hope most, they find hope. When people need peace most, they find peace. Maybe you believed before you ever saw it and that is why you were invited to see."

Kelly processed this for some time. "I think there's more," she finally said.

"How so?"

"I'm not just willing to believe. I long to believe."

"Well, we have something in common then. Because I feel the same way."

18

Chapter Eighteen

Kelly's life had become a whirlwind of strangers coming and going in a kaleidoscope of emotions. Like oil on canvas, the vibrant colors of tears, laughter, wonder and awe blended into a beautiful, wondrous painting.

But Kelly still had a job to do and bills to pay. Byron was ready and waiting at the curb Wednesday morning. He jumped into the back seat before Kelly could open her door.

"Looks like you're all ready to go," she said. "Today is the big day."

"As ready as we'll ever be. We're going to switch our video with the school's anniversary video. It will show up on the big screen in the auditorium at exactly 11:04. After that, I'll take the microphone and get a nice speech in—my closing argument, you could say. The jury will take it from there."

"Don't forget; your dad is coming."

"That part makes me nervous." Byron took a swig of Coke and wiped his mouth on his coat sleeve. "I don't want to…disappoint him. It's not hard to do. Let's face it: I'm not a real lawyer. I'm just a kid. I don't know how to give a great speech like Dad. He's been on CNN, Fox, Good Morning America, The Today Show. He's been in *The*

Wall Street Journal, The Times. He always knows exactly what to say to a big audience." Byron offered a crooked smile. "But one-on-one? Now, that's another story."

"Byron, you are your father's son. That's clear in a lot of ways. But you are also your own person. You have your own gifts and talents, and you are going to do just fine today. Don't compare yourself to anybody." Kelly was lecturing herself with that comment.

"I sure hope you're right."

"I know I'm right, and guess what? I have the afternoon off. I'm going to be there too."

"You got off?" Byron brightened. "How did you do it? Dad doesn't believe in time off. I could be as sick as a dog and still going to school. Unless I'm on my deathbed, I am fully able to sit in class and hold a pencil. That's what Dad thinks anyway."

"Well, maybe he's changing." Kelly met Byron in the mirror with a wink. "It's a very special day."

Byron folded his arms across his chest. "Dad changing? That'd never happen."

"Why not? You're changing, Byron Irving. And I can't wait to see it." Kelly watched for his reaction. "By the way, after your case closes and we're done celebrating, I have something I need to show you."

But Byron wasn't listening. "Sure, whatever." He retrieved his notebook and was rehearsing his speech. He mumbled to himself, and every now and then, his pointer finger shook the air.

"It's at my house," Kelly said. "We'll stop by there after your polo match tomorrow? Just for a few minutes?"

"Sure."

Kelly dropped Byron off at school and he leaned inside the Rolls before closing the door. "I learned something by watching those trials down at the courthouse," Byron said. "Nobody likes people who are too perfect or pretend to be. We all root for the underdog. I guess it's okay to maybe have a weakness or two because kids can relate? That's what I'm hoping anyway."

"I like your thinking. I'll see you later. And, Byron, like I said, I really need to show you something later. It won't take long."

But Byron had more important things on his mind. He joined his two friends on the sidewalk. They strode into school together, three heads held high, three shoulders back.

This would be a day that Byron would remember forever. Kelly knew special days didn't disappear; they grew stronger and more meaningful as time passed. Byron Irving would be an old man someday, retelling this story to his grandchildren. This wasn't only a day for victory.

This was a day for a voice.

Kelly would have to wait a little longer to show Byron the puddle. There was still time.

Meanwhile, she had a few hours until Marcus was ready for pickup. She returned to the garage in hopes of finding Mr. Perez. He had not been at work this morning, which was very strange. Mr. Perez never took time off, other than during the snowstorm. Kelly found him in the break room, busy cleaning his locker. "Hi there," she said.

He glanced behind. "Hello, Ms. O'Sullivan. Back to clean the automobile and refill the drink station, we can only hope?"

Kelly watched Mr. Perez stuff papers and clothing into a large leather luggage bag. "What are you doing?" she asked.

He refused to be distracted. "I am officially retiring, much to the delight of the entire Irving family."

"What are you talking about? Mr. Irving doesn't want you to leave." Kelly's heart catapulted. Had she done something to jeopardize Mr. Perez's employment? She knew Mr. Irving's ego was fragile, and although everything seemed fine, she had been shocked by Irving's reactions before. "Did something happen?"

"Yes, something happened." Mr. Perez shoved a few freshly pressed shirts into a side pocket.

"I'll talk to Mr. Irving," Kelly reasoned. "I realize I haven't followed all the rules, but that's not your fault. I'll explain everything."

"My retirement has absolutely nothing to do with your skewed version of the driver position requirements."

"But you never mentioned retirement before. When are you leaving?"

"Today."

"Today?"

"Today. Shall we repeat the word a fourth time? Perhaps it will have a resounding effect the fourth time around." He saluted the air.

"You were leaving today...without saying goodbye?"

Mr. Perez dropped his luggage with a purposeful thud and turned to face her. "Life tends to make sudden turns and stops, without a blinking signal, without a yellow light. I had a bit of shocking news. According to my physicians, it seems I don't have much time remaining on this earth. Although..." A blank expression crossed his face as he became lost in thought. "I really had nothing planned with the remainder of my life, other than work, of course. But I always enjoyed this position. It was...enough. Some people...they dream of retirement. They waste their years, longing for what is to come and dismissing what is already here. There is a life lesson therein, somewhere." Mr. Perez snapped out of his trance and looked directly at Kelly. "Ah, here it is: Never accept a position unless it brings you fulfillment and satisfaction." His lips flattened.

Kelly inserted, "Or you desperately need the job. There's a good reason."

"I am fully aware that is why you became a driver. I saw it on your face that very first day. That pitiful expression of defeat mixed with sheer determination. A juxtaposition of wills, so to speak. You earned this driver position because you met the credentials, albeit minimal. You were the first woman driver and the first person to ever succeed, apart from myself, of course. You have earned your due respect. And that, Ms. O'Sullivan, is the very best accolade of them all. You must remember that when I am not here to remind you."

"What are you saying? I'm never going to see you again?"

"Nope."

"What about Dad?"

"Nope."

"Proper English, please?" Kelly gently teased the old Mr. Perez back again.

"Nope. I've been using your crass form of negative the past few days, and I have come to appreciate its rightful place within the English language." His hands danced like a symphony conductor's. "It has a sort of pizzazz, an inherent sarcasm. In any event, I have adopted it."

"I suppose retirement gives you freedom to do and say a lot of things." Kelly softened. "At least, that's what my dad always says."

"Retirement has absolutely nothing to do with my acceptance of slang. I heard it all before somewhere in the 1970s. It is this dismal diagnosis that has changed me forever. Quite literally. A death sentence, if you will, possesses the power to do many things."

Kelly shifted her weight. "I'm so sorry."

"Why ever would you be sorry?" Mr. Perez returned to packing. "It's not your fault. Unless...could it be? I would love someone to blame. A scapegoat would be ever so satisfying."

"Mr. Perez, do you really have to leave today?" Kelly asked. "Can't you stay a little while longer?"

"Are you referring to my presence in the parking garage or life in general? Ah, what does it matter? I will not be missed. I am not married. I have no children. Mr. Irving will quickly hire my replacement. Everyone is replaceable. Did you know that? Perhaps you would like to be promoted to garage superintendent?"

Kelly ignored his cynicism. "I'm going to miss you."

Mr. Perez straightened to face her. "Ms. O'Sullivan, that is very kind of you and just the perfect thing to say at a time like this, but let's face it—you barely know me."

She shrugged. "I'll miss you." Her words choked.

Mr. Perez became lost in thought again.

Kelly stepped closer. "My dad gave me a message for you."

"Oh? Whatever might it be this time?" Mr. Perez returned to packing. "Whatever his debate, it doesn't matter any longer. Simply tell him...tell him...he won. The end."

"It's nothing like that. It's something very important. What Dad's asking of you...it's not a favor for him...or me...it's something for you. I promise you won't regret it."

"What does this favor entail exactly?" Mr. Perez narrowed his eyes.

"He wants you to come to my apartment. West 134th in the basement."

"Sounds simply divine. I cannot wait to see the darling place. I'm sure it's absolutely charming."

"Just knock on the door. Dad will be there. He'll let you in. He wants to show you something."

"What might this something be?" Mr. Perez raised open hands. "A Christmas gift? Perhaps a miracle of some kind? Miracle on 134th Street?" He dropped his arms. "How absurd."

Kelly inched closer still. "Will you go?"

Mr. Perez brushed both hands against his pants. "Seriously?"

"I promise you won't regret it."

"Fine." He shooed Kelly away to give himself some space. "What do I have to lose?"

"Wonderful. Thank you so much."

Kelly watched while Mr. Perez finished packing. He slammed the locker door with a clang. "I believe you have somewhere to be?"

"I do. I need to clean that car and get back to work." Kelly moved to the door. She stopped, one hand on the doorknob. She couldn't leave quite yet. She turned back.

Kelly met Mr. Perez squarely in the eye. They lingered this way for a long while. Kelly was learning that sometimes words were not necessary.

Finally, she opened the door. "I'll tell Dad you're coming."

But Mr. Perez did not respond. Kelly could feel his eyes upon her as she moved through the garage toward the Rolls.

There were times in life when you knew it would be the last time you would ever see someone again.

And there were times when you wished you had known.

19

CHAPTER NINETEEN

Kelly and Marcus entered the auditorium as the assembly was beginning. Marcus wore his usual pressed suit and starched tie, and Kelly wore Mom's Irish wool blazer with a narrow lapel and gold claddagh buttons. It seemed that jacket was destined for stressful days.

The auditorium resembled a theatre and was primarily used for high school musicals and plays and talent shows. The stage was elevated, front and center, with red velvet draperies pulled to each side. The seats surrounded the stage in a semicircle with two upper-level balconies. The students had already settled in as Kelly and Marcus took their places in the back row.

The headmaster, Dr. Barrett, stepped up to the podium. He was not what one would expect from a headmaster of a very elite private school in Manhattan. He had shoulder-length hair that he continuously battled to control by tucking frizzy strands behind each ear. He wore a double-breasted blazer and a pair of ripped, faded jeans, and he spoke, quite purposefully and obviously, using teen lingo and every outdated slang acceptable by the urban dictionary but not found within Merriam-Webster. He thanked the teachers for a *stellar* fall semester. *Time to spill the tea.* He outlined the class achievements thus far. *No cap, these are real numbers.* He displayed the sports trophies earned, the science competition awards, and the academic excellence banners, calling them his *drip*. He then confessed he was going to *flex* a little and offered himself a few accolades in regard to school safety and the school's longtime mission to uphold certain values and standards. He asked if anyone wanted to give him a *clap back,* and when he got no response, he added something about not being *cheugy*—whatever that meant. Then he rallied them with *Okay, Gen Z, let's get started!*

Next, a pianist took the stage. This student had recently won the National Solo Competition and performed his star piece for the school. Of course, no student was listening but instead was texting, gaming or chatting. Then three students were recognized for their significant achievements in engineering, mathematics and music, earning them summer internships at various universities throughout the nation.

Kelly's heart beat faster. She glanced at Marcus, but he seemed calm and collected. Kelly felt as though she were about to give the biggest speech of her life rather than Byron. She wondered what Byron was doing right now. Was he standing just offstage in the shadows somewhere? Were his palms sweating? Was his heart pounding as ferociously as Kelly's?

Or maybe not. Maybe this was the very moment Byron Irving had been waiting for all his life, and he couldn't wait to have a voice.

Finally, a large white screen lowered onto the stage, preparing for today's presentation, and Kelly elbowed Marcus. "Here it comes."

Headmaster Barrett introduced a commemorative video highlighting the school's achievements from its establishment to the present—a proud seventy-five years as the reigning private educational institution in the Northeast, coveted by many privileged families but attended by few. "Man, have we got a lot to celebrate, *crew*, or what?" Barrett exploded with an excitement his audience did not share. "I am *high key stoked* right now. So, what we have here is a little video we had made. It's pretty basic but really huge. Just posted it on YouTube yesterday. We have it on Snap and Insta. It's going to go viral. You are *G.O.A.T.* Can't wait for you to see it. *Slay!*"

Marcus whispered in Kelly's ear. "This basic but really huge video cost over fifty thousand dollars."

"That is outrageous."

"Barrett didn't think so. He's the star of the production."

Headmaster Barrett snapped his unruly hair into a ponytail and continued, "We're going to be showing this video to all the new kids and parents. We're using it to let people get our *vibe* around here. I'm trying to get a few of the television stations to pick it up. The link is on our web. Share it on social media, *squad*! It's all yours."

"That'll be the day," Mr. Irving whispered.

"Dim the lights and *skrrt*!" Barrett sat in a folding chair on the right side of the stage, crossed his legs and folded his hands expectantly.

The room went inky black.

The screen lit stark white.

Somebody threw a ball of paper at the screen.

Headmaster Barrett stood, hands on his hips, glaring out at the crowd, and somebody threw a ball of paper at Barrett.

The video began, and it was not at all what anyone was expecting.

The picture was shaky, wobbly, clearly filmed by hand and by mobile phone. It depicted a recognizable locker area at the school. Three older boys, wearing the school uniform, were laughing and joking. The audience was smiling, chuckling; they wanted in on the joke, too.

Suddenly, the comedy turned tragic. A smaller boy was seen, down on all fours. The auditorium went silent. Headmaster Barrett motioned wildly toward the video control booth, demanding the video be shut down. But Kelly knew the technicians were Byron's friends, and there was no stopping them now.

"Bark." The commanding voice on the screen was followed by a barking noise that filled the auditorium, echoing off the walls and into the students' ears. The acoustics were purposefully pristine in this theatrical space. Nobody was missing a sound.

The three older boys clipped a dog collar around a smaller boy's neck. Then they attached a leash to the collar and proceeded to drag the boy all across the linoleum school floor. This went on for two, maybe three minutes. Name-calling, beratement, psychological degradation—more familiar at an army enlistee boot camp or a fraternity pledge ceremony—were used for one purpose only: to break.

Kelly watched Headmaster Barrett. He was absolutely stunned, flabbergasted. He shouted to the control booth but to no avail. Finally, he stood motionless, his mouth gaping.

"Why you so little, Byron?" The older boy's voice. "Can't you grow any more than that?"

"Yeah, you got short little legs and arms." The second bully spoke now. "You look like you're in first grade. Are you a real boy? I don't think so. Just pretendin' to be real."

Raucous laughter on the screen caused the room to fall deadly silent.

"He acts like a little girl. Don't ya? Maybe you are a little girl. You can be our baby sister. No, I got a better idea," the video continued. "He's so little. He can be our pet."

Then it got worse.

One bully removed Byron's eyeglasses and tossed them to the ground. The second pushed Byron to his knees. "Whatcha doin', Bingo? You're a dog. A little furry dog with a pink collar. Bark, Bingo, bark now or you'll be sorry."

Byron refused.

They dragged him across the floor, back and forth like a dead mop. He didn't cry out. He didn't beg. He did absolutely nothing.

Kelly's stomach twisted. She glanced at Marcus. His jaw pulsed; his fists clenched. He looked as if he might jump out of his seat and dive onto that stage. Kelly rested her hand on his forearm, and Marcus reached for hers, gripping it, squeezing tight.

The video depicted the three bullies, doubled over with laughter. But it wasn't real laughter. It was artificial, forced laughter. Something was off. Something didn't feel right.

On the screen, Byron clambered to his feet, the leash dangling from his neck. "I see you. I know who you really are," he said strongly, firmly. "There's something wrong with you. Something screwed up in your brains. Maybe you were hurt, and now you want to hurt somebody else. Maybe you're just plain mean, and it feels good to be mean, to watch somebody else hurting. Maybe you're really afraid of me or maybe you're jealous of me because I don't pretend. I am who I am. You're trying to hurt me, but you do it in secret because you know it's not right. Normal people don't feel good about hurting other people." Byron looked at the floor where he'd been dragged. "Or even dogs."

Kelly turned away. She couldn't bear to watch. She felt the grip of Marcus's hand on hers with renewed force. She looked at him. He was the perfect example of controlled, but in his eyes, something more. Not hate, not vengeance. A desperate longing for justice.

Byron's cool voice chilled the auditorium. "The only thing I know for sure is you will never be happy. You'll never have a good relationship because you don't have it in you. You don't care about anybody but yourselves. You don't know how to care. I think you *wish* you could feel something, but you can't, and for that one reason, I feel real sorry for you. You need help."

A tear dropped from Marcus's eye, and he let it fall. Kelly knew it was not only the scene unfolding before Marcus that broke his heart, but also that Byron had been suffering with this secret for months, and Marcus had never known anything about it. All his stealth surveillance, the hidden cameras around his home, and his efforts to keep Byron safe had been useless.

It was up to Byron now to prove his case, but the bullies didn't seem to comprehend what was transpiring. They had been hit swift and hard by Byron's words and they widened their stances, unfazed by the verbal attack. But Byron wasn't concerned with them any longer. He spoke to the hidden cameras. "And any of you who just sit by and watch somebody get bullied, let it go, ignore it. Well, what you're doing is really being a part of it. Silence is a side. Silence is a choice. Silence is a voice. And pretending it isn't happening doesn't make it go away. It only makes it worse."

Kelly felt the pain in her own heart. There were some things on the video she hadn't noticed right away. Like how Byron's pants had slipped down and his white underwear was showing. Like how Byron's hands were clenched into tight fists. How the sweat dripped from Byron's brow and blended with his tears.

Byron was beaten and battered, but his voice rang steadier and stronger than ever before. "All throughout history, there came a time when one person, one voice, stood up against evil. All you really need is one. Well, that voice is me. I am one."

In the video, the bullies descended upon Byron with vengeance, their wide backs closing in around him. Arms swung; legs kicked.

The video ended. Abruptly. Suddenly. Uncomfortably.

The room went jet black again. Not a sound. Not a sniffle. Not a cough.

Footsteps crossed the stage—hard-soled shoes.

The lights came back on.

But it was not Headmaster Barrett at the podium this time. Barrett had not moved from his shocked stance on the side of the stage.

Byron Irving stood at the podium. He looked so small up there. So skinny. His glasses had slipped down his nose. His jacket was a little too big. His pants baggy. He pressed his mouth to the microphone. A screech shrilled from the speakers.

Byron pointed to the empty screen. "That, Headmaster Barrett, is also Madison Academy."

Silence. All mobile devices had been abandoned to laps. All eyes were glued to that stage.

"I have something to say." Byron's voice was a little shaky but determined.

There was a tangible awareness in the auditorium that Byron deserved to speak, and Byron sensed this. No more whispering or gossiping. All eyes were glued to Byron Irving, and he seized this rare opportunity to have a voice. *One opportunity,* Kelly thought. *We fight, all our lives, to be heard, but very rarely is anyone listening. If we could only get their attention, for a few minutes, how we could change the world...*

Surprisingly, Byron didn't talk about the video, the bullies, the physical and emotional wounds. He spoke about something else.

"I have a friend." Byron cleared his throat. "Her name is Rose O'Sullivan."

Kelly's eyes pooled before another word was uttered. She felt Marcus's arm around her shoulder, pulling her in tight.

"I believe that my friend Rose dreams of the things we already have. She dreams of getting herself dressed and riding the subway to school. She dreams that, someday, she can sit in a real classroom with other kids her age. That she can have a real teacher. You all know what a teacher is—that person who stands up in front of the class and tells us all sorts of wonderful secrets about the world. That person we take for granted and make fun of and think is super boring and useless. We skip school and count the days until summer. We can't wait for Fridays. We hate Mondays. All stuff we take for granted.

"My friend Rose dreams of going to school. I think she dreams there might be another girl sitting beside her in class. Maybe she looks over at that girl, that girl looks back at her, and they see something in each other that they like, maybe something they have in common. Maybe they're curious because they're total opposites. Because different is okay. Different is good. They see each other. It's that simple. And one of them says to the other, 'Hey, you want to hang out after school today? You want to go see a movie? You want to go to the game tonight?'

"My friend Rose dreams of having a friend. Just one. She dreams of being able to run. To be able to go outside in the bright sunlight and run around all day long if she wants to. Maybe she can even play a sport. She doesn't have to be good at it. She just wants to be part of a team. She wants to hear the coach say, 'We got this. We can do it. Let's go.' This school makes us take gym classes and sign up for at least one sport and all we do is complain about it. We hope it rains or the gym teacher gets sick. The truth is, we are able to play a sport. To run, to jump, to throw a ball.

"Do you see what I'm saying here? Rose hopes for everything we already have. The stuff we take for granted. The stuff we complain about. The stuff that we think is boring and stupid. She would love to sit next to the kid that you think is a total loser. The one who isn't really good looking and doesn't wear the right clothes. Maybe he's the little guy, like me. Maybe she's the shy girl, like you-know-who. Maybe she's not confident and outgoing. Give her a break, will you? She's only a teenager. She's got the rest of her life ahead of her, and she doesn't have to be everything right here and now. And anyway, maybe she doesn't like your idea of everything right here and now. Maybe she wants to be different. Why can't we all be a little different? Why do we have to be the exact same? The truth is, trying to be the same—well, that's what I call boring and maybe even...cowardly.

"I would say that my friend Rose is different. She is only three years old. She's had migraine headaches since she was born. In other words, her head hurts real bad, pretty much all the time. It stops her from doing a lot of things, but she tries anyway. Even with the pain, she fights for the life you and I already have. She longs for it. I think she dreams of it. I know she will dream of it, soon enough.

"So, why am I telling you all this? Because I believe with all my heart that someday Rose is going to be able to go to school, and when she finally gets there, I want kids to be nice to her. I want them to welcome her and say 'hi' and 'Come join our lunch table' and 'Come try the soccer team.' I want kids to say 'I like your hair,' or 'That dress is cool,' or 'Great shoes,' even if her style is not what you're wearing. *Especially* if her style is not what you're wearing.

"I want kids to see Rose when she finally walks through that school door and to treat her like somebody who deserves to be here. Like somebody who matters. Because Rose matters. We all matter. Every single one of us.

"I got news for you. We are all different. Every one of us. But you know what? We're all the same, too. We all have things we're dealing with. We all have stuff. We hide it. We pretend it's not there. We deal with it in lots of different ways, but we all got something. It comes with life. Do you know what somebody once told me? They said, 'You have to keep fighting. Keep believing.' Don't ever let anybody take that hope from you."

A heavy hush swept into the assembly and hovered above and around them.

One lone student seated in the center of the auditorium stumbled to his feet and began to clap, slow and steady.

Marcus and Kelly joined in.

Then two girls in the far corner.

Then a few more people down front.

Headmaster Barrett did not move from his place. He remained at the far end of the stage, stunned.

Soon the entire auditorium was standing in applause, offering shouts of victory, hoots and hollers and whistles. Hands shot up. Papers flew through the air.

Everyone was cheering. Everyone but the three big boys depicted in the video. They sat motionless in their seats.

Surprisingly, nobody berated those bullies. Nobody tried to attack them, push them, shove them, or even speak to them.

They were completely and totally ignored.

Headmaster Barrett, however, found them and had them escorted out through the crowd.

Byron walked off stage.

Kelly turned to Marcus. She shouted above the revelry. "Now *that* is how an expert trial attorney closes his case!"

Marcus grabbed Kelly and spoke in her ear. "I would really like to meet your daughter, Rose."

Kelly nodded. "She will be at Byron's polo match tomorrow. She loves the game."

Kelly and Marcus followed the crowd into a large open lobby. The students were riled up with the excitement of Byron's speech and the early dismissal from school. Headmaster Barrett must have known it would be impossible to get any of them to focus now.

Byron spotted Kelly and Marcus in the pack and waved. Byron pushed toward them but was delayed by pats on the back and hugs and selfie photos and thank-yous. He maneuvered through the crowd until he stood before them. He wasn't smiling, but an aura of contentment flooded his countenance.

Kelly bent over and hugged Byron. She whispered in his ear so only he could hear. "What you said about Rose..." She squeezed him so tight. "It was so very wonderful. Every single word of it. She is going to do those things and more. I hope she grows up to be just like you, Byron."

Marcus grabbed Byron into a bear hug and held tight.

"I'd like to invite you both to come to my apartment tomorrow," Kelly told them. "After the polo match. Sort of a celebration. I'll have dinner."

"Are you cooking?" Byron smiled.

"Yes, I'm cooking, but the real reason is I need to show you something."

"What is it?" Byron's curiosity piqued.

"You'll see."

"Will Rose be there?" he asked.

"Yes, she sure will."

"We would love to come to dinner," Marcus said.

20

CHAPTER TWENTY

When Kelly returned to her apartment, she was exhausted in the very best way. It had been one of the most amazing days of her entire life, and she couldn't wait to tell Dad. But much to her surprise, she could not even get close to her front door.

A throng of people crowded around her apartment entrance, down the sidewalk and around the corner. All shapes, sizes and colors of people. Some bedraggled and sick, some healthy and strong. Some chatted in groups, sipped coffee or checked their phones. Some stood silently, patiently, with expressions of hope. Some wore designer hats or scarves, while others wore faded, ripped hoodies and sweatpants. Some were bareheaded, letting the winter wind sting their cheeks, and some were wrapped head-to-toe in fur, their faces hidden within. Kelly immediately thought of Byron's speech: We're all different; we're all the same.

Kelly gently wove toward the front of the line. "Sorry, pardon me. I am not cutting. I live here." No one minded. No one questioned.

"One at a time." Dad's voice on the other side. "Please wait your turn."

"Dad, it's me. Let me in."

"Kelly? Get in here. We had a big morning. You wouldn't believe the people coming through this door. We had a guy who told me he just rang the morning bell on Wall Street, some heart surgeon from Sloan Kettering, that guy who runs that famous pizza joint in the West Village, a man who told me he's been homeless for six months and living under an overpass, a girl who said she's working at a strip joint, and—oh, wait until you hear this one—a cabbie. I knew the guy from my years on the road, recognized him right away, and..."

Kelly searched the room for Rose. She was seated beside the twinkling Christmas tree, playing with a puzzle. The place was quiet and peaceful, unlike the bustling scene outdoors. Kelly went to Rose's side and almost tripped over a pair of shoes.

"You'll be happy to know I'm making everybody take off their shoes," Dad said. "Keeping the place as clean as I can. Can you believe all these people? A big news crew showed up here this morning. I didn't let them in. They came for all the wrong reasons, looking for a hot story, their next big comedy show. I told them it's about time for some good news for a change and to get lost. A couple of 'em came back later without their cameras and without their smirks and I welcomed them in." Dad motioned toward the long line forming outside. "All I know is, we'll get them all in here—the ones who need to be here. Don't ask me how..."

Kelly wasn't arguing. "Okay, Dad." She lifted Rose into her arms and sat with her in the chair by the window, hugging her, loving her. Kelly's attention turned to the elderly woman stooped over the icy fog, gazing inside. When she was finished, the woman lifted herself to her feet and addressed Dad. "Thank you so very much."

Dad led her to the door, where she slipped back into her shoes before leaving. At this point, Dad admitted the next person. "Next in line. Come right in. There ya go, buddy. Shoes off, please. That's the way."

This guest was a young man, maybe in his mid-twenties. He wore a leather jacket, leather pants, and a tattoo of a lightning bolt across his forehead. He held a single bill out to Dad. "That's an even hundred," he said.

"We don't want your money, son," Dad said.

"I can pay."

"Not for this, you can't." Dad pointed toward the ice. "Go ahead."

The man surveyed Kelly's one-room apartment, the worn sofa, the mattress on the floor beside the tree, the rickety kitchen table. "Looks like you could use it."

"My friend," Dad said kindly. "The stuff in life that really matters can't be bought or sold, and to try only makes you look like a fool. You'll see what I mean in a second."

The man shoved the bill into his pocket. "So, what do I do?"

"Go on over and take a look."

"That's it?"

"That's it."

He kicked off his combat boots and padded over to the frozen puddle. He squatted before it, then looked from Dad to Kelly, then to Rose, and back to the ice. He shifted onto his knees, leaned forward and peered inside.

This young man, like every other person Kelly had witnessed looking into the ice, responded the same as the rest. No words, no shock, no surprise. A sense of peace flooded his face. He was reluctant to remove his eyes. He didn't cry, although some did. He didn't laugh, although some had done that too. His expression revealed serene contentment, a look that said, *I should have known*, or *I knew all along*, or *How how did I ever forget*, or something like that.

After about three minutes, the man stood and straightened his jacket. He walked toward the door, put his shoes on, turned to Dad and said, "I'm sorry."

"Nothing to be sorry about. Not here. Not now. Merry Christmas."

Rose yawned and snuggled into Kelly's chest. "Dad," Kelly said. "How long are we going to let them inside? Rose is getting tired."

"Let's give it a couple more hours. I'll tell them we're closing the doors because of the baby, and they can all come back tomorrow. Oh, and Kel." Dad left his position at the door temporarily to draw closer to Kelly. "I almost forgot something. A couple people were here today. They wanted me to tell you."

"Carolyn?"

"Yeah, a Carolyn, for one. She didn't say much. She seemed like a nice woman. She was a little worried about getting her feet dirty on the concrete floor, and I told her it was either that or nothing, and once she got over the fact that this wasn't the Four Seasons, she did just fine. Oh, and our friend Perez was here."

"He came."

"He sure did. He wasn't his old self. Didn't feel like talking, or I should say arguing, but that was okay. Before he left, he gave me a message for you. He said, 'Tell Kelly I saw her in the ice.'"

Kelly was not surprised. She thought of someone else. "Did a Claire come?"

"No. Nobody else."

Dad gave his notice to the crowd outside. "Shutting down in two hours, folks." Then one by one he allowed about twenty more people into the room. After the last guest, Dad shut the door, turned the deadbolt, and fell onto the sofa, exhausted. "I think I'll stay the night if you don't mind. Too tired to ride that subway."

"That would be fine." Kelly placed the sleeping Rose on her mattress by the tree and lay down beside her, pulling the blanket over them both, snuggling Rose closer. "You know where the blankets are."

"Sure do. Good night, girls."

"Good night, Dad. We love you."

"I know that. And I love both of you more than the air I breathe. But I suppose you already know that too."

Rose's steady breathing signified she had quickly fallen fast asleep. Kelly thought of Byron's speech again, trying to remember every word. She pressed her mouth against Rose's ear and whispered, "You are going to a real school someday."

Kelly felt Rose stir slightly, but she continued talking. "You are going to be on the swim team. I think you would make a great swimmer. Maybe polo, like Byron. You are going to make some wonderful friends. I can't wait to meet your friends. They can come here after school to play. I'll have snacks for all of them. I'll buy some games too. Sometimes, you girls will decide to ride your bikes to the park. I'll let you go, if you're in a group, but you'll have to take your phone with you so I can check up on you. I'll give you some money for pizza or an ice cream, too, and..." Kelly soon drifted to sleep, too. The last thing she remembered was Mr. Perez's words when they first met. *Yes, Mr. Perez, hope is a glorious thing.*

21

CHAPTER TWENTY-ONE

O n Thursday morning, Kelly dressed Rose in her pink snowsuit, her dark sunglasses and her earplugs. Rose was very pleased to climb into her stroller. She knew where they were headed well before Kelly announced they were going to see Byron play polo.

Rose clasped her hands in absolute delight. "Hurray."

And this made Kelly so very happy.

Dad promised to manage Kelly's apartment and welcome the guests to view what everyone was now referring to as the "Miracle on 134th Street." Of course, the landlord had stomped down the stairs, hands on both hips, demanding to know what was going on down there and threatening all manner of legal recourse and eviction. Dad had led him inside and showed him exactly what had been going on inside that one-room garden apartment, and that was the end of that. In fact, the landlord was now shoveling snowy pathways through not only the front sidewalk but all sidewalks several blocks down to be sure everyone had a safe place to stand.

"Take your time, you two. Have some fun." Dad seemed more pleased than Kelly that the two of them were going on an excursion.

He kissed Kelly on the cheek and then Rose. "Christmas miracles happening all around."

But Rose was on a mission. "Go, Mom!" She sat in her stroller and kicked forward like a miniature Napoleon charging into battle.

"It looks like I'm being bossed around by a three-year-old." Kelly feigned agitation.

"Sure looks that way. Those terrible threes. Reminds me of you."

A three-year-old with strong opinions and desires was exactly what Kelly was hoping for.

She could not contain her smile as she hailed a cab. Rose was mesmerized by the sights and sounds outside her car window, the holiday decorations, the people rushing about, the storefronts, the lights...the city of New York. Kelly took the time to explain everything Rose saw. Rose's eyes were wide and wondering, and she repeated Kelly's words. Words like "Macy's" and "Santa" and "deli" that Rose had never used before because she rarely ventured outdoors.

They arrived at the Athletic Club, a place that was beginning to feel like home, and Kelly envisioned Rose and herself attending lots of games here from now on, maybe even a few practices. She had even called the office and inquired about swim lessons and open swim times. Kelly's goal for the new year was to get Rose inside that beautiful blue water.

Kelly and Rose took their same seats on the metal bleachers above the pool. The pungent scent of chlorine and the players' echoing shouts felt familiar and somehow comforting. Rose insisted on sitting beside Kelly on the bench again. And Kelly's smile continued as she watched Rose's legs swinging back and forth with anticipation.

Kelly pointed to Byron at the goalie net. "There's Byron right over there. Do you see him, Rose?"

But Rose had already spied her friend and was not taking her eyes off him. "Hi, *Bywin*." She waved excitedly.

Rushing footsteps shook the bleachers as Mr. Irving raced in. "Am I late?" He slid into the row behind Kelly.

"No, they're just getting started."

"I had a little problem getting a ride down here. My driver called off today, and I had to hail a cab."

"That driver of yours—asking for all these days off? You should fire her."

"I already tried that," Mr. Irving scoffed. "The trouble is my family likes her too much."

Mr. Irving had been in such a rush to get to the pool that he hadn't noticed Rose, sitting beside Kelly. In his socially awkward way, he blurted, "Is that your daughter?"

"Yes. Rose, I would like you to meet Mr. Irving."

Mr. Irving leaned forward to see Rose better. "She's a doll. You'd never know she had all those problems."

"Mmhmm," Kelly said. "She's a living, breathing doll, and she can hear you."

Rose turned back to squint at Mr. Irving, and Kelly could tell Rose was deciding whether she liked him or not. It was the exact same reaction Kelly had upon first meeting the man.

"Rose," Kelly explained, "Mr. Irving is Byron's dad. Can you say hello?"

Rose was satisfied with that explanation. "Hello." She swung her attention back to the game.

Mr. Irving backtracked. "That was an ignorant thing to say. I tend to blurt rude things out now and then. I always have. It seems to work fine when you're the CEO. I'm supposed to make my subordinates feel uncomfortable, keep them off guard, but in the real world, I look like an idiot."

"Don't apologize. You were being truthful. But..." Kelly lowered her voice and leaned closer to Mr. Irving. "Rose is changing. She is doing amazing things now." Kelly flicked her eyes onto Rose and back again. "If you could have seen her a few months ago...We could never go anywhere like this before."

Mr. Irving considered Rose, as if he was able to see into the past and understand the hurdles, the failures, the triumphs. Maybe he was.

The game began and all attention shot toward the pool. Byron's stance was set to high alert, protecting the net. The opposing team approached, and he defended the goal with vigor, punching the ball away from the net, slicing it and spinning it in a new direction.

Kelly turned to see Mr. Irving's reaction. Surprisingly, his expression resembled that of all the other dads at the pool today. He was just another proud father watching his son win a polo match.

"I told you." Kelly clapped as Byron saved the goal from a downward spike.

"I never saw a polo game." Mr. Irving joined the applause. "Do you know it's considered one of the toughest sports out there? They say it's a combination of swimming and basketball and football. He certainly didn't pick something easy."

Byron lunged into the water, blocking another attack, and Rose joined the clapping with all her might. She didn't understand every move that was transpiring in the water below, but she knew it was Byron's job to keep that ball out of the net.

The players kicked and dove and sprang into the water, battling for control of that little ball, and in the excitement, Kelly had forgotten to watch the clock. Twenty minutes had passed, and Byron had not checked himself out of the game yet. She understood. The opposing team brought some fierce competition, and he couldn't abandon his post, but soon...

Kelly monitored the clock mounted to the far wall. Twenty-five minutes passed, then thirty, and now Kelly was becoming concerned. This team would do just fine without Byron for fifteen minutes, and Byron knew it. Winning or losing was not Byron's greatest concern. Byron's health was paramount, and he was clearly winded. Kelly didn't want to alarm Marcus. She attempted to discreetly wave to Byron and point toward the clock. Byron caught her eye several times but blatantly ignored her.

What did he think he was doing? Byron had promised his father and his doctor he would take himself out of the game to catch his breath. Why was he breaking that promise now?

"Mr. Irving," Kelly began delicately.

"I know." He rested his forearms on his knees, as if to see more clearly. "The question is why?"

"Maybe to prove something?"

"To who?"

"His father has never seen him play before."

"That is ridiculous. He's got nothing to prove to me."

"Maybe you should go down there and talk to him."

"He'd be appalled if his father marched down there to reprimand him. I can't go down there, and he knows it. He's testing me, that's what he's doing, but I'm not falling for it."

"I can go," Kelly offered.

"You could. You're probably the only one who could get away with it. But he'll be livid with you, too. This isn't about a polo match. This is about Byron exerting his independence. No different than him skipping school."

Kelly turned to face Mr. Irving. "Maybe this is about Byron want-ing to be a part of a team, to live a full life."

"Is it?"

Now forty-five minutes into the game. The hands on the clock were moving too fast. Kelly stood. She was going down there to have a talk with Byron. If he never spoke to her again, she didn't care.

Just then, the coach blew his whistle for a time-out. All players stopped, swam to the pool sides and waited for instruction. Byron's coach approached his team, but he didn't address all the players—only Byron. Byron moved his head from side to side in response. He was refusing to be pulled from the game.

"What is he thinking?" Kelly thought aloud.

"That is about enough!" Mr. Irving slapped his knees and stood. "The problem is not the asthma anymore. The problem is Byron's belligerent refusal to obey authority. He must do as the doctor in-structs. He must not tax his lungs, he must take the medications, he must be diligent in self-care if we are going to have any chance at...at..."

Irving refused to finish his sentence. A chance at what, Kelly won-dered? At living?

Irving started again. "I should have called that doctor myself. I tried, but he was on some sort of vacation. I should have demanded he phone me from whatever sandy beach he was lounging on, slap that margarita out of his hand and give me the exact physical restrictions for the playing of this sport. I should have made Byron sign an agreement."

"This is not a corporation you're running. It's a teenager."

"A teenager whose brain is not fully developed."

That fact was becoming more obvious by the minute. Kelly deflat-ed. "Go down and talk to the coach. It doesn't matter if Byron gets mad. He's not keeping his side of the bargain." She slipped her arms into her coat sleeves. "Do you want me to come?"

"I can handle it."

Irving clanged down several sets of metal steps to the pool deck, and Byron noted his approaching. Kelly motioned frantically for Byron to get out of the pool, but he wasn't interested in Kelly or Rose anymore. His full attention was on his father, and Byron was welling with anger.

Irving pulled the coach to the side. They spoke at length for several minutes. During this time, the players on both teams and the parents in the stands were equally curious and impatient. They knew this time-out had something to do with the goalie, the only player the coach had spoken to, but why?

The coach shook Irving's hand, then approached Byron, who was still clinging to the pool sides. The coach pointed a stern finger. His voice was raised. Kelly couldn't decipher the exact words, but even Rose knew it wasn't good news. She bit her lower lip.

Byron placed both palms on the pool deck and hoisted himself up from the water. He retreated to the bench, where the coach continued to berate him in front of the other players. The coach waggled an angry finger from Byron to the goalie net to the bench to Irving, over and over again. His teammates focused anywhere but the altercation, studying their hands or looking the other way.

Byron hung his head in shame. But more concerning was how winded he was. Kelly could see his chest heaving. Byron had no business staying in that game. Ignoring his condition was not the way to solve it. Fighting against it, battling it, waging war against it—yes. But ignoring it—no.

Suddenly, a boy from the opposing team stood. He wore a red cap, a different color than the other players on his team. Maybe team captain? His face contorted with rage. He shouted something at Byron. Byron stood in return and shouted something back. Then all players on both teams stood. Voices rose, cursing, a few obscenities, some name-calling. Some of the words could be heard even this far up in the bleachers, and Kelly put Rose's earplugs back in, but Rose pulled them out. Even Rose wanted to know what was happening down there.

The player with the red cap held the polo ball in his hand. His teammates were shouting, "Do it! Do it!" He pitched the ball, hard and straight, at Byron. It struck Byron in the center of his chest. Byron fell backward onto the tile floor with a thud. His teammates retaliated and charged the opposition. The players shoved and punched and wrestled, slipping across the slick deck surface and toppling into a pile of raging teen hormones. Byron, somewhere at the bottom.

The crowd went absolutely wild. Kelly stood, but she still couldn't find Byron inside the ruckus. "Come on," she said to Rose. "We're going down there." She lifted Rose into her arms and clamored down the metal steps. But every other parent in the pool area had had the same idea. They converged upon the scene, and Kelly was suddenly lodged within an angry mob.

A whistle blew, over and over again. The coach mounted the bench, barking orders, trying to gain control of the riotous scene, but nobody was listening. Players tumbled back and forth across the benches. Some splashed into the pool. A few dads entered the scuffle with harsh words and shoves of their own.

Kelly spied something bright red on the floor. Smeared blood.

From within the tumultuous brawl, one man fought his way free from the crowd. He moved toward the rear of the pool. It was Mr. Irving. He was carrying Byron in his arms. The pool management tossed a blanket over Byron and led them to the emergency exit.

Kelly pushed through the crowd. "Let me through! Let me through!"

Irving saw Kelly and shouted, "They're taking him to the hospital." His face shadowed in fear.

"I'm coming."

"There's no room. Meet us there."

Kelly stood helplessly as she watched the paramedics place Byron on the stretcher and attach an oxygen mask over his nose and mouth. The ambulance doors closed. Through the car's rear window, Mr. Irving could be seen at Byron's side. Red lights flashed an alarm. Red, like the Christmas lights on the street, like the red lights on Kelly's tree, like the boy's red swim cap, like the red blood on the tile floor.

Happy and sad, mixed up together, all the time, everywhere in this world.

22

CHAPTER TWENTY-TWO

K elly shouldered through the double doors and raced down the hospital hallways, Rose still in her arms. The scent of disinfectant and the fluorescent lighting had always irritated Rose's headaches. Before every hospital visit, her medications were increased to soothe the harsh stimulants and prevent an episode. But not this time.

Rose bounced up and down in Kelly's arms with every step. She clearly sensed the tension in Kelly's limbs, noted the frantic expression on Kelly's face, and Rose began to cry.

"It's okay, Rose. Shhh, don't cry." Kelly pulled her closer. "We're going to see Byron."

Kelly burst into the overcrowded waiting room to find Mr. Irving in the corner chair, head between his knees. She drew closer, kneeling at his feet. "What happened?"

"They're working on him right now." He spoke without raising his head.

Rose had stopped crying. She was observing Mr. Irving. She climbed out of Kelly's arms and drew closer to him, resting her cheek on his knee. Irving could not ignore that tender gesture, and he combed Rose's red hair with his fingers, just like Kelly always did. Then he lifted Rose onto his lap, holding her against his chest.

Rose snuggled into Mr. Irving. This hug wasn't for Rose. This hug was for Irving.

There had always been something about Rose. Something special. Maybe it was because she had been a child sequestered to one room of pain for her short three years on this earth. Maybe because she sat idly most of her day, looking out the window or at the pages of a book. Or maybe because she often lay in her bed for hours on end, staring into the room, watching Kelly move about. Rose had been in the world, but not a part of it. Three years of observation had allowed Rose to understand things that a typical three-year-old might not.

And most of all, Rose knew what was needed when nothing else would do—the tender expression of love from one person to another. It was without cost, but it was also so very, very valuable. It was everything.

Kelly followed Rose's lead and sat beside Mr. Irving, holding his hand. The three huddled together in a little ball for quite possibly over an hour.

A nurse appeared at the doorway several times, calling out different family names, and the parent or spouse was then directed to the hospital room where their loved one had been transferred. They would meet with the physician and learn the diagnosis and the prognosis—in other words, the good or bad news.

Finally, "Irving." A robust nurse appeared with one hand bracing the open door and one foot in the waiting room.

"Here." Mr. Irving stood, still cradling Rose.

"Come with me."

"Can I bring these two?" Mr. Irving was obviously referring to the child he was carrying and the woman clinging to his side.

"Are they immediate family?"

"Yes."

"How are they related?"

Irving told a little lie. Kelly believed in truth. She always told the truth. But sometimes, like this very instant, a lie seemed to be okay. She needed to see Byron, and Byron needed to see Rose. Rules and regulations had been drawn up by hospital board members seated around a big conference table. They believed they were choosing the best solutions under the worst circumstances, but they could not possibly consider every circumstance, and that was why, sometimes, rules were meant to be broken.

Mr. Irving's words both shocked and comforted Kelly simultaneously. "Yes. They're family." But maybe that wasn't a lie after all.

They were taken past the ER, down a long hallway, and up an elevator to the fourth floor. The sign read *Intensive Care Unit*. This was not a recovery room where Byron would rest awhile and then be able to return home. This room meant there were serious unresolved medical problems.

They found Byron wrapped in a cloud of white sheets. Wires protruded from his chest and arms. There was a clear tube in his nose and a wider tube in his mouth, both taped down tight. His glasses were resting on the bedside table. His eyes closed. His clothing and shoes had been stuffed inside a clear plastic bag.

Mr. Irving set Rose gently on the floor, and the three encircled Byron's bed.

Byron's doctor appeared from behind. "Mr. Irving, I got here as soon as I could. I flew home this morning. He's on medication to sedate. He might open his eyes, but of course, he can't communicate. The ventilator will breathe for him. He had a very significant eosinophilic asthma attack. He is unable to breathe on his own."

"Is he in any pain?" Irving's voice cracked.

"No."

"When will he breathe on his own?"

"I don't have an answer to that. Some irreparable damage has been done to the lungs. We're awaiting the CT scan results now. I'm not sure what triggered this. The records showed he was in a swimming pool?"

"He was playing water polo." Irving's tone abruptly turned combative. "You cleared him for it! This is all your fault."

"I did no such thing. I never would have authorized something like that."

"But Byron said…" Irving's mind was unraveling the truth. "Wait a minute…he never phoned you?"

"No. Not that I know of. I can check with my nursing staff, but whether he called or not, I never spoke to him or any of my nurses about water polo. I would never approve of something like this. It's far too strenuous."

Mr. Irving watched Byron sleeping. Deep, cleansing breaths were pushed in and out of Byron's lungs by the ventilator. The hissing of the machine parts replaced the sound of Byron's breaths. "He wanted to play that sport."

"The air in an enclosed pool," the doctor reasoned, "is moist and humid. That wouldn't be the problem. That would actually help. But the sport itself, the shortness of breath…I wouldn't risk it."

Kelly longed to speak but said nothing. Guilt welled up within her like a boiling pot of dirty water until her throat choked. Kelly had supported Byron's playing this sport. She had driven Byron to water polo practice after school, secretly, discreetly, purposely disobeying Mr. Irving's direct orders, and Mr. Perez's as well.

What had she done?

Mr. Irving defended his son, even now. "He was the goalie. He was taking breaks. Except today. He wouldn't take a break today."

"If he was taking breaks, that could be another matter altogether. But I would have to observe the sport, the environment, the oxygen demands before ever authorizing anything like this. This attack was much worse than any of the others. His lungs were already very weak. He lived with a lot of limitations. A sport like that would place undue stress upon an already fragile situation."

Kelly had not been aware of the severity of Byron's illness. She had assumed he was capable because he had been playing water polo for months. And because Byron wanted this sport so very badly. Tears clogged her vision, and she turned away from the doctor and Mr. Irving momentarily. Even the most honest and well-meaning attempt to help someone was pure ignorance without all the facts. She had no defense. She had no excuse.

Mr. Irving caught the doctor's use of past tense. "What do you mean, *he lived with a lot of limitations*?"

The doctor remained stoic. "I cannot give you a false sense of hope."

"What are you saying?" Mr. Irving demanded.

"I won't know anything definite until the diagnostic results are in, but the prognosis is not good."

Kelly backed into a corner, holding Rose tightly in her arms. She suddenly felt vulgarly visible, like the uninvited guest, the instigator of the disaster, the perpetrator, the assaulter...the murderer. Guilty and convicted without a word spoken.

What had she done?

The room fell still. The beeping of the heart monitor, footsteps in the hallway, the whizzing of air through the ventilator—in and out, in and out. Kelly watched the doctor's movements, the slightest turn of his mouth, the flicker of his eyes. She wanted him to say something more, to change his mind, to take it all back.

A ball had struck Byron in the center of his chest. Why wasn't anyone talking about the incident that incited his inability to breathe? Wouldn't that contusion have made an already tenuous situation far worse? Kelly shook her head, criticizing herself for trying to sidestep blame. Byron had not taken himself out of the game. He was severely winded. He was pushing himself to live a full life, exactly as Kelly had advised him.

What had she done? She wished she could turn back time to weeks ago. Back to the moment inside the limo when Byron had first confided in her. She wished she could warn him *not* to play polo, to refuse to drive him downtown, to report his secret jaunts to his father.

Mr. Irving was right. Mr. Perez was right. Kelly was not qualified to be a mentor, a psychologist, an advisor. She looked from Mr. Irving to the doctor, then to Byron and back again. She longed to find adequate words to apologize, but any apology would be insufficient and inappropriate. She longed to confess that this was all her fault, to release Byron, a fourteen-year-old boy, from any wrongdoing the doctor or his father might place upon him, but even that seemed weak and insignificant.

The doctor said, "I'll leave you alone." He shook Mr. Irving's hand and closed the door.

But when Kelly and Mr. Irving turned back to Byron, they found a far different sight. Rose had climbed up into the hospital bed and was lying beside Byron, her arm wrapped around his chest and her head against his shoulder.

Mr. Irving wiped his eyes with his bare hand.

He motioned Kelly toward the hallway, and she followed.

He shut the door behind him.

He took a step toward Kelly until their bodies were just inches apart, their noses almost touching.

Kelly trembled with guilt and shame and sorrow that she could not contain even if she tried.

Irving lowered his chin and held her gaze, purposefully, intently. His nostrils flared.

His voice turned deep and raspy. "Get out of this hospital. Do not let me see you anywhere near my son ever again, not within ten feet of my home, not near my parking garage, not anywhere near any of my automobiles. If you try to contact my son in any way whatsoever, I will make sure you never find work in this city again as long as you live."

Kelly opened her mouth to say something, anything, but no words came. She couldn't blame Mr. Irving. He was defending his child. The exact same thing Kelly had always done for Rose.

Irving turned toward Byron's hospital room and added, "I'm filing a restraining order. I'm going to hand deliver it with my lawyer present so there is no question whatsoever that you will never come near us again." Then he swung back to face her. "I'm going to shove that restraining order in your hands, and maybe, just maybe, you will finally understand that we never asked you for any of this. All this meddling and intervening in things you don't understand. I lost my girlfriend because of you. I lost my dog walker because of you. Mr. Perez is retiring, and I have a gut feeling you had something to do with it. And now, my son. You took my son away from me. If I ever hear of you working as a driver for any family in this city, in this state—strike that—in this country, I'll report you to the authorities!"

Kelly released a half nod in agreement with his harsh decision. She was still on Byron's side, she would always be on Byron's side, and this decision was the best thing for Byron.

23

CHAPTER TWENTY-THREE

Kelly had not slept much during the past few days. She hadn't eaten much either. None of those things mattered any longer. They were the unimportant trivial stuff of life, the bare necessities. Her sole purpose was to love little Rose now. Rose seemed so sad. She understood that Byron was hurting, that Kelly was hurting, that Mr. Irving was hurting, and Rose was hurting too.

Kelly had given Dad a couple days off. He planned to buy a few gifts for Rose and pick up a fresh turkey. This gave Kelly some time before giving Dad the bad news. But some things in life cannot be procrastinated forever. Whether you wanted them to come or not, they came. Today was happy and sad all swirled together into one beautiful, ugly painting. Today was Christmas, and dad would be returning with arms loaded with gifts and a heart loaded with joy.

But it was tainted now, because of Kelly. She was the first person in the O'Sullivan family to be fired from her driver job. The first person in her family to bring ruin to the family she had been working for. The first person in her family to disobey every warning from her father and her employer. The first person in her family to bring shame upon the O'Sullivan name.

And...Dad would be hurt by all of this, too. He would be so disappointed. Dad had one child, Kelly O'Sullivan, and that girl couldn't seem to get it right.

To make matters worse, Kelly would have to give notice to her landlord. She couldn't afford the rent any longer. She and Rose would have to move in with Dad for a little while until Kelly could get back on her feet.

And Kelly would have to let Mrs. Andrews go, too. The wonderful, amazing Mrs. Andrews who had brought so much joy and hope into their lives. Kelly could no longer afford to pay her either.

But Christmas came. Despite it all and maybe because of it all, Christmas was here.

Kelly sat at the kitchen table, watching Rose eat a late-night dinner of sliced bananas and raisin bread. Any sort of Christmas celebration would have to wait until tomorrow, because of the crowds still gathered outside. But Kelly knew now what really mattered in this life—not the big dinner or the gifts or the decorations. Oh, those were wonderful *extras*, as Kelly now referred to them. All that really mattered was that sweet little girl sitting before her. And Dad, of course.

And Byron. Byron had never left Kelly's thoughts and prayers. Was it possible to pray every minute of every hour of every day? Kelly now knew that it was.

After a long day of welcoming almost one hundred visitors, Kelly ushered a young woman out the door, just as Dad returned, his arms loaded with packages. "Sorry I'm so late. Train shut down. Some sort of safety issue. How's it going? You getting all those folks in here okay? I'll take it from here on out." He checked his watch. "Almost nine o'clock. We'll give them until midnight, then we're closing up shop."

It was time to tell Dad. *But why now? Why here on Christmas night, of all times and all places?* Kelly only knew that she had waited long enough, and it was time to share her secret. Maybe *release* was a better word? The carrying of a burden was lighter with more hands. Kelly had learned that raising Rose.

She tried, but she was unable to open her mouth to offer any greeting whatsoever. She couldn't speak without a flood of tears and emotion and pain exposed. She simply nodded and smoothed a few strands of Rose's hair.

"What's goin' on, Kel?" Dad slipped out of his coat and left the packages on the floor. "You can talk to me. What happened? I knew I shouldn't have left you two alone so long."

Tears welled in Kelly's eyes.

"Is it our little Rosie?"

Kelly shook her head.

"Is it that line of people? Somebody do something out there?"

Kelly shook her head again.

"So, you don't wanna talk about it? That's okay. I get it. But I'm here when you're ready. Whatever it is, we'll work through it. You, me, Rose. Together. We'll work it out."

Kelly felt a lump form in her throat. She swallowed hard.

Dad slid a chair close to Kelly. "Life is a struggle. But you already know that, don't ya? Life is hard. The sad and happy come our way, switching places every day, sometimes every hour. I can't erase that sadness for you, but there is something I can do. Sometimes I got the power to do only one thing: love you. I love you, Kel. Rosie loves you...Mom loves you."

With that truth, Kelly found the strength to speak. "I know that, Dad."

"I know you know."

"It's the only thing that's keeping me going."

A pounding at the apartment door drew Kelly, Dad and even Rose's attention. This wasn't the normal gentle knock of visitors coming to and from this apartment. This knock was angry, demanding...convicting.

Dad stood. "I'll get this one."

Kelly knew exactly who it was. "No, Dad. I'll get it. It's something I need to do." She heaved her weary body from the chair, but Dad blocked her pathway with an outstretched arm.

"Not with your old dad here, you won't. You go ahead and sit yourself back down." He swung the door open wide to a man wearing a black suit, red tie and expensive designer shoes. Behind him was a similar-sized man, positioned like a bodyguard and wearing basically the same outfit.

Marcus Irving was still simmering with anger as he threw his chin toward the street. "What's that long line about? Where is Kelly O'Sullivan?"

Dad defied his rudeness. "I'll be asking the questions from here on out. Who do you think you are and what do you want with my daughter?"

"Dad." Kelly stood. "That's my employer, Mr. Irving." Kelly glanced at the second man behind Irving. "And his lawyer."

"*Former* employer," Irving shouted at Kelly.

"No need for shouting on Christmas, Irving." Dad wasn't a driver anymore. He was a father and a grandfather. "What do you want here? Don't tell me you came to see our puddle, because you sure don't look like you got it in you."

"Puddle?" Irving tossed a look of disgust at Kelly's impoverished apartment. "What on earth are you talking about?"

"I'm talking about the reason for that great, big line outside." Dad thumbed at the waiting crowd. "Why do you think all those people showed up here on Christmas night? Like they got nothing better to do?" Dad scoffed. "They came to see something." He pointed to the frozen mist in the center of the room. "They came to see that."

Irving's gaze dropped to the ice and held.

"That's not the reason Mr. Irving is here." Kelly approached Irving and took the paper from his hand. "He's serving me with some kind of a restraining order."

Irving seemed unconcerned with his legal documents temporarily. He spoke without removing his attention from the steamy mist. "What the hell is this place?"

"Just the opposite, Irving," Dad swiped the paper from Kelly's hands.

Kelly softly intervened. "I can handle this, Dad." She turned to Mr. Irving. "This is my home. Rose's and mine."

"You live down here?" Irving did not conceal his disdain.

"Yes, it's called a garden apartment. And Mr. Irving...as long as you're here...I'd like you to see something. It will just take a minute." Kelly gestured to the frozen puddle.

"What is that thing?"

But before Kelly could respond, Irving's lawyer shouldered past Irving and stepped forward. He removed his shoes and looked to Dad for permission.

"Go right ahead, my friend." Dad offered an open palm toward the ice, and the lawyer hesitantly accepted.

"What do you think you're doing, Williams?" Irving's outrage flared.

"Let him be," Dad cautioned. "You got no authority here."

Irving watched his obviously prestigious, high-paid lawyer kneel before the icy mist and stare into its glossy surface. Kelly felt the weight of time as the lawyer lingered, slightly longer than the others. When he was finished, he rose from the floor, slipped into his shoes and opened the door.

Irving snatched the lawyer's jacket collar. "Where do you think you're going?"

"You're on your own with this one, Marcus."

"You'll regret this."

Williams wrenched free from Irving's grasp. "Following you here today is the best thing that ever happened to me."

"You're fired!"

"No need to fire me. I already quit." The lawyer turned on his heel and closed the door behind him.

Irving snarled at Kelly. "I don't need him anymore, anyway. You got your papers. Don't come near my family ever again or I'll see you in court."

But before Kelly or Dad could respond, Rose answered on behalf of all of them. She slipped from her kitchen chair, an innocent smile gracing her face, and skipped over to Mr. Irving. Rose grasped Irving's hand within her tiny palm and pulled him toward the ice.

Even Mr. Irving couldn't be angry with little Rose. "What is it, Rose?" he asked.

"Come," she said. "Come see."

"I—I don't have time for all this." Irving worked to gently release her grip, but Rose wouldn't allow it. "Come see *Bywin*." She pronounced Byron's name as best she could.

"Byron? What the—?"

Rose pointed to the ice. Mr. Irving looked from Kelly to Dad, then to Rose, and back again, but there was no reason for cajoling or convincing. Either Irving longed to peer inside the icy mirage...or he did not. Either he was desperate and hurting and willing to believe...or he was not.

Irving's curiosity got the best of him. Or maybe, just maybe, Mr. Irving needed this moment as much as Kelly had, as much as Dad had, as much as any of the hundreds of visitors who had been drawn to this apartment during a snowstorm at Christmastime had.

Irving shuffled toward the ice. He stood above the fog, arms crossed, gaging, wondering, deciding. Finally, he knelt. He glanced back at Kelly and Rose and Dad.

Kelly offered a single nod.

Irving pressed his palms to the floor and leaned forward. He peered into the icy sheath on Kelly's cement floor, that little patch of city water that had frozen solid and refused to go away. It had come, it was here, and it would be gone when its purpose was fulfilled. It had come at Christmastime, and when Christmas day was over and done the ice would melt back into a puddle of city water, once again. Dad knew that; Kelly knew; even little Rose seemed to know.

Now it was Mr. Irving's turn.

Tears slid down Irving's cheeks as he was enveloped within the mist and gazed into the frozen water. Kelly knew what he was beholding: everything he had already known within his heart but had somehow forgotten in the rush of life. Everything that ever truly mattered was being laid out before him. So simple. So concise. So true and good and real.

Marcus Irving was witnessing the exact opposite of everything he had worked for and coveted. Kelly suddenly understood that when people said things like "It's the little things that matter" or "Stop and smell the roses," they had no idea what wisdom they were uttering. *Why do we search for the grandeur? The prestigious title? The shiny new car? The fancy house?* Those things would mean nothing if we were left all alone in this world. If we were the only person on the face of this earth, none of those things would matter, and we would be longing for that one thing—that simple, powerful gift that everyone carries but often dismisses as trivial and mundane.

We would be longing for exactly what Marcus Irving was seeing inside that frozen mirage.

Irving took his time at the icy puddle, and like all the other guests before him, he did not want this moment to end.

But Dad spoke. "Time's up, Irving. We got a long line waiting out there and only a few hours left."

Irving pressed the palm of his hand to his lips and then transferred that kiss delicately onto the ice. He held his hand in place for several seconds.

Finally, he stood. He inched slowly, each step with trepidation, each step with apprehension, until he stood directly before Kelly. Tears stained his unshaven cheeks. His lips quivered. His eyes closed and his head trembled. Irving clearly longed to say something but could not find the words.

Kelly knew that feeling. She carefully reached for his hand and held it within her own for several minutes. Irving's hand was large and smooth, his only work involving paper and a computer and a pen. His hand was damp and cold and limp, a shadow of the man he once pretended to be.

Kelly held Mr. Irving's hand tightly within hers.

He accepted her invitation and returned another. He wrapped his arms around Kelly, and she fell into his embrace. Her shoulders shook with sobs.

"I'm sorry," she whispered in his ear. "I'm so very sorry."

Irving leaned back to view her.

"Can you ever forgive me?" she begged.

"There is nothing to forgive," Irving said. "I'm the one who owes *you* an apology. For everything. For all of it."

Dad backed away from the tender scene. Kelly had not explained her dilemma, but Dad understood that words needed to be spoken, forgiveness rendered and accepted. Dad lifted Rose into his arms, and she rested her head on her grandfather's shoulder, watching her mother and Mr. Irving's exchange.

But Kelly needed to ask Marcus Irving something. She needed to solidify the meaning of what he had witnessed, especially right here and now, on this very day, with Byron lying in that hospital bed, fighting for his life.

"What did you see?" Her question was kind and gentle.

"I think you already know."

"I do, but I want you to say it."

Marcus swallowed a couple of times. All eyes were upon him, even little Rose's. He raked a hand through his buzz cut and loosened his tie.

"I saw myself first...my own reflection in the ice, and I suppose you already know, but I don't look so good. I'm broken, I'm guilty, I've hit rock bottom. But not only that. I'm also furious and frustrated at the absolute powerlessness that I feel with my son lying on that hospital bed. There is not one thing I can do. Nothing!"

Marcus knit his hands, gathering himself before continuing. "But then I saw something more. I saw people. All the people I love. The people...who love...loved me. They moved in close and surrounded me. They were holding me up, carrying me, lifting me. There were dozens of them..." He choked back tears. "All holding my hand. Every single one of them. I know that doesn't sound possible, but they were."

He swallowed harder. "The strangest part, the most incredible part, was seeing the people I hadn't seen in many years because they're not with us any longer. They passed away, gone from this world. But you know something? I've never stopped missing them. I've longed for them, needed them. They were there, in the ice. I saw...I saw...my grandmother. Not the old woman I knew, but the younger version. The person I only remember from photographs. She was so vibrant and healthy and beautiful, just now, and she was grinning down at me like she used to do when I would visit her as a kid." Marcus slumped into a kitchen chair and lifted his eyes to the ceiling, lost in thought. "I'd run up those front steps and across her wide porch and slam that screen door, knowing she was waiting for me. She'd bend down and give me a big hug, squeezing the air right out of me, and I knew, I always knew, even from a very young age, that that woman loved me.

"I saw her now. She ruffled my hair. She wasn't sad or worried or afraid, like I am. She was filled with this aura of peace. She smiled at me, and then she reached out and held my hand.

"She didn't say a thing. I didn't say a thing. No advice. No messages." Marcus dragged a hand across his tired face. "The only thing that mattered was that my grandmother...that she...loved me. No—strike that. That my grandmother *loves* me. She still loves me just as strong, even though she's gone from this world."

Dad sat Rose at the table with her crayons. Then Kelly and Dad addressed Marcus. Their eyes were filled with tears, but hope lit their faces. "What else did you see?" Kelly asked.

Marcus buried his face in his hands and took several deep breaths before answering. "I saw...I saw...my wife, Carole. I don't like to talk about her much. She was so sick at the end. Whenever I think about her final days—her broken body, her pain and suffering—I put all that out of my mind. I try to remember the healthy her, the woman she truly was." Marcus shot Kelly a stern look. "My wife was not her sickness. This is something I've learned through all that suffering. Carole was not a sick woman; she was a woman who was sick. That cancer did not define her. It did not describe her. It was beside her somehow, like an enemy fighting against her. But inside Carole's battered body, inside her very soul, the real Carole was still there, alive and healthy and vibrant.

"I saw her in the ice. She was standing above me. She was holding both of my hands, looking straight into my eyes. She didn't look upset, or sad, or anything like that. She was so strong, so beautiful, so peaceful, and she had this look in her eyes...you know...I always wondered about that. Does my wife still love me? *Can* she still love me? But now I know that...she does. She loves me. She still does." Marcus broke into a silent cry.

Kelly and Dad remained still, and even Rose stopped coloring, giving Mr. Irving time, waiting patiently.

Finally, Marcus composed himself again. "You know something? I realized for the very first time that it's not Carole who has the power to love me forever. It's love. Love has the power. Am I making any sense here?"

Kelly nodded, and Marcus continued.

"My wife didn't say a word. My grandmother either. They've given more than enough advice during their lifetimes. It's my life, my turn now, and it's up to me to live it. We all get that one chance, that one shot.

"But they did give me something even better. This force was flowing from them to me and back again like a windstorm, like a wild hurricane...like that snow storm we just had." Marcus stood. "I finally understand that love doesn't weaken or fade...or die. The only thing love does is somehow get stronger."

Marcus approached Kelly. "And something more..." He did not try to hide his tears. "I saw you, Kelly. I saw you and your daughter, Rose. You were holding my hand too."

Kelly's body softened.

"And..." Marcus's words lifted lighter, softer. "I saw all kinds of children from all over the world who were suffering from asthma, just like my Byron. We may never meet them, but we have this connection, this unity, like we're fighting the same war on different battlegrounds." His expression shifted to excitement and surprise, as if he had just discovered a rare cure. "We're not alone in this fight. Something bigger than this sickness is banding us together, uniting us, strengthening us."

Kelly surrendered a pent-up breath that she had been holding for days. "Yes, yes. We talk about love as if it is a silly thing, a Valentine's Day Cupid's arrow kind of thing. We say things like 'I love your new car' or 'I love the sunset,' and that's fine, but it's making us forget what love really is. It carries us. It connects us. It holds us and comforts us. It strengthens us. I don't know why I never saw all this before either. We had it all along. We took it for granted. We underestimated it. We even...ignored it. I guess you could say that love is everything."

"Absolutely." Marcus smeared a palm across his wet cheeks. "I saw Byron. He was hugging me so tight, and he was smiling up at me. I love that kid so much. He knows how much I love him. I could see it in his eyes. I've done the best I could with Byron since my wife passed. I know I've made some mistakes, but I always loved him, the only way I knew how. I'm not perfect." Marcus's voice fell below a whisper. He wiped his nose with his jacket sleeve. "I guess we all know that by now."

Even Rose felt the raw emotion in the room and stood beside her mother, holding tight to Kelly's pant leg. Kelly felt uplifted and renewed with Rose's small gesture, with Marcus's confessions, with Dad's guarding eye upon the tender scene. It was a new feeling, a fresh feeling, despite the sorrow and loss. *Happy and sad at the same time?* No, something much stronger than that. Some might call it joy. Kelly knew now that joy was different from happiness. *Happy* sounded like the word *happened* because it depended upon the things that happened that day or hour.

But Joy just existed all on its own. It didn't care if the world around it was filled with sadness and defeat and turmoil; the world's conditions didn't affect joy. The world wasn't powerful enough.

Kelly's dad spoke up. "Can I say a little something here? I am the oldest, and somewhere I once heard that old age comes with wisdom. Well, sometimes in this great big world, we can feel like we're the only person going through hard stuff, the only one who knows what pain feels like, but we're not. Rosie keeps going over to that frozen puddle and saying, 'Kids.' She sees other kids her age who are suffering from headaches. I'm sure of it. Your son, Byron, and our little Rosie are not the only kids who are hurting in this world. Someday our kids are going to grow up and meet some of those other kids who suffered just like them, and they're all going to band together and go out there and find some cures. It's love that finds the cure. Not hate. Oh, sure, we all hate sickness, but hate isn't strong enough to do much of anything but cause more pain."

Kelly wrapped her arm around Dad's shoulder and squeezed. "Thank you for that, Dad."

"Oh, I'm not done yet," Dad said. "I'm just guessing at this, but I really believe love is a gift that we've had with us all along, but sometimes we get so busy we forget we have it. That's right. I said it. Love is power. It's bigger than all of us. It didn't come from this world because this world is too broken, too beaten up, and everything just goes and dies off here. But love...love comes from someplace perfect...someplace eternal. And this little patch of ice filled with the stuff? It's...it's nothin' short of a miracle."

Kelly whispered, "A miracle on 134th Street."

"That's exactly what I'm trying to say here, as hokey as it might sound. This thing is a miracle that came when we needed it most. It's Christmastime. There's no coincidence in that. Love is a gift."

Irving blew his nose on his pocket square, gathered himself, buttoned his overcoat, and straightened his tie. He paused at the doorway for a long while before he said, "I better get going." He twisted his mouth, working to get the words out. He addressed Kelly. "I'll see you after the New Year then?"

Kelly questioned.

"Back at work," Irving clarified.

And in one instant Kelly's life changed, once again. A sudden flip, an upside-down twist and turn of events. But this time, the change was hinged upon something that was in her control, in Irving's control. This time, life's circumstances were not storming down upon Kelly's head and pushing her into a shadowy dark corner with no way out. This time, change was hinged upon one very difficult choice.

Forgiveness.

Mr. Irving had chosen forgiveness, and because of this one difficult decision, good had come.

Kelly made the same choice in return. Because when all of her guilt and pain washed away, Kelly was still left with some hurt of her own. Irving was not unlike Damean in a lot of ways. Irving's actions had conjured up a lot of painful memories.

She glanced at the frozen puddle. But then there was love. Love for Rose, love for Dad, love for Byron...love for Mom. And that love seemed to cover up all the evil and wash it away somehow. Kelly made a tough decision in return. She would not allow all of those hurtful moments to keep hurting. She would not allow all of those hurtful moments to ruin her future.

"Yes," Kelly said. "I will be there."

"You're going to have to manage the garage for a while, too. Until I find a new supervisor."

"That's fine."

"It'll come with a raise, of course."

"Thank you."

"No. Thank you, Kelly O'Sullivan, for everything. The good and the not-so-good. For all of it." He took the paper from Dad's hands and tore it to shreds. Into tiny little pieces, one-by-one. It took some time to change a restraining order into dozens of fluttering snowflakes, but Irving was patient. He obviously wanted that sheet of paper, the ink upon it, and even the memory of the thing completely destroyed.

When he was finished, Irving opened the door and did not turn back when he said, "Please come and see Byron as soon as possible. Rose, too. He would like that. I know he would...He needs that."

The door didn't have time to close before the next visitor entered. One after another, they were drawn to the small apartment, on Christmas night, longing for something, for anything, other than what was outside in the dark.

The next few hours passed quickly. Kelly had kept Rose up late, hoping for a little Christmas Eve celebration, but time had swept far too swiftly. The last knock on the door, the last visitor came and left. Dad checked his watch. "That's a wrap. It's almost midnight. I suppose it's too late for that turkey and those gifts."

"Tomorrow," Kelly said. "There's time for just one more thing before this day is over. Something I've been curious about. Something I need to know."

Kelly knelt before the ice. "Rose. Come over here, sweetheart."

Rose ran to Kelly and snuggled against her. "I want you to look inside that puddle, Rose. With me. I'm going to hold you in front of me and I need you to look inside. Like you always do. Can you do that for me?"

Rose yawned but obeyed.

"What are you up to?" Dad asked.

"You know exactly what I'm doing," Kelly said.

Rose knelt down with Kelly behind her. They gazed into the frozen mist together, mother and daughter. Kelly held Rose tightly against her chest, cheek to cheek. She kissed Rose softly. "Go ahead, sweetheart."

The icy fog began to shift and reshape like a warm breeze colliding with a frigid day. An image gradually appeared, blurry at first, clearer with the love that passed between Kelly and Rose and back again.

Finally, Kelly saw them. The children. Hundreds and hundreds of children from all around the world. Some carried crutches, some wore casts, some had cuts and bruises within their hearts and within their bodies. Yet they were all holding hands, each and every child, loving each other through it all. And a greater love, not from them, but from somewhere bigger, stronger, more powerful swept in and around and through them. Uniting them. Comforting them. Strengthening them. This love filled the ice, the children, Kelly and Rose, and the entire apartment with hope.

A cloud settled over the ice and the image abruptly sifted and filtered and changed. Two new faces appeared. The faces of Kelly and Dad now, in the ice. They were holding Rose's hands. Loving her. Simply loving her, because sometimes that is enough. All the time—love is enough. And that love, once again, flowed stronger and mightier than ever before. It was as if a gale force wind was storming into them and around them and through them. Into their very hearts and souls.

Swiftly and suddenly, a fresh fog emerged, creating and forming something new. They saw a healthy, young, vibrant woman, wearing a dark wool dress. Her black hair was pinned atop her head. She wore no makeup, no jewelry. But something in the twinkle of her eyes, something in the slight up-turn of her lips.

Kelly knew this woman. Kelly had loved this woman all of her life. This woman had loved Kelly since the second she was born—Kelly's mom. Rose's grandmother.

And the memories rushed in as the warm breeze coated the ice with a soft, clean wash of something familiar, something different, something that did not begin here but had come.

Rose noticed Kelly's tear-stained face and Rose brushed those tears away with her chubby, little fingers, one by one. "Don't cry, Momma."

Kelly shook her head. "I'm not crying, Rose. Not really. These tears are just the opposite of crying."

Kelly's mother, like all the others, did not speak any words. Sometimes feelings were everything, and the feeling that swept from Kelly and Rose to Mom was stronger than any words ever spoken. Kelly instantly understood that this was where words came from. This was where life began. This was how people became human. How people united, relationships flourished, and life held meaning and substance and purpose.

This was Love.

And there was a sweeping gust of love in return, lavished upon Kelly and Rose, swirling in and around and over and through them, until they were brimming with the thing. Until the amount of love within them flooded the tiny apartment and the street beyond.

Just then, Kelly heard the church bell strike midnight. *Twelve bass gongs, twelve resonating heartbeats, twelve tears, twelve laughs, twelve wonderful symbols that time goes on, whether we agree or not. We are here, and then we are not here. But we leave something behind and we carry something with us, forever and ever and ever. It has no past, no present, no future. For this something existed long before us and long after us. It is contingent upon nothing. It simply is...love.*

Twelve bass gongs signaled the ending of Christmas Day. And the beginning of a new day.

The image of Kelly's mother began to fade. Slowly, softly, gently. The vision was blurry, then only a stroke of color, here and there. A blue, a turquoise, a gray. Then a cloud, a steam, a mist evaporating, dissipating. The ice began to melt, swifter than any ice before. It was releasing its frozen hardness. Its cold outer shell. Its pride. Its unforgiveness. Its anger.

Kelly finally understood: *The melting of a frozen heart.*

The water shimmered and twinkled, clear and clean at first, then gradually fading to the same old puddle that had been there before. The familiarity of the thing, the steadfastness of the thing felt comforting somehow. Yet Kelly and Dad, and even little Rose knew. That puddle was not the same. It would never be the same again.

And then, just because, Kelly whispered, "We love you forever, Mom."

Dad stood behind them. "It's gone."

"No, Dad. It was here all along and it always will be. We just forgot to see it."

"Like Christmas Day," Dad thought aloud. "Here and then gone, but with us forever."

Kelly stood to face Dad. "This was...this is...a Christmas gift."

Then Kelly turned her attention outside, past the window, but further still, upward, onward, to someplace far away from here, but also very close. To that place where love reigns forever. Toward the eternal, heavenly place where powerful things like faith, hope and love run free and wild and reckless and strong. To the place where love was created and born and exists, apart and separate, yet present and united with us forever.

"Thank you," Kelly said. "For the everlasting gift."

ABOUT THE AUTHOR

Chris Storm writes stories about women in jeopardy, women over-coming and women triumphant. She has lived in 10 different towns across the U.S. including the deep bayou of Louisiana, the remote Appalachian hills of West Virginia, the foot of the Adirondack Mountains of New York, the abandoned steel mills of Pennsylvania and the touristy coast of Florida. All of her books are set in places where her family has lived; and may be visited and investigated as authentic and odd and mysterious and...wonderful. "There is something amazing about every place, if you are willing to find it."

She now lives in the Carolinas with her husband of forty years and is the proud mother of two adult children, one sweet grandbaby and two mischievous grand pups, Ralphie and Hank.

Her motto: "Read a novel; because within those mysterious pages, filled with interesting people and far-away places, you will discover something of you—something lost, something buried, or, maybe, just maybe, something you never knew."

Website: ChrisStormBooks.com